Craks in a Marriage

BARBARA BARRETT

Craks in a Marriage

Copyright © Barbara Barrett 2018

Published by: Barbara Barrett

ISBN: 978-1-948532-00-6

Published in the United States of America

This book is dedicated to both my Florida and Iowa mah jongg groups. They have provided me with hours of entertainment and enjoyment and have been my support groups as my writing career has progressed.

Chapter One

"**M**ah jongg!" All five feet six of Kat Faulkner bounded from her chair. She clapped her hands together like a child waking on Christmas morning.

"No kidding?" Seated across from her, Micki Demetrius played with the overgrown, oblong jade bauble on her ring finger, her latest impulse buy, and waited for her friend to rack her tiles and prove her win before revealing her own hand.

On Kat's right, Marianne Putnam pushed back an errant strand of graying red hair as she delayed racking her tiles as well. "I hope you've done it, hon. Remember the last time you tried that hand and got your ones confused? We all got so excited for you, we showed our tiles before we discovered your error, so no one won."

Kat's smile said it all. "This time I've got it. See, two flowers and 2018 in all three suits, bams, dots and craks."

Sydney Bonner, on Kat's left, the unofficial leader of the foursome, checked the assembled tiles against her card of official standard hands. Of all fifty-one winning hands on the card, this one was worth the most. One could not achieve this hand using any joker, or wild cards. Sydney rarely went after one of these, let alone was lucky enough to receive the right tiles, so she hadn't bothered to learn them. "They check out, Kat. Congratulations."

Rising to congratulate her friend, Sydney turned to the other three tables of women in the room. "Hey, everybody. Kat got the seventy-five-cent hand."

In seconds, the other twelve players flanked their table for a glimpse of the near-impossible hand.

Beaming, Kat added, "I've been trying to get this one forever."

"Let's take a picture." Micki grabbed her phone from her purse and held it up to frame the shot. "Smile, Kat. Let me see if I can get the tiles in the picture too."

Once the picture was taken, Sydney, Micki and Marianne each paid her seventy-five cents. "I hope you remember your promise to take the four of us to tea if you ever got this hand," Sydney reminded her.

"I did, didn't I?" Kat turned to Marianne. "You set up the time and place. I'll make good."

"That's the only positive thing I can say about today," Micki said. "I was down to my last three quarters. Your win cleaned me out."

"About time you got your comeuppance. You've been the big winner the past three weeks," Marianne pointed out.

Kat jiggled her newly-won two dollars and twenty-five cents in her hand like she'd been penniless before her win, despite the fact she was a multimillionaire. "Send me a copy of that picture, okay, Micki?"

"Already emailed it."

"Thanks."

"Send a copy to me too," Sydney said. "I'll make sure to include it when I post today's results."

"Oh, Syd, you don't need to do that." Kat's hopeful

expression indicated she didn't want her friend to listen.

"Nonsense! How often does this happen? Not very." Sydney answered her own question. "This is a Big Deal. We have to treat it as such." Despite her friend's growing popularity singing pop, soul and blues tunes of contemporary female singers at area clubs, Sydney knew Kat would love this kind of attention. She rarely was the big winner at mah jongg but kept coming back each week for the love of the game.

"Can we get back to play now?" Olivia Schwimmer at the next table asked rather pointedly. "I might not have had a seventy-five-cent win going, but my hand was still looking pretty good."

Good old Olivia, the consummate competitor. Jokers seemed to gravitate to her, and more jokers increased the odds of winning. However, Sydney didn't recall Olivia ever getting a mah jongg with this hand. This was jealousy, pure and simple.

Just for that, why not prolong this break even more? "Hold on a sec, Olivia. Before everyone starts up again, let's discuss our location the third week of next month. We need to find somewhere else to play, because the community center staff have to set up this room for some evening festivity that day. Where should we go?"

"How about your village clubhouse, Sydney?" Marianne asked.

Sydney had been afraid someone would mention the Sleepy Palms clubhouse. "I can ask, but I think that new men's card group has dibs on it." She knew that because her husband, Trip, had recently organized the group as another way to fill his retirement time.

Marianne made a clucking sound. "That's right. I forgot because that's one of Beau's golf days, or he would've joined."

"You can come to my place," Kat offered.

"You sure, Kat?" Marianne asked. "We're always intruding on you."

"I don't mind. I love having the company. All that space goes wanting most of the time."

Olivia released an audible sigh, loud enough for everyone to hear her frustration. "If that's settled, can we resume play now?"

"In a minute." Sydney couldn't resist keeping this ball in the air just a little longer, now purely to antagonize the impatient player, because this next part could easily be done later by email. "Everyone who plans to play that day needs to get her name to Kat at least twenty-four hours in advance, so she can let the people at the gate know."

"Okay, okay. We all know the drill. Now, can we please get back to play?" Olivia's raised voice signaled she had reached the limit of her tolerance.

Better get this show back on the road. Sydney had had about as much fun annoying Olivia as she could justify to her conscience. "Let's get going, everyone." She reclaimed her seat and drew a pile of tiles toward her to start setting up her wall.

"Why did you tell them I needed twenty-four-hour notice for the gatekeeper at Mangrove Estates? They'll be happy if I call them with the names a half hour before the session," Kat said.

Micki inclined her head as well. "You're a wicked woman, Sydney Bonner." A saintly smile curved her lips.

"She had it coming." Sydney kept her voice low. "She couldn't stand our taking even a minute to recognize Kat's big win. She could just cool her jets a little while longer."

"A wicked, *wicked* woman," Micki reiterated, nodding.

Sydney fixed her friends with her most innocent of expressions. "Who? Me? Or Olivia?"

The rest of the afternoon passed with less excitement. Several more people got mah jongg, but mostly the twenty-five-cent variety.

Sydney lagged behind the others to pack up her set. With the addition of the acrylic "sliders" that attached to each tile rack so the player could easily move her wall of tiles into the center of the table in the course of play, the items in her carrying case had to be arranged just so in order to close the case.

As she arrived in the parking lot, she noted Olivia outside her SUV, two spots away from her own. Sydney couldn't avoid hearing part of the conversation. "You could have given me more than two hours' notice. Once again, I'll have to invent a reason for your absence. This has to stop, Paul." Her voice had risen.

Syd and Trip were attending a dinner that evening with Marianne and Beau. Was that call in reference to the same event? She thought back on the social activities of late in which she'd been involved—the symphony, the local theater group's latest show, the auction to support the high school orchestra. Serendipity Springs, the jewel of central Florida, wasn't that large a town; one tended to run into friends and acquaintances often. She loved that about the place. She remembered seeing Olivia at two recent affairs, but Olivia's husband, Paul, had only been with her once. But then, how many times had Trip begged off accompanying Sydney to some shindig?

She arrived at her two-story, four-bedroom home in the Sleepy Palms section of town wondering if she had time to get in a nap as well as shower before she had to dress for the night's festivity. It was the monthly Serendipity Springers dinner. The Springers was a social group for residents over fifty. She and Trip more than qualified.

One never knew how these monthly dinners would go. Seating was luck of the draw, or rather, what seats happened to be unoccupied by the time one arrived. As much as every person over fifty she knew resented being stereotyped as a senior citizen, they couldn't help themselves when it came to the dinner hour. Usually, over three-fourths of the group showed up at least fifteen minutes in advance, many as early as a half hour. She and Trip were rarely part of that group, Trip because he didn't subscribe to the group's "early bird gets the worm" mentality, and she because, once Trip made up his mind to be unique, he couldn't be dissuaded, so she just went along.

That's why she'd suggested Marianne and Beau come with them. Didn't matter how late one was—even if right on time—when seated with your dear friends.

As it turned out, the nap didn't happen. Trip had other plans.

Her bed, her lovely site of temporary respite, had disappeared underneath a sea of clothing. On closer inspection, the pile turned out to be the jackets in which her husband had performed his old barbershop routine. At least four—his favorite with red and white stripes, a bright green with the multiple snap-on collars that could be used for Christmas, St. Patrick's Day and the first day of spring, a sapphire blue sequined number and the plain black one for formal occasions—were spread out on top of one another.

Custom-made Halloween costumes joined the barbershop paraphernalia: a pirate jacket, white blousy shirt and pants, a caveman animal skin and a kilt and sash.

"There you are," he said, entering the bedroom from their walk-in closet. Over six feet tall, retaining most of his hair, though it was now mostly white, and with a square jaw and cleft chin, he still looked pretty good to her, despite her frustration over the cluttered bed. "I've been doing inventory. Don't I have more costumes somewhere? I thought I was a cowboy once. Also, a firefighter."

"What are you looking for?" She didn't mention the location of the other two costumes, which had gone to a charity garage sale last year. With his permission, of course, although she'd asked just before he'd dropped off to sleep.

He stopped rummaging through the pile long enough to glance at her. "The Springer men have decided to put on a variety show as this year's fundraiser for the hospital's heart wing. They convinced me to chair the thing."

Convinced. Right. Her spouse jumped at any chance to occupy his time. Three years into retirement, he was still seeking new meaning in his life. His Springer brothers knew this and took flagrant advantage of him. She gestured toward the mess preventing her nap. "What's with all this? You're planning to do a one-man show?"

He paused a millisecond, as if considering this new thought. "Good idea. Maybe someday. But for now, just nudging the old brain for ideas."

"You couldn't make a list from simply perusing these items in the closet?"

"Sorry. I'll put everything back as soon as I'm done. I'm aware we have to pick up the Putnams in an hour."

She allowed herself one last longing look at her side of the bed. "Let me grab my clothes for tonight, then I'm off to my shower."

Two minutes later, as warm, comforting water streamed down on her from the showerhead, Sydney attempted to calm her breathing. Though she was happy Trip had a new interest, tiny fingers of dread poked her brain. Trip's "projects" rarely proceeded in a vacuum. Sooner or later, she'd be pulled into the vortex of his schemes, er, plans, when some minor detail he'd forgotten suddenly blossomed into a major predicament.

Breathe, girl. This will be fun. Uh-huh, like the men's fashion show he arranged last spring. He'd convinced a major department store to provide the wardrobe. Everything from tennis togs to tuxedos. Another department store got wind of the event and convinced him to let them contribute their casual wear. When the first contributor heard about their competitor joining the festivities, they bowed out a week before the show. Though Trip scrambled to fill the holes, she'd been the one on the phone for two full days schmoozing and cajoling other men's clothing concerns in the area to join the party.

A talent show could be even more complicated what with finding acts, soliciting backers, advertising and rehearsals. A lot of balls to juggle. Plus, he'd probably be working with the same cast of characters, who would now be singing, dancing, telling jokes or whatever, instead of simply modeling clothing. Did the man never learn?

Chapter Two

*A*pparently, Paul Schwimmer was able to change his plans and make it to the dinner with Olivia after all. Had Sydney not overheard their earlier conversation, she would have had no inkling trouble brewed beneath the surface of that marriage. Olivia hung on her husband's arm as they entered Leonardo's, one of the town's premier restaurants, after the Bonners and Putnams arrived. Only two seats remained, and, to Sydney's distress, they just happened to be at her table. Olivia smiled lovingly into her husband's face as he pulled out a chair for her.

Marianne leaned closer to Sydney. "She sure seems to have changed her tune since a few hours ago. It nearly killed her to see Kat get that big payoff."

Sydney lowered her voice to a whisper. "Although Olivia likes to win, she doesn't like to see the same happen to others." The round table was large enough and the room chatter loud enough to muffle their exchange.

"Wonder what old Paul has done to crank up her smile."

Remembering Olivia's earlier exchange with her hubby, Sydney wondered too.

Privy to none of his wife's recently acquired knowledge about Olivia, Trip went into host mode, even though they'd only taken their seats minutes before. "Haven't seen much of you two lately. What's been occupying your time?"

Olivia opened her mouth to respond, but her spouse beat her to the punch. "Busy time of year, fall. Snowbirds returning to the fold, tourists starting to swarm. Monitoring my various investments keeps me occupied." His reference to the Schwimmer wealth not so subtle, the guy didn't even mention his family taking up his time.

Apparently, that was Olivia's department. "Our statewide holdings keep Paul on the road a lot. I'm fortunate he was able to free up his schedule tonight." Her saccharine tone belied the anger Sydney heard only a few hours earlier. Though she'd never put Trip's attentiveness to her, or lack thereof, in the same category as what seemed to be the case with Paul Schwimmer, Sydney had to admit, she'd cover for Trip just the same. Mercy, she had done so several times over the years, but for what she considered less offensive reasons than being gone all the time.

"Too bad you couldn't free up your schedule for the trustee meeting at church last week." The male half of the fourth couple at the table, Don Martin, shot a sideways stare at Schwimmer.

"Couldn't be helped," Schwimmer said.

"What night was that, Paul? Tuesday? Wednesday? Thursday? You were gone all three nights last week." Olivia's face seemed to have frozen into a permanent smile.

"Tuesday," Martin replied. "The board is approaching the end of the church's fiscal year, and you and I have some things to discuss. Soon."

"Sure, sure, Don, as soon as I can find time."

"Find it."

An awkward silence descended on the table. Taking Schwimmer's lead, everyone, with the exception of Martin, perused their menus. Even he finally gave in and opened his, just as their waiter arrived.

The rest of the evening passed in relative civility. Martin didn't participate much in the table discussion, and when he did chime in, he adopted the same chitchat style of everyone else.

While the rest were still eating dessert and lingering over coffee, Schwimmer rose, and though not forcibly, still managed to "encourage" Olivia to stand as well. "Early day tomorrow, so we'll take our leave. Great dinner, everyone."

On their way to the restaurant's entrance, Schwimmer stopped at another table, where more members of their group were seated. "Well, well, McGraw. Heard you were under the weather. Must've had a swift revival."

His voice carried far enough for Sydney and those remaining at her table to overhear. Cole McGraw, the current Springer president, mumbled something, kept his head down. Schwimmer bent his head toward the man and said something more in a much lower tone, which Sydney and the others couldn't hear. Though her arm was still entwined in his, Olivia appeared to separate herself from her husband's conversation while she nodded to other members of their group at the next table.

As quickly as he'd pulled up, Schwimmer continued his departure, Olivia faithfully following in his wake. Within two minutes, McGraw and his wife, Annalise, took their leave as well, McGraw almost throwing a wad of bills at their waiter.

Martin harrumphed. "The man can find time for his

golf buddy but not his church." Within the next five minutes, he and his wife left also.

Marianne turned to Sydney and Trip, blue eyes wide. "Was it something we said?"

$$\boxed{D}$$

"I was so glad Kat won that hand yesterday," Micki told Sydney as they drove to their monthly coupon clipping meeting the next day. Town residents contributed grocery store coupons from their Sunday newspapers to their committee, which cut and prepared them for submission to a national organization that converted their value to underwrite the grocery bills of military families.

"Like she needed the two dollars and twenty-five cents she collected from the three of us." Sydney kept her tone light so her passenger would realize there was no, well, little envy in her statement. After a lifetime of living frugally supporting her ailing mother, Kat, a single woman, had won a national lottery shortly after her mother's death. The windfall had allowed her to move to Florida from Illinois, buy a huge home in the most fashionable area of Serendipity Springs, Mangrove Estates—although the town had no rundown sections— and live the good life.

"She could use the boost. She's nervous about her next singing engagement, although I don't know why. The more she performs, the more she relaxes and enchants her audience."

Micki tended to be the least sentimental of Sydney's three close friends, though she had a soft spot for Kat. Like herself, Micki was tall and thin, though unlike Syd, who'd let her hair go silver, Micki wore hers dark with a streak of gray on one side. She hailed from New York

City. Brooklyn. She'd taught high school English for most of her career, until the cold winters got to her. She'd relocated to Florida and taught the same subject in a town half an hour from Serendipity Springs for three years before retiring. These days, Micki freelanced, writing magazine, newspaper and blog articles, which helped augment her pension, which only went so far to support Micki's rather audacious lifestyle.

"You've done wonders getting Kat out of her self-imposed box."

"Yeah, well, I don't mind prodding when it comes to her getting out, spending some of her lovely lottery money and God forbid, meeting men. But you're the one she seeks out for personal advice."

The others had also just arrived at the small conference room at the community center when Sydney and Micki stepped into the room. Three other women and one man, a husband who seemed to go everywhere his wife went, occupied the room. Johnny Bayliss had stifled their talk—gossip—the first few times he'd sat in, until he'd voluntarily shared a tidbit about two of the men with whom he played petanque, a game similar to bocce. From then on, the floodgates were open, with Johnny a major contributor to their information sharing.

Today he bounced in his seat, seemingly eager to share his latest nugget. "Somebody in this town is playing around with somebody else's husband."

Though Sydney relished a snippet of info about the private lives of the locals, she tried to avoid gossip that would hurt others. Tough yardstick to discern sometimes. Johnny's statement throbbed with the potential to fall into that category. She'd listen to get the facts. At least, that's what she told herself. She'd let the others do the fact-gathering.

One of the other women took the bait. "Who're the somebodies? You gonna tell us?"

"Only know the lady in question, if you want to call her that," he replied. "None other than the town's former beauty queen and current best-selling real estate agent, Periwinkle 'Peri' Dawson." He clamped his mouth shut and surveyed his listeners for their reactions.

Micki waved a hand. "Old news, Johnny. Everyone knows Peri's a flirt."

Johnny twisted around to face her. "Flirting's one thing. Having an affair with a married man is something else."

"How do you know this?" the first woman asked.

"Heard it from someone who should know."

"In other words, this is pure speculation," a second woman said.

Johnny straightened his shoulders. "More than. Just can't reveal my source."

"Now you sound like someone on a TV gossip show," the second woman replied.

Johnny pursed his lips. "Don't want to get anyone in trouble."

"Except Peri Dawson," Micki said.

Johnny pulled out his stack of coupons from a storage bag and went for his scissors. "Never mind, then."

Johnny's wife entered the fray. "Don't be like that, John. Like her or not, Peri Dawson is a respected member of the community. Her commissions may outdistance everyone else, but she's also very generous with her time and money with several charities. If a story like this is unfounded, it could hurt her reputation."

"Okay, okay," he conceded. "I heard this from one of my fishing buddies who lives upstate. He's been thinking of relocating here and was in her office going over some listings when she stepped into the hall to take a personal call. When she didn't let it go to voicemail or excuse herself for an emergency, my friend got curious, so he opened the door a bit. She was making plans to meet someone at a motel on the outskirts of town. 'What about your wife?' she said, and followed up with, 'Oh, you naughty boy.' Didn't sound like any client to my friend. Unless he wanted her services for something else."

"Based on that fragment of a phone call, your friend concluded she was having an affair with a married man?" Sydney asked. She hardly knew the woman, but in all fairness, Johnny's account was inconclusive. "One who lives here in town, no less?"

"Ah, shucks, ladies. Didn't know I'd get the third degree just for letting you in on this bit of news. Next time, I'll get written confirmation of all the facts before sharing some juicy piece of information."

"Now we've hurt your feelings," Micki said. "We must sound like hypocrites to you, since we rarely pass up a good piece of gossip. But an affair with a married man is a serious thing."

"Guess I get what you're saying. Just wanted to fit in. You all must wonder why a guy like me even comes to these hen sessions."

"Hey, all men are welcome here, Johnny," the first woman said. "Don't feel you have to gossip with us to fit in."

"That's what I told him when he ran this story past me earlier," his wife replied. "But like he says, he really enjoys being here."

After a few more minutes reassuring Johnny they wanted him to remain with the group, the subject was dropped, and everyone went back to clipping.

Only after Sydney and Micki were back in the car did Sydney bring up Johnny's claim. "Just between us, do you think Peri Dawson is having an affair with a married man from here in town?"

"I don't like the woman, Syd. It would be very easy for me to jump on Johnny's bandwagon, but not on such flimsy information. Even Peri Dawson deserves the right to be presumed innocent until proven guilty."

"That's very high-minded of you."

"Maybe. Mainly, though, I don't want to be quoted as furthering this story."

"So, we're not going to share this with even Kat or Marianne?"

Micki scooched farther into the leather seat back, today's ponytail swinging. "Now who's being high-minded? Let's just agree to resist temptation to bring them in on this as long as we can. And if the four of us just happen to be alone some night and imbibing some of Kat's fine wine, who knows?" She favored her driver with a cherubic grin. "A girl can only keep so much from her besties."

Chapter Three

Sydney spent the next few days finding excuses to avoid the house. More to the point, avoid Trip and his latest project. Her husband was a man possessed as he attempted to come up with the "perfect" theme for his variety show. "Gotta find something that's never been done. Something that'll draw a wide sector of townsfolk."

"Why not pick something with a proven track record?"

The look he gave her with those hazel eyes said he couldn't believe she could be so dense. But he said, "Diminishing returns, babe. Can't count on hitting it out of the park a second time. Got any ideas?"

"Me? You must be desperate."

"No, I respect your opinion. You see things from a different angle than I."

"What have you considered and rejected so far?"

He recited a lengthy list.

"Not much left."

"Yeah. Everything I've come up with, some other group has already done it."

They'd been down this road before. She'd learned the hard way that her role wasn't to suggest the ultimate great idea. Instead, he needed her thoughts to shake loose the logjam in his brain, eventually resulting in his brilliant inspiration. "How about a sampler highlighting the best of the best from the other groups' shows? You know, a sort of nod to everyone else in town to pull in that wide sector you want."

"Hmm. Interesting. Kind of like a review."

"Okay. You could call it that."

He rubbed his jaw, scratched behind his ear. "Yeah, but that'd be like stepping on everyone else's toes. Like we can do it better."

"Not if each group has their own representative."

Trip massaged the back of his neck. "If we invited those groups to participate, we could bill this as a community-wide event." And he was off, the idea now officially his, since he'd put his spin on it. She didn't need to stick around, although he was barely aware of her presence by this point.

She had nothing planned for today, except cleaning the fridge. Surely there was some better way to invest her time? Something away from the house? There was always the fitness room at their clubhouse. Or the pool. In the end, she grabbed her digital reader and headed for the local coffeehouse. Even if she wound up sitting by herself, it was such a nice day, she could find an outside table and read in the sun.

The coffee establishment was located in the heart of downtown. A grillwork fence surrounded the courtyard, which provided patrons a certain amount of privacy while observing passersby. A laurel oak in the center favored them with shade. One of her favorite places to visit. After she'd picked up her skinny vanilla latte, she opened her reader and brought up the latest cozy mystery by a new author someone had recommended to her.

She treasured these times. Alone in the midst of others, a tasty beverage and a mystery to solve. A literary mystery, anyhow.

She'd barely finished the first chapter when she heard sirens approaching. Ten seconds later, the sheriff's car sped by, blue lights blazing. A few beats later, two more sheriff's cars followed. All three vehicles proceeded down the street, turned the corner by the town's main lake and headed to the end of the street, where they abruptly stopped, lights still oscillating. Because they were over two blocks away, she couldn't see much, although she could make out rapid movement toward the nearby woods that flanked the lake.

Had someone been hurt on the walkway? Passed out or had a heart attack? If so, the EMTs should be showing up soon as well. Although she didn't see herself as a rubbernecker, her curiosity outweighed her desire to continue with her story. Not when a real-life emergency was on tap.

She closed her reader, flung her coffee container into a waste receptacle and slipped out the gate, walking as nonchalantly as possible toward whatever the action was across the lake. Serendipity Springs was generally a quiet town. Its residents liked it that way. But a constant diet of tranquility could at times be...too tranquil. When momentary excitement invaded their lives, people tended to drop everything and go investigate. Sydney was joined in her faster-than-usual stroll around the lake by several shoppers, store owners and tourists.

The proprietor of the exclusive doggy treats store caught up with her. "What's up?"

"No idea," Sydney replied. "But it warrants three sheriff's vehicles."

Two deputies attempted crowd control after they'd

put up temporary barriers prohibiting further civilian progress toward the woods. "What's going on? Did someone get sick on the walkway?" Sydney asked one.

"Don't know yet, other than the sheriff ordered the rest of this path closed."

At that point, an EMS vehicle pulled up, and three people streamed out. They took off for the woods carrying various pieces of equipment.

"Hey, guys, what's up?" one of the onlookers called. The EMTs just kept going.

But a jogger who'd apparently been coming down the path from the other direction slowed as he passed the barrier. Several of the curious surrounded him like ants discovering a discarded piece of fruit. Sydney shouldered her way into the crowd. "Body over there in the bushes," he managed to gulp out. Body? That meant... How grisly.

Apparently, the rest of his run was more important than sticking around to get more details, because he took off a minute later while the rest of the gathering speculated about what had happened and who it could be.

Sydney stood around with the rest of them waiting for more news. After another fifteen minutes, an official-looking state car arrived. Two plainclothes guys got out, one carrying a large suitcase-type bag, and shot off without speaking with anyone. Ten minutes later, the first of what would turn out to be three TV crews from Orlando arrived, double-parked and shut the street down to one lane. The crowd continued to grow, although Sydney wandered a few feet away to snatch room on a bench while there was still space.

A woman she vaguely recognized from church settled next to her while still holding on to the leash of a white terrier. "Do you think whoever's lying over there was killed? Pixie and I just came off that path minutes before all this ruckus erupted." She slammed a hand to her heart. "We could've run into the killer ourselves."

Sydney shot the woman a searching look. "Killer? Surely not. We don't have murders in Serendipity Springs. We thrive on our dull little lives."

"You think someone just collapsed on a run?" the woman returned. "If they did, I certainly didn't see them go by me. Pixie would've launched into a barking fit if she even sensed someone nearby."

The woman's words sank in. "You didn't see anyone else?"

"Other walkers? Yes. And a couple bikes sped by, nearly knocking us over. But no one was down, bent over or even limping."

Then "the body" had to have been out of sight, somewhere off the path but close enough for someone to have found it. She recalled there being a couple of setbacks along the path. A smaller one was constructed for bird-watching. The larger was a boardwalk path that ended in a rectangular platform surrounded by benches for viewing the flora and fauna.

She considered going home. She'd been gone a little over an hour. But she couldn't bring herself to leave yet. Whoever the authorities had rushed over to save or whatever could be a tourist out enjoying the town's sights or someone staying at the hotel on the other side of the lake. But it could also be a local. Someone she knew. She had to find out.

She didn't have long to wait. Within minutes, the sheriff himself returned to the barriers and motioned for the crowd to reassemble. "A woman who is staying at the hotel was exploring the nature path back there and spotted a body in the undergrowth several feet from the path. The body is that of a white male in his fifties or sixties, but we haven't determined yet either his identity or cause of death. We ask for your cooperation as we remove the body by backing away and giving the EMTs space to come through."

Shortly thereafter, two EMTs appeared and hauled a gurney with a bagged body to their vehicle. Expressions shuttered, they spoke to no one. In seconds, they loaded the body and took off.

Members of the media surrounded the sheriff. Sydney wasn't close enough to hear what he said, other than to observe him shaking his head. Finally, he told everyone there'd be a press conference later in the day, once next of kin had been notified. No time was stated.

Not much more to be learned here. Since she'd parked her car near the coffeehouse, might as well return there. See if any of the customers had gleaned more information about the incident than she had.

As she entered the courtyard, she spotted Olivia Schwimmer seated by herself across the way. She'd seen enough of the woman for this week. She really didn't want to make nice when she was still so curious about Olivia's call to her husband. But avoiding the woman would be too obvious.

"Hi, Olivia. I see you enjoy this courtyard too."

The other woman glanced up from her paperback. "Oh, hello, Sydney. I was just grabbing a few minutes to read this month's book club selection."

Yay! An out. "Oh, then I won't keep you from it."

"No, please join me. Do you know anything about what's going on around the lake? I couldn't hear anything, but I could see a crowd gathering."

Resignedly, Sydney sank into a chair across from Olivia. "They found a body off the jogging path."

Olivia's eyes widened. "Really? Did they say who it was?"

"Not yet. Don't even know if it's someone who lives here or a tourist. The sheriff's office is handling it."

Olivia shook her head, as if attempting to accept the sad news. "I guess we have enough seniors in town that someone was bound to have a heart attack on that trail someday."

If that's what happened. But Sydney let it go. No need to speculate. "They are attempting to identify the person and then notify next of kin. They have to do that before they'll release further information to the public."

Olivia's cell rang. "Hello? Yes, I'm Olivia Schwimmer. Yes, he's my husband. Where am I now?" She mentioned the name of the coffeehouse. "Yes. There's someone here with me. Okay. How soon?" She hung up, a very strange expression covering her face. "That was the sheriff's office. They want to talk to me and asked that you stick around."

Shards of ice sliced into Sydney's heart. She bit a lip to keep from saying anything, but she knew what was coming. What crazy twist of fate had selected her to be here with Olivia at this moment?

Olivia closed her book, stuck it away in her purse. She pursed her lips, folded her hands. "This isn't good, is it?"

"We don't know that yet, Olivia. Try not to think about it for now. Maybe you should go back to your book?"

"Can't concentrate. All I can think about is their suggesting you stay with me. That means I'll need someone to keep me calm when they tell me whatever it is they have to tell me." She raised moist eyes toward Sydney. "For your sake, I'm sorry that role fell to you. But I'm glad you're here."

"Don't worry about me. Can I get you anything? Water? Another coffee?"

Olivia waved away the suggestion. "Oh, no. My stomach is churning already."

When the sheriff arrived, he seemed to zero in on their table. Sheriff Richard Formero had been elected two years ago when the former sheriff retired. Prior to that, he'd served as deputy for five years here in this county and for several years before that in an adjacent county. Tall, broad-shouldered like a former swimmer, he removed his cap as he approached Olivia, revealing a crew cut of dark hair sprinkled with a little gray. Only then did Sydney notice that the smattering of patrons who were there a few minutes before had left. The staff appeared to have migrated to the back room.

"Mrs. Schwimmer?" he asked, staring at Olivia. "Olivia Schwimmer?"

Olivia started to rise, but he gestured for her to remain seated.

He briefly glanced at Sydney, then back to Olivia. "I regret to inform you that your husband, Paul, met with a fatal accident earlier today."

"Fatal? Meaning he's…dead?" she returned.

"Yes, ma'am, that's correct."

"How? Did he have a heart attack or something?"

He bowed his head slightly. "We found his ID in the wallet that was on his, uh, body. But we need someone to formally identify him. Until we know for sure this is your husband, I can't tell you anything more."

"You want me to identify him?"

"Yes, ma'am, but if you don't think you can, perhaps," here he turned to Sydney, "your friend?"

Please don't let her say me. I'm no good around dead people.

Olivia focused pathetic eyes on Sydney. "Could you, please, Sydney?"

"But I hardly knew your husband." Sydney struggled to find a way out. Olivia might not be her favorite person, and Olivia's marriage might not be as perfect as she pretended, but she didn't deserve to learn of her husband's death this way or be alone when she identified his body. What if they'd found Trip over there in the woods? She wouldn't want to face this on her own. "I'll go with you. How would that be?"

"Okay. Thank you."

The sheriff and a deputy escorted them to the morgue. Sydney had never been to this part of the hospital, although she knew of its existence. She gripped Olivia's cold hand in hers as they entered together, she needing as much support as the other woman. They were taken to a small anteroom with one window. It was covered on the other side with a closed drape.

"If you'll stand here, ma'am?" He indicated a spot just in front of the window. "The, uh, body will be brought to the other side. All you have to do is tell me whether or not this person was your husband. Okay?"

Olivia gulped and closed her eyes briefly, as if praying for strength. Or perhaps praying the body she was about to view was not her husband.

The drape opened. On the other side, a body covered almost completely in a white sheet, except for part of the face, was laid out on a table.

Olivia gasped, placed a hand to her mouth and folded at the waist. Tears that had hung near the surface throughout their wait for the sheriff and then the ride to the hospital now poured forth freely.

"Mrs. Schwimmer?"

She nodded. "Yes, that's him. That's my husband, Paul."

The sheriff gave an almost imperceptible nod to someone behind the window, and the drape closed.

All Sydney could think to do was pull the new widow into her arms. Olivia came willingly and continued to sob into Sydney's shoulder. The sheriff stood stiffly a few feet away and allowed Olivia time to react.

As Olivia sobbed, the sheriff produced a couple of tissues and handed them to Sydney. Finally, the tears came less ferociously. Olivia sniffed several times, then accepted the tissues and blew her nose.

Olivia turned to the sheriff, her eyes rimmed in red. "Now that I've identified him, can you tell me what happened? Why was his body wrapped like that?"

The sheriff released a breath. "Your husband was hit on the back of the head, hard, with a yet-to-be-determined blunt object. He fell forward into a shallow pool of water, which is where he was found. The medical examiner will have to determine whether he drowned or had already expired when he hit the water."

Olivia simply stared at the man, attempting to process his words. Sydney was further ahead.

"You mean…?" Olivia asked.

The sheriff nodded. "Your husband was murdered, Mrs. Schwimmer."

Chapter Four

The fact that she had known a murder victim hit Sydney all at once. Had she not been there to support Olivia, she might have given in to her nausea and dizziness. Only by focusing on the new widow was it possible for her to get through this surreal situation.

The sheriff offered to drop Sydney off at the coffeehouse to pick up her car before taking Olivia home, but surprising herself, Sydney begged off, choosing instead to accompany Olivia home.

"That's very kind of you, Sydney, but you've already gone well beyond the bounds of our acquaintance accompanying me to the hospital."

It would be so easy to agree and head home, but as much as Olivia might prefer to be alone, someone needed to stay with her right now. She had to be in some level of shock. Sydney couldn't justify leaving her on her own. "I'll respect your need for space and stay in the background, but I'm going with you."

The sheriff agreed to have his deputies bring both cars from downtown to Olivia's house.

Once they reached the Schwimmer house, Olivia

excused herself and retreated to her bedroom. Sydney let her go. A few minutes later, she wondered if that was the best decision. Would a depressed Olivia become suicidal? Sydney made a quick search of the kitchen, telling herself food and beverage would be a good excuse to check on the woman. By the time Sydney reached the bedroom, Olivia had showered, changed to loungewear and was toweling off the long brown hair she usually wore in a bun.

Sydney stared a second longer than necessary at the woman, relieved by her relative calm. "I made myself at home in your kitchen. Here's some tea and a sandwich."

"I couldn't possibly eat or drink anything right now. But thank you."

"Okay. Perhaps later?" She noticed the clothes Olivia had been wearing earlier lying on the floor and bent to retrieve them.

"Don't!" Olivia shouted. Then she relaxed. "I'll get those later. They probably should go to a dry cleaner." Her voice resumed a more normal tone.

Sydney left them alone, as ordered, but not before she saw a small patch of what appeared to be blood along one sleeve.

"I'll take care of calling my children. I don't want them to hear about their father on the news, but I have no idea what to do for funeral arrangements. It would be a big help if you could go online and find a list of what to do."

Though surprised that Olivia had apparently come out of her shock, the request was something Sydney could handle. "Sure. Can I use your computer?"

Olivia led her to Paul's office and turned on the laptop and printer. Sydney set to work while Olivia returned to her bedroom. She was back within ten minutes. "My daughter will be here within the hour. She's only thirty minutes away, but she had to make arrangements for someone to cover her sixth-grade class the next several days. My son lives in Atlanta and won't be here until tomorrow."

"I'm glad you got through to them both, although it couldn't have been easy."

"Yes, well, their father wasn't always their favorite person, but he was their father, and in the end, that's what counts."

Strange statement. Maybe the shock hadn't passed after all. Sydney sidestepped the reference to Paul. "Here are a couple lists I printed for you. First thing, you'll need to select a funeral home. Perhaps your daughter can go over the rest with you when she gets here."

Olivia settled into a chair. "Before she or anyone else arrives, we need to talk." She leaned closer. "I need your help in another way. I'm a proud woman, Sydney. I don't like to rely on anyone else to solve my problems, but at the moment, I'm not in a position to do that."

Caught off guard, Sydney set down her lists, not sure what was coming. "Solve your problems? What are you talking about?" As soon as the words were out, she wanted to retract them. What was she getting herself into?

"When the sheriff pulled me into his office earlier and you waited in the outer room, it wasn't just to console me. He said there were questions about Paul he needed to ask right away."

"Questions?"

"About Paul's life. People who might bear him a grudge. People to whom he may have owed money or insulted. I told him I didn't know of anyone like that, although as a businessman in our community, he may have stepped on toes at times."

Where was she going with this? Maybe she just wanted to talk, vent. "I've never been personally involved in, uh, situations like this, but I guess that would be the kind of thing the sheriff would need to know to start his investigation."

"His *investigation*, yes. Then he started asking about Paul and me. Our marriage. Our relationship."

Uh-oh. Sydney remembered the telephone call she'd overheard. Oh, God, the sheriff wouldn't talk to Olivia's friends and acquaintances, would he? What would she tell him if he did? She wasn't one to skip over the truth. "I guess that would be part of his investigation as well."

Olivia gripped her hands in what looked like a steely prayer. "I didn't kill him, Sydney. You have to believe me."

"Okay?"

"But things haven't been what I'd describe as happy between us lately. The sheriff is sure to uncover some of that. If he does, he might stop looking for the real culprit and tie it all on me."

"But if you're innocent, how could he make the charges stick?" Sydney blurted out her question, flabbergasted at the woman's statement.

Olivia glanced away, as if not wanting to face her directly. "I can't believe I'm saying this, but I suspect Paul was being unfaithful. I was about to confront him, as soon as I had more definite proof."

Sydney opened her mouth and closed it just as fast. What could she say? What was she supposed to say?

"I know. You're surprised. To our friends and the rest of the community, even to our children, we seemed like the perfect couple. No cares in the world. So supportive of each other."

Maybe not *that* perfect, but until recently, Sydney would have agreed with the statement. "I, uh, had no idea." Okay, sometimes she did stray a *tad* from the truth. When it would hurt someone else if she was too frank.

"Paul had a straying eye. Probably part of aging. Had to prove to himself he still had the old charm. For all I know, this might not have been the first liaison. He wasn't as careful hiding things this time. That's all."

Sydney's mind skipped around, trying to connect loose ends in Olivia's words with other observations of late. Would Olivia kill Paul over an affair? Sydney couldn't dismiss the possibility, despite Olivia's claim of innocence. Olivia had admitted she was a proud woman. No doubt about that from her play at mah jongg. Would she stand by and let the man cheat on her? What if he wanted a divorce? Would she allow that to happen? Probably not. But the idea of Olivia bashing him in the head didn't wash. She might be a woman who took action, but she was precise, methodical. If she decided to off Paul, she would do it in a less sloppy way that wouldn't lead back to her.

"Did you tell that to the sheriff?

Olivia pressed her lips together. "No. Like I told you, I only suspected Paul of playing around. If he was seeing someone else, let the sheriff discover it on his own."

Sydney wondered what she'd do if she were in Olivia's place. Not that Trip would ever cheat. If for no other reason, although there were plenty of others, the man was too busy keeping himself busy in retirement to have time to mess around. "You need to prepare yourself, then. Because Sheriff Rick Formero is no pushover. If there's something to find out, he will."

"That's why I need your help."

"What? How?" This conversation was getting weirder and weirder.

"I need to spend the next few days with my children

getting through the funeral and handling the estate, but I doubt the sheriff will back away from his investigation during that time. I need for you to help me discover who really did kill Paul."

Had she heard the woman correctly? "I'm not an investigator."

"That's just it. No one would suspect you of gathering information for me. But you and those cohorts of yours probably know everything that's going on in this town. Use that talent to help me clear my name."

Chapter Five

Sydney wasn't ready to go home yet. Not with Olivia's bizarre request so fresh in her mind. Instead, she summoned her three friends to the local café. While she waited for them to arrive, she updated Trip by text, not yet ready to mention Olivia's bizarre request. She tried to down a burger without much success.

"So, tell us all about it," Marianne probed as soon she settled into Syd's booth. "Who found him? Is it true, he was killed? How did Olivia react?"

Sydney moved a pickle around her plate with her fork. How much should she reveal? The sheriff hadn't exactly sworn her to secrecy. "For once, Olivia's tenacity stood her well, although that was probably the shock more than anything. I don't think it totally sunk in that her husband was gone, even after she identified his body."

Kat gasped. "They made her do that?"

"Someone had to. She tried to get me to do it, but I didn't know the man that well. Since their kids both live out of town, it would have taken longer to wait for them to arrive."

"Is it true, he was killed? It wasn't an accident?" Micki asked.

"I guess I can tell you that much. Yes." She related what the sheriff had said about someone bashing in Paul's head. "From what little interaction I'd had with him, he wasn't the nicest guy in town. But no one deserves that."

"We've never had a murder here in town," Marianne said. "Is the sheriff's department up to investigating this?"

"I saw people who appeared to be from the state Office of Criminal Investigation show up at the murder site with various equipment," Sydney related. "So, the sheriff's office isn't on their own."

"Plus, they get enough practice with the foul play in the rest of the county," Micki added. "We've been lucky here in the Springs, but it was bound to happen someday."

Kat shivered. "Ooh. Don't say that, Micki. This is a good town. People here don't murder other people."

"Maybe it was an outsider?" Marianne suggested. "Someone who did business with Paul Schwimmer."

"But knocking him on the head?" Sydney couldn't get past the way the man had been killed. "They don't know exactly what was used yet. They referred to it as a blunt instrument. But surely someone wasn't carrying it on their person when they went after him. You don't go walking around town carrying a baseball bat, unless you're on your way to a game. My guess is they picked something up along the way, a log or maybe a rock."

"What about a walking stick?" Marianne suggested. "Or maybe there was a petanque game under way about the same time. The petanque field isn't that far from the woods where he was found."

"We can speculate on the actual weapon later," Micki said. "You've got something else on your mind, don't you, Syd?"

Sydney breathed in what could be her last full breath

for a while. Her relationship with these dear women was on the brink of change. No matter what they decided to do, their lives would be different after today. "I went home with Olivia, thinking someone needed to be there until her family arrived. Before I left, she asked me and the three of you to essentially go undercover to find out who murdered her husband." Met with open mouths in response, she went on to recount Olivia's reasons for needing their help.

"But we're not professionals," Marianne argued. "We may all have had respectable careers before retirement, but none of us has any experience in law enforcement or investigation."

"That's what I told her."

"And her response?"

"Sure you want to hear?"

Marianne nodded, although she wrinkled her forehead.

"Apparently the four of us have a certain reputation. At least with Olivia. Supposedly, we know everything that goes on in the Springs."

Micki sat back, blinked. "Whoa. Really? Boy, is she mistaken."

"I tried to tell her that, but I couldn't dispel her impression of the four of us."

Marianne called the question. "So? Are we going to do it?"

Sydney took a sip of coffee. "That's why you're here. I'm still trying to decide. Every ounce of good sense tells me to say 'no, thanks,' but she sounded so desperate. I can't forget the appeal in her eyes."

"What if she really did kill her husband? Why would she want us looking into the case? How would we serve her purpose?" Marianne asked.

Syd remembered the spot of blood she saw on the sleeve of Olivia's jacket and the woman's harsh reaction when Syd tried to pick up the garment. If she and the others agreed to do this, that blood needed to be explained first. "I keep coming back to that question myself."

"If we did this, is there any way she could shift the blame to us?" Micki wanted to know.

Sydney gave the question some thought. "Well, she wants us to keep our investigation on the down low. Would we look suspicious if somehow what we were doing were revealed?"

Micki still needed to be convinced. "Maybe she could make it look like we resented her so much we set her up by murdering Paul ourselves and then worked behind the scenes to make her look like the killer."

"That's so far-fetched. Do you really believe she could sell that?" Marianne replied.

Micki shook her head. "Well, no. I was just playing *what if*."

"Let's say we agree," Kat said. "How far do we take it? What if we not only clear her name, but we also figure out who killed Paul? How do we protect ourselves?"

"From the killer or the law?" Marianne asked.

"Both, but especially the killer," Kat replied.

"Gee, Syd, the more we play around with this, the scarier it seems," Marianne said.

"I know. But I wish you could've talked with Olivia yourself. She's scared and hurt and grieving all at once. I hate to walk away from someone going through all that."

Marianne picked up the abandoned pickle on Syd's plate and nibbled on it. "Look, guys, since she referred to all four of us, we either all agree to do this or we're out."

Kat crinkled her eyes. "I don't know, Syd. I don't

want to be the one holdout who keeps the rest from investigating, if that's what you all want, but this feels so unlawful, even if it's not. I've got relations I've never heard of vying for my winnings. I don't want to give them any excuses for having me declared incompetent."

"We don't want that for you either," Marianne agreed.

"Then, I guess we should drop it," Sydney said.

Kat held up both hands. "No, wait. That was the old fraidy-cat me. You've all taught me to stick up for myself, as well as step out of my self-imposed walls."

"But your point about keeping what we're doing from the real killer still bothers me," Micki said. "How do we guarantee our own safety?"

"First, our investigation can't look like an investigation," Sydney stated. "Whatever info we gather has to come from other means, like what appear to be casual, spontaneous conversations."

"You mean like sitting next to someone at a concert and saying, 'So, who do you think murdered Paul Schwimmer?'" Micki asked.

Marianne rolled her eyes. "Of course not. First, we develop a list of all the people who've recently interacted with Paul Schwimmer. Like last week, Syd and I sat at the same table as the Schwimmers at the monthly Springers night out. Don Martin and his wife were also at our table, and if I recall correctly, Don was upset with Paul for skipping a church trustees' meeting."

"That's right," Sydney responded. "Paul got so upset, he made Olivia leave early, but as they left the restaurant, he also had words with Cole McGraw. So, for starters, we could put those two names on our list, then figure out how we could discuss something else with them and work in their blowups with Paul Schwimmer. Or at least listen to what others have to say about them."

"Or we could just make a list and hand it over to the sheriff," Kat suggested.

"Olivia's worried the sheriff won't look beyond her, if and when they uncover the affair," Sydney said.

"Then we need to add the mistress to the list," Marianne said. "She seems like a prime suspect to me."

"If she even exists," Micki replied. "We've only got Olivia's misgivings to go on. She could've invented the woman to throw suspicions away from herself."

"If there was a mistress, we first have to figure out who it was," Sydney said. "That could prove to be just as difficult as identifying the murderer."

They spent another half hour speculating about possible suspects but were unable to come up with more. Finally, they agreed to talk with Olivia before deciding whether to take the case.

Chapter Six

When Syd called Olivia the next morning to set up a meeting, she learned that Olivia and her daughter, Lilith, had gone to the funeral home and wouldn't be home for a few hours. With time on their hands, they decided to start their sleuthing at the monthly meeting of the Serendipity Springs Women's Club. Even though they still hadn't made a decision, they could test out the ease with which they could extract information from others.

Only Sydney and Micki belonged to the group; the other two trailed along as their guests. As soon as word spread that potential new members were in their midst, Kat and Marianne became the hit of the day. Almost to a woman, everyone wanted to court them.

Annalise McGraw, Cole's wife and the club president, approached them first. "Katrina Faulkner, delighted you could join us today. I hope this means you're considering membership. We do such good work."

"So I've heard," Kat replied. "I understand you're debating whether to form a ladies' chorus. I might be interested in being part of such a venture."

"That's right, you sing locally, don't you?"

"On occasion," Kat replied. In front of cabaret audiences, shy, retiring Katrina Faulkner morphed into quite the chanteuse. Even Annalise McGraw seemed aware of Kat's reputation.

Apparently satisfied she'd adequately welcomed the newcomer, McGraw moved on and continued to work the crowd.

Kat turned to Sydney. "As many times as Annalise and I have been thrown together socially, this is the first time she's spoken directly to me."

"Not to burst your bubble, but she's trolling for new members, especially rich ones like you."

Kat's shoulders slumped as they took their seats. "That again. As much as I appreciate the lifestyle my winnings afford me, it's things like that which almost make me regret winning the lottery. Almost."

Sydney felt a tapping on her shoulder. The woman seated behind her leaned in. "I heard you were with Olivia Schwimmer when she learned Paul was dead."

Gossip alert. Fortunately, Sydney had already given thought to her standard response to this question. She wasn't here to provide information. Her task was to gather it. "Yes, I just happened to be seated with her when the sheriff found her. So shocking."

"So? What do you know about the investigation?" the woman wanted to know.

"No more than you, I'm sure. I only know the Schwimmers socially. How about you?"

The woman seemed taken aback to have her question redirected at herself. "Me? I know them enough to speak to when I run into them at social gatherings, but that's all. Now that I think about it, Olivia and I were on the same committee at the library last year. She was a real stickler for detail, if I recall."

"You didn't know Paul?"

"I, uh, steered clear of him. I guess I shouldn't speak ill of the dead."

A bell sounded in Syd's head. This might be her first clue. "You've got me curious. Why did you keep your distance?"

The woman seemed to consider her reply. "Even when they'd be together at some event, he always seemed like he was there on his own. Like he was single, if you know what I mean."

"Did he ever come on to you?"

The woman snickered. "Me? Heavens, no! I assumed being near his age, I was too old for him. But if an attractive younger woman happened to be in the vicinity, his eyes appeared to change. Brighten, like I remember from the bar scene years ago before I married."

More of the group were taking their seats. The meeting would start soon, but Sydney's interest had been piqued. "Lech?"

"Not quite so sleazy," the woman replied. "Paul Schwimmer was a player. He could be smooth at the same time he was making an improper suggestion, so a woman would come away wondering if he'd propositioned her or not."

"The meeting will come to order," Annalise McGraw pronounced from the dais.

Sydney tuned out most of the meeting, her thoughts revolving around this latest information about Paul Schwimmer. His eye for younger women fit in with Olivia's suspicions. Although the "younger" part was new.

Fifty minutes later, following a twenty-minute business meeting and a half-hour program about the new women's center, Sydney and Kat were back on the prowl. They split up, agreeing to meet in the lobby in ten minutes, about all the time they had before everyone went off to their own lives.

Sydney spotted one of the women who usually played mah jongg with Olivia clearing the refreshment table and offered to help put away unused napkins, plates, and cups. "Are you planning to go to Paul Schwimmer's funeral day after tomorrow?"

The woman, Clarissa White, paused, as if not sure of her response. "I guess so. For Olivia's sake. I know she can be a real pill at times, but no one deserves to lose their spouse so young and in such a tragic way."

"Good. She needs the support of friends right now."

"You think so? Olivia's always seemed so self-contained, happy with her own company."

"Perhaps that's just a sign of shyness," Sydney suggested.

"Or fear of saying too much." Clarissa carried the unplugged coffee urn into the small kitchen just off the meeting room. She had more to say when she returned. "My husband and I haven't been close friends with the Schwimmers, but they do play in the same golf league. Whenever I'd see them together, they acted like two people on a blind date, polite but uninvolved."

Clarissa's observation added one more dimension to the Schwimmers' relationship. "See you at mah jongg," Sydney said once they were finished. She left to find the others.

At the sandwich shop just down the street from the community center, where the Women's Club meeting had taken place, the four of them reconnoitered and compared notes. "Did you know Trip has asked the Women's Club to participate in his show?" Micki asked Sydney.

"He and I talked about approaching other groups in

town to get more participants, but I didn't know he'd actually proceeded with the plan. I don't recall that topic being discussed during the business meeting, although I admit I didn't listen very well."

Micki leaned in. "Well, according to Trina Hopkins, who's vice president, Annalise McGraw tabled discussion of Trip's proposal at their executive board meeting, saying she needed to consult the bylaws first to determine if such collaboration is allowed."

"You're kidding," Marianne said. "Is that her way of turning him down without actually saying she's not interested?"

"That's what Trina suspects," Micki replied. "Apparently under her watch, Annalise has big plans for the organization, and she doesn't want to dilute the impact by promoting fraternization with other groups in town."

Kat raised a palm. "Fascinating as this discussion is, it's not adding to our investigation."

Micki shook her head. "That's where you're wrong, Kat. Isn't one of the possible suspects on our list Annalise's husband, Cole? Why do you think she's so intent on making Women's Club rock this year? Things aren't so great at home. At least that's Trina's theory, although Trina may still be smarting from Annalise besting her in the election last spring."

Sydney considered. "Was Trina just speculating, or did she mention anything specific?"

"Something about Annalise needing to throw herself into her organizations because Cole's out on the golf course so much."

"Oh, c'mon. We're all in that position," Marianne said. "Well, those of us who are married. It's one of the perks you and Kat don't even realize you have."

"That's such a relief. I'm so glad there's no man in my life so I won't have to complain about him being on the course so often," Micki said. Was that envy speaking?

"Did Trina say who Cole golfs with these days?" Sydney asked, looking directly at Marianne. Would her friend remember a certain gossip session starring their two spouses? She and Marianne had been complaining about some imagined slight at their weekly mah jongg game when the guys interrupted.

"We can top that," Beau had said. He'd gone on to describe Cole McGraw's elaborate efforts to lower his golf scores without anyone knowing. They'd used Cole's three-week absence, when he and Annalise took a river cruise abroad, to bring in a new fourth.

Micki raised a brow. "Ah-hah. You've connected the dots. Cole's been playing with none other than Paul Schwimmer. Although Trina's husband hasn't been part of that foursome, apparently he overheard a weird conversation between Paul and Cole in the locker room about a month ago. She couldn't remember all the details, but it had something to do with Cole's score that day not matching the score Paul thought he should have."

Marianne blinked, then returned Sydney's stare. "Interesting."

"I saw that look pass between the two of you," Kat said. "What do you know that we don't?"

Sydney filled them in on their husbands' story about Cole McGraw's cheating. "Of course, there's a formal procedure for handling that at the club, but the guys didn't want to push it that far, if they could avoid it."

"Do you think Paul was less forgiving than your husbands?" Kat asked. "If he threatened to formally protest Cole's scores, would that be reason enough to murder him?"

"Could be," Marianne responded, "if more than embarrassment were involved. Like if Cole planned to run for some kind of office. Cheating at golf might not look too good on his resume."

"He already is president of the Springers," Kat said.

Micki made a face and rolled her eyes. "As difficult as it is to get anyone to hold that office, I doubt golf score tampering would get him thrown out."

"I meant something like state representative," Marianne answered. "Anyway, keep his name on the list."

Sydney sat back, folded her hands. "Not bad for one morning's work. We managed to unearth more dirt on Cole McGraw, as well as Paul himself. What next?"

"What do we know about their children?" Marianne asked.

Kat asked, "You think they might be suspects?"

"Her daughter is already here, and the son should be on his way. When we talk to Olivia and if we decide to do this," Syd said, "we can ask about her children then."

They didn't have long to wait. Olivia called while they were still at the sandwich shop and said she and her daughter were back home. She also urged them to hurry, because the sheriff had already called while she was at the funeral home. That was enough to put him off for the moment, but not for long.

Since they didn't have time to prepare any food on their own, they purchased what they could from the sandwich shop to take to the family.

Olivia and Paul had moved into the two-story Mediterranean-style house shortly after the town was established twenty years prior. Though obviously expensive and quite elegant, the furnishings didn't appear to have been updated since then. Mauve and hunter green dominated the color scheme.

A woman Syd didn't recognize answered the door. "Hello?"

"Hi. We play mah jongg with Olivia and thought we'd bring some food by. I was with her yesterday when she got the news about her husband," Sydney said.

"Oh, come in. I think she's expecting you."

All four proceeded to the kitchen to drop off their offerings. A younger version of Olivia sat at the kitchen table going through a photo album. She glanced up at the women's arrival, eyes red.

"Oh, sorry to disturb you," Kat apologized. "We'll just put away our items and leave you alone."

"You're not disturbing me. I haven't seen my father much the last few years, so I was reliving old times through these photos. My mother won't let me do much more to help her. This food is a godsend, since I'm not much of a cook, and I want to make sure she's eating properly. I'm Lilith, by the way. You're…"

Micki took the lead with introductions. "We play mah jongg with your mother and know her from several other groups to which we belong."

The daughter turned her attention to Syd. "I recognize your name." She tapped her chin with her index finger. "I know. You were with Mother when…" Her eyes clouded, and she was unable to finish her thought.

"Yes, that's right. She asked me to go with her while she, uh, dealt with the authorities. Then I brought her home and stayed with her until your neighbor arrived."

"Right. The neighbor on the other side has been here today. They must be communicating on their own, taking turns. They show up, leave, and shortly thereafter, someone else shows up. I thought you were the next in line."

"Your mother is expecting us. How is she doing?"

"Why don't you ask her yourself?" Olivia stood in the doorway, a parody of a smile on her face. Her bun was back, but it looked mussed, and her ivory complexion had gone pale. The stylish dark gray pants, off-white pullover and light gray cardigan could not disguise her strain.

Instinctively, Sydney went to her and offered a brief hug. "We dropped off some food items."

"That's very kind of you all. My daughter-in-law offered to take over the cooking for a few days, but with two toddlers in tow, I'm sure she'll be happy to have some items to fall back on."

"Do you suppose we could all talk in the den I used yesterday?" Sydney asked.

"Follow me," their hostess said.

Chapter Seven

"*I* wasn't sure if you would actually do this," Olivia said once she'd closed the door to the den.

"We're here because I told you we'd come. Whether we continue to look into Paul's death remains to be seen," Sydney replied.

Their hostess lifted a brow. "What does that mean?"

Sydney took a seat, followed by the other three and then Olivia. "Here's what concerns us. We've never done anything like this before. We have limited access to the same evidence the sheriff will be gathering. We don't want to alert anyone else about what we're doing. Those conditions may be beyond our abilities."

"But you're still going to try, aren't you?"

Sydney eyed her three companions before answering. "Yes, we'll give it a try, if you are prepared to let us investigate our way."

Olivia opened her mouth to respond, but Sydney cut her off. "You need to be completely up front and honest with us about your marriage, what you know of Paul's business dealings and his personal relationships. Can you do that?"

"I can't be part of the team?"

"Your role is to let us do the investigating and the interrogating. There may be times when you'll have to gain information for us firsthand, but we'll determine those situations. You are not to do your own investigating. Do you understand that and agree?"

Olivia had taken the office chair behind the massive desk. Now, though, she shot up and leaned across the desk. "I'm supposed to go about my everyday life like nothing has happened and wait for you all to come to me?"

Marianne jumped in for Sydney. "Your everyday life as you knew it no longer exists. Your husband was taken from you in a most violent way. You have no other choice but to be cooperative with the sheriff and his deputies, because you want to find your husband's murderer. To do more than that may raise questions."

Olivia sank back into her chair. "I hear what you're saying, but I'm afraid the sheriff is only going to look as far as me."

"He's a capable man, but he has little experience with murder. He may call in outside help from the state," Kat said.

"Is that a good thing?" Olivia wanted to know.

"It should mean they won't glom onto the first person that comes to mind, the spouse," Micki said, "but it also widens the circle of people getting involved in your private life. That's another reason why you need to remain above this. Let us do the legwork."

Olivia ran both hands through her hair. "I get that, yes. But I want to be kept in the loop."

"Which we'll do as much as possible," Sydney said, "but we're concerned in a moment of panic or frustration with the authorities, you'll let it slip that you've involved us. It's imperative we be able to do our thing unnoticed, because we have a much better chance of learning things that way."

Their hostess folded her hands on the desk, studied them for several beats.

"You could always hire a professional investigator who knows what she's doing," Micki suggested.

Olivia shook her head. "No, I don't want to advertise I have need of someone to prove me innocent. It may come to that, but not now. Let's try it your way." She paused, as if considering what she'd agreed to. "Where do we go from here?"

Sydney took the lead. "Do you have any ideas who might have wanted your husband dead?"

"Paul irritated several people recently, myself included. But wanting him dead? No. Obviously, someone did kill him, but I'm not aware of any threats he received."

"Give us more specifics about the people Paul irritated," Micki said.

Their hostess appeared to go into herself, as if reconstructing a list of her husband's detractors. Unfortunately, the only two she could come up with were the same two they'd already identified, Don Martin and Cole McGraw.

"How much do you know about Paul's business dealings?" Sydney asked.

"I rarely got involved, not that I wouldn't understand things—I have a business degree from Florida State— but he preferred to keep most of that to himself. He retained most of his files here in his office, if you want to see them."

"The sooner the better," Sydney said. "I suspect the authorities will be taking them any time."

Olivia unlocked a couple of filing cabinets off to the side, and Kat, who'd once served as executive assistant to a CEO of a major corporation back in her home state of Illinois, began going through them. The others resumed their questions about the other possible suspects.

"What do you know about the situation with Cole McGraw?" Marianne asked next.

"I only know the name because Paul kept repeating it the night he'd discovered McGraw had been shaving points from his score. Paul might be a ruthless businessman, but he detested cheating. At least at golf. Men are weird like that. A couple of strokes deducted from a score, and they're ready to fight the Crusades. But stepping out on a wife now and then? Not considered cheating, as long as you don't get caught. At least, that's what I suspect he felt."

"We'll come back to that comment later, but first, do you know if Paul did anything about McGraw?" Micki asked.

"He stopped playing with him, but I don't think he brought formal charges at the club. I'm guessing he spread the word in more subtle ways, maybe cost McGraw some business deals. Paul didn't want anything to do with him after that."

Marianne took her turn. "What was the big deal about Paul's missing the church trustee meeting that so incensed Don Martin?"

"From what little Paul told me about that situation, I would've thought Don Martin would have preferred Paul's absence. Paul questioned some expenses that had been approved by Martin. On paper, they apparently looked legitimate, but when Paul pushed for more documentation, Martin dragged his feet."

"You're right, your husband's absence would have worked in Martin's favor," Marianne said.

"Except Martin had been pushing for Paul to increase

our annual contribution to the church. As if we don't already give more than our share. I guess Martin had planned to corner Paul the night Paul didn't show."

The three of them were silent while they each finished their notes. Kat was still busy going through Paul's business files.

"Wouldn't there be copies of recent trustee budget reports in Paul's files?" Kat asked. "If we could find those, maybe we could identify what Paul was questioning."

Sydney played with the idea. "Maybe he even emailed his concerns to Martin.

"I'll turn on the computer," Olivia offered, "but I'm not sure I have the passwords to go further. The same with his phone."

Sydney and Marianne tackled the laptop. Paul had apparently been very careful with securing his private information.

"Don't you use this laptop too?" Marianne asked.

"Well, yes, I have on occasion but not often. When I have used it, I got in through my own passwords."

Sydney released a frustrated sigh. "I don't suppose he kept his passwords in a separate location off his laptop?"

"If he did, I have no idea where. But he tended to write important things in a few notebooks in his desk for easy reference." Paul kept a neat desk, with only his laptop, a few pens, a blank pad of paper and a dictionary resting on its surface. All three drawers on the right were locked, as were two of the three on the left. Only the top left and center drawers were open, and they netted very little.

"Foiled!" Marianne said, the frustration in her tone echoing the disappointment they all were feeling.

"Maybe not," Olivia said. "For as careful as he appeared to be about his private dealings, Paul could also be forgetful. It's possible he kept things like passwords nearby, easy for him to find when he couldn't remember them."

Marianne went to the two open drawers. The center drawer was a jumble of office supplies: pens, pencils, erasers, paperclips of various sizes, and to their delight and hope, several pieces of paper. She dumped them on top of the desk, and both she and Sydney went through them one by one.

"Nothing," Sydney said, finishing her pile.

"Me, either," Marianne added.

Olivia went through both piles herself. "Hmm. That's not like Paul. There must be something somewhere."

Sydney flipped through the dictionary, thinking a loose slip of paper might fall out. Nothing. Not to be defeated, she began looking up specific words: computer, laptop, private. No go.

"Do you suppose he'd go for the obvious?" Olivia asked. "Password."

Sydney went to "password." Nothing. She eyed the rest of the page. There it was, on the facing page, just a little less obvious.

She tried the code on the laptop and it immediately opened. She glanced at Olivia. "Good guess."

Sydney, with Marianne and Olivia looking on over her shoulders, did a search of emails sent to "Don Martin." Several notes popped up in the queue. She went to the earliest and pulled it up. Just a confirmation of an upcoming board meeting.

She went through a few more. Not much of interest until she landed on one from the previous month. "Don, going over church budget update from last month. What is the Seiler Corporation?" A week later, a similar note appeared. "Don, haven't received your response to my question last week about Seiler Corporation. Internet search nets nothing."

"Seiler Corporation?" Marianne repeated. "Did Paul ever mention them to you, Olivia? Or suggest he was having difficulty getting a response from Don Martin?"

"Paul rarely shared any of his dealings with me," Olivia said. "Even those concerning our church, but now that I think about it, he insinuated something about Don as we were leaving the Springers' monthly dinner last week." She stood, rubbed her chin. "I'm trying to recall his exact words. Something about Don's time on the board being limited, if not his time as a free man."

"That sounds ominous," Sydney said. "Did he elaborate?"

Olivia shook her head. "No. I tried to follow up, but he just brushed it off. Said, 'Never mind.' He used that phrase with me a lot lately. Seems like we shared so little in recent years."

Sydney considered pursuing the comment but decided to leave it alone. She suspected Olivia hadn't realized what she'd said and, if questioned about it, would back away. Better to wait until they gathered more information about Paul Schwimmer's life on their own.

Sydney searched Paul's email inbox. "The only thing here from Don Martin must have been sent the day after the last board meeting, because he's asking Paul why he didn't attend."

Sydney furrowed her brow. "That's strange. Don apparently didn't respond to Paul's emails about this Seiler group, but the minute Paul didn't show for a meeting, Don followed up."

Olivia swathed a hand through her hair. "That is strange. Paul missed several board meetings during the last year, supposedly due to schedule conflicts, but I don't recall Don ever checking up before. Or anyone else on the board, for that matter."

"Do you think this note is significant?" Micki asked.

Olivia's forehead crinkled. "Possibly. But even if it is, what can we do about it?"

Sydney pursed her lips. "For now, all we can do is take note of it. But it certainly doesn't eliminate Don Martin as a suspect."

"What about Paul's church board files on the computer?" Marianne asked.

"Can't find a folder specifically for the church board," Sydney said.

"Do a search of his email files, then," Marianne replied. "Who's the board secretary, Olivia?"

"Corinne Weller."

Sydney keyed in the information. "Nothing under her name. Let me try the church's name." The few seconds before the laptop responded seemed like an eternity. "Damn. Nothing." Sydney stared at the computer screen. "This doesn't make sense. Either Paul moved anything he received from the board secretary to a separate folder named something else or someone or some other entity was sending the board info. Or Paul deleted all board communications. Not likely."

Marianne, the closest they had to a computer guru, returned to the list of email folders. "There's got to be something in here he used for board communications." She ran her finger down the list. "It's all so general. Family. Business. Hobbies. Miscellaneous."

"Wait. Back up," Olivia said. "Check out 'Hobbies.' Paul had to be talked into serving on the board. When they finally convinced him to participate, he offhandedly referred to it as his new *hobby*."

Marianne discovered three sub-lists when she clicked

on Hobbies. "I don't see anything that sounds like a church board here. Bridge. Golf. Tennis."

Olivia leaned over her shoulder. "He's never played bridge. Wait. Our church is located on Bridge Street."

Sydney, who'd traded places on the computer with Marianne, now leaned over her other shoulder. "That could be it!"

"It's locked. We need a password," Marianne said.

"Try the one we used before," Sydney said.

"No luck."

"Where's that dictionary?" Sydney asked. Marianne shoved it across the desk top to her. Sydney turned to the B section. "Okay, here's 'bridge.' Nothing. Same as before. No entries on either of these two pages."

Kat joined them. "How about 'church' or 'board'?

"No."

"Trinity. That's the name of our church," Olivia said.

"Bingo," Marianne said. The password worked. "We've struck pay dirt, ladies. All the board minutes for the last several months are here, and there's a separate section for various reports, including the financials."

Sydney turned to the widow. "With the sheriff on the way, I'd like to send myself copies of as much of this as I can in the next few minutes."

Olivia bit a lip. "All of that? I know you need to go through it with more time than you have now, but it's confidential."

"We'll respect that as much as we can. If we find something that has to come out, we'll let it come through you, if possible, since as his heir you'd have access to it." She wasn't sure of the legality of her assurance, but the information in these documents could be what Olivia needed to clear her name.

Olivia took a few seconds to consider, then agreed.

"I'll do it," Marianne said. "I'm probably faster at this than the rest of you." Without waiting for consensus, she started typing. "I've deleted the note I sent to Sydney with the files attached from this computer," she said once she'd finished. "Any IT person could probably find it, but they'd have to be looking for it first."

"You're probably ready to talk about me as a suspect," Olivia said when their eyes all found her again.

"Tell us why you think you are and why you think the sheriff might stop looking once he gets to you," Sydney said.

Before she began, Olivia raised her shoulders and took a breath. "I believe Paul was cheating on me. How do I know? Mainly suspicions. He'd be gone on business several nights in a row, like the night he missed the church trustee meeting. In the past, he usually finished his business on the road in one or two nights. In the last few years, he was frequently gone an average of three nights a week."

"Did you ever attempt to verify his whereabouts?" Sydney asked. It was a difficult question to ask, but they needed to know.

"A couple times. I called the places he told me he'd be staying. He was always checked in, but that didn't mean he was there."

"Then why…" Marianne pursued.

"Why did I assume he wasn't there? Because someone would mention seeing him in town on one of those days. Usually very innocent comments, but after I'd heard these comments more than twice, I began to wonder."

"Did you ever confront him?" Micki asked.

"I never had any hard evidence, and I didn't want to make an issue until my suspicions would stick. To be honest, I didn't want to disturb my comfortable lifestyle.

Paul's money came from the family wealth. I might have gotten my fair share in a divorce, but I wasn't ready to fight him."

"Did you ever have him followed?"

"No. I considered it, more than once. But like I said, I was a coward."

That statement put an end to follow-up questions. An awkward silence ensued.

"You see why I'm the most likely suspect. I had the most to gain by his death," Olivia said, as if she could tolerate the silence no longer.

Kat was the first to speak. "In your mind, perhaps. But other than to us, have you voiced these concerns to anyone else? Your children, perhaps?"

"No. Like I said, I couldn't prove anything. We'd grown apart. Although we still slept in the same bed, we rarely had relations any more. I've not told the kids that, although I think they may suspect."

"This next question is prying but necessary," Sydney said. "How does his will provide for you and the children?"

Olivia considered. "My children and I meet with the lawyer the day after the funeral, but I already know most of it. I inherit this house, our bank accounts and all liquid assets and any holdings other than the Schwimmer land. The children inherit equal ownership in it, although decision-making authority goes to Donovan, as the male child. So sexist. There's probably a copy of the will somewhere in those files, so you can see for yourselves."

Marianne put into words what Sydney had been thinking. "In other words, you stand to gain quite a bit. Which could be viewed as a powerful motive for murder, if it appeared that situation might be about to change."

"You mean, if a divorce was in the works?" Olivia asked.

"Right. But if no one else suspected he was messing around, divorce wouldn't be likely," Micki said.

"Unless he promised his mistress it was," Olivia added.

The three of them exchanged a look, joined by Kat over at the files. Sydney put their thought into words. "This is the first time you've mentioned he was cheating with one person in particular."

Olivia offered them a wide-eyed expression. "There's a difference?"

"Uh, yes," Marianne replied. "Cheating with anyone he happened to hook up with would be considered one thing. The man couldn't keep his business in his pants. But a mistress says he'd moved on to someone else. Someone who might be entertaining hopes of replacing the current Mrs. Schwimmer. You."

"Oh," was all Olivia could utter.

She really hadn't perceived the difference? They seemed to have gone as far as they could at the moment. Sydney said as much to Olivia and the rest. "We'll look into the information you've given us today and will get back to you in a day or so. Let us know immediately what the sheriff asks and takes from your home as evidence. Do you have an attorney yet?"

No, she hadn't had time to even consider the need for one. Should she find someone?

"As soon as you can," Micki advised. "Be prepared. If you don't know of anyone, try Colette Brownley. She's a defense attorney I interviewed for an article I wrote on women in law."

"Okay. Thanks," Olivia replied.

One more thought occurred to Kat as they prepared to leave. "We'd like to talk to your children while they're still in town to get their read on what happened to their father. They may have noticed more than you think. You need to be prepared for their observations."

"I hadn't thought of that. Yes, I guess it's okay to talk to them. But won't you have to tell them what you're doing? You said you wanted to keep your role quiet."

"Not if we approached them as friends who are concerned about how you're faring."

"All right, then."

All right, indeed. They'd made progress with this meeting. They still had no particularly great candidate as murderer, but they'd learned a lot more about Paul Schwimmer, the man.

One item still bothered Sydney. She asked the others to wait in the living room while she talked in private with Olivia.

While Olivia seemed taken off guard by the request, Sydney struck with the question she'd been wanting to ask since the day before. "If we are to eliminate you as a suspect, I need to know about the blood on the jacket sleeve you wore yesterday."

"Blood?" Olivia appeared to be unaware of what could have been telltale evidence. Or she'd been ready for this question.

"As soon as you got home, you took a shower and shed the clothing you'd been wearing. When I went to pick up the pile of discarded clothes, you told me not to, but not before I saw a splotch of red on the sleeve."

"Oh, that. Strawberry jelly from the stuffed doughnut I had at the coffee shop. Dripped on my jacket before I realized there was another hole in the doughnut."

Plausible, although Olivia was usually so fastidious, it didn't strike Sydney she would be so messy with her food. "Could we see it?" Olivia's response could be telling.

"Sorry. Lilith and I dropped it off at the dry cleaner on the way to the funeral home." Her smile didn't waver.

It would be just like the woman to address stains on her clothes immediately, even in the midst of funeral arrangements. On the other hand, if it was blood, even if it wasn't Paul's, she'd be just as anxious to remove it. Net result: That niggling doubt still remained. "Oh," was about all Sydney could reply.

She and Olivia were just rejoining the others when the doorbell rang. The sheriff. The four investigators clustered together in the living room. They couldn't very well leave without him noticing them, so the best they could do was appear to have stopped by to check on Olivia.

Though an eyebrow lifted slightly when he noticed them, Sheriff Rick Formero quickly regained his composure. "Ladies? Didn't expect Mrs. Schwimmer to have company."

"They stopped by after you called, Sheriff," Olivia said. "We play mah jongg together, and they wanted to see how I was doing. They were just leaving."

"Right," Micki said, edging toward the front door.

Marianne took Olivia's hand. "Call us if you need anything."

Kat hugged Olivia.

Sydney pulled up last. "Sheriff," she said as she went by him.

The four made their way to the car at a slower pace than usual, attempting to appear nonchalant yet relieved to have completed the social call.

Chapter Eight

No one spoke until Sydney, who was driving, turned the corner. "That was close," Micki said, her breath coming in gulps.

"He couldn't possibly suspect we were there for any reason other than to check on Olivia," Marianne said.

"Can we go to your place, Kat?" Syd asked. "We have a lot to process, and I don't want Trip walking in on us at our house."

"First, tell us why you pulled Olivia aside when we left the office," Marianne said.

Though she wasn't totally convinced by Olivia's explanation of the stain, Syd didn't want to weaken the others' belief in the woman's innocence. Not at this point, anyhow. Plus, Olivia's reason for the stain was at least plausible. Now that they'd all committed to this clandestine investigation, she owed her friends the truth, so she recounted seeing the splotch on Olivia's jacket and Olivia's response. Nonetheless, she didn't mention the tiny doubt that still lingered in her own mind.

The others appeared to accept her account.

"How many computers do we have with us so we can split the task of reviewing the files? Kat asked.

"Mine is here in the car," Sydney replied.

"I brought my digital reader with me," Micki added.

Marianne grimaced. "I could run home and get mine. Wish I'd thought to bring it."

"No need. I've got a laptop and desktop," Kat told them. "We should be fine.

Once settled in the office of Kat's mansion, they switched on their devices but turned first to their meeting with Olivia. "While it's fresh in our minds, let's list what we learned today," Sydney said. "I'll start. We have her permission to contact her kids, although we'll have to couch that in terms similar to what I proposed. Concern for her. We've already met the daughter, Lilith. I didn't pick up any bad vibes between the two or on her part alone. The son and his family should be there by now. Maybe one or more of us could take in the visitation and talk to the kids then."

"You and I can't go, Syd," Marianne said. "We're attending the high school play with our husbands tomorrow night."

"I can go," Kat volunteered. "Want to go with me, Mick?"

"Sure," Micki replied.

Sydney turned to Kat. "With that settled, let's talk about Paul's files. What did you find, Kat? Anything of note?"

"Only had enough time to scan the contents, although I did locate his business receipts for the current year. Focused only on motels and hotels. There were several for three-day stays, but that doesn't tell us anything. He could have paid a day ahead and snuck back to town, or someone could've joined him for part or all of his hotel stay. They were all for king-size beds."

Sydney let out a big sigh. "Darn! I don't know what I

was hoping you'd find. Especially with so little time. I doubt we'll get another chance to see his files."

Marianne consulted the pad of paper she'd used to take notes. "The only other item I've got here is that what she told us about Don Martin and Cole McGraw matched up with our findings. Nothing new."

Kat held up a hand. "Wait. There was one new item concerning Martin. He was pushing Paul to up his financial support of the church. That could mean something."

"Too bad we don't know anyone else on that board who could shed some light on that point," Micki put in.

Marianne shook her head. "If the church is in need of money, I doubt if anyone on that board would tell us until they're ready to admit as much to their congregation."

"Suppose it's more than expenses outrunning revenue?" Sydney said. "Olivia told us Paul questioned some expenditures Martin had approved. Could he have been using church money for his own purposes?"

"That's a pretty serious allegation," Micki returned.

Sydney tapped her pen against her notepad. "Supposition only. Say Martin had major bills he couldn't pay. Maybe he used church money, relying on Paul's increased contribution to cover it."

"Then he had to get rid of Paul before the missing money came to light," Kat speculated.

Sydney chewed through her theory. Did it hold water? "What a paradox. Martin needed Paul's money, but he didn't need Paul pushing to know more about the expenditures." Then an idea came to her. "Say Martin followed Paul on his walk so he could make his play for the money. But Paul was having none of it, not only refusing to up his donation but also guessing Martin had used church funds for his own purposes. Martin had to shut him down. Immediately. Without thinking it through, he grabbed a log or a rock and bashed in Paul's head."

"That could be it!" Marianne said.

"Sure worth pursuing further," Micki added.

The review of the board of trustees' files went quickly once the documents had been split four ways. Micki received all the minutes for the last year. The financial reports were divvied up amongst Sydney, Marianne and Kat.

"So far, they've hardly mentioned the budget at all in the minutes," Micki said. "But I've only read through the first two months."

"Here's something we didn't know," Kat said, sitting forward. "Don Martin apparently was serving as church treasurer a year ago when this report was prepared. I wonder if the board appoints its own treasurer rather than assigning that role to another church member."

Sydney glanced up from the report she and Marianne were studying. "He also signed as treasurer on this report four months ago."

"Does that mean he was the one paying the bills?"

"Let me check the church's policies and procedures manual. I think I saw it on the church's website," Sydney said. "Ah, here's what we're seeking. Bill paying from the central budget is done by the office staff for ongoing building and program expenses previously approved by the board. The treasurer must sign off on anything outside the list of approved items or above the approved amount."

Marianne put down her cookie. "In other words, the treasurer has a lot of discretion."

Kat gazed up from her computer. "It's at least possible for Don Martin to have redirected funds."

Micki harrumphed. "Embezzled, you mean." Having made that pronouncement, she and the others went back to perusing their respective documents. "Oh-oh. I'm back in June, halfway through their fiscal year. Don Martin noted that, although the overall year-to-date expenses were well over half the budgeted amount, the board shouldn't be alarmed. That was typical. Several annual bills come due the first three months of the year."

Kat nodded. "He's right. I'm going over the June financial report now. I see what he meant. Operational expenses are at seventy percent."

Sydney pulled her paper and pen closer. "How much would that twenty percent overage be in actual dollars?"

Kat screwed up her face, doing the math. "Just under two hundred thousand."

"That's a few pennies," Micki said.

"I'm skimming through the list of individual checks issued. Hold up, here's the first reference I've seen to the Seiler Corporation. That's the one Paul questioned, right? There's a check here for five thousand five hundred dollars."

"Not huge but still significant," Sydney said. "What's it for?"

"Miscellaneous supplies," Kat replied.

Marianne sat back in her chair. "Possible. They might be gearing up for the fall program, or there could have been a mid-year sale. These reports don't seem to include individual receipts. Are they retained separately?"

"There's probably a ledger somewhere," Kat said. "Most likely electronic, these days, but the receipts would have been scanned into it."

Sydney blew out a breath. "We can only drill down this far."

"Do we have enough to make a convincing case that

Martin is a suspect?" Marianne asked.

"Let's keep going to see if there are further comments in their meeting notes and pay particular attention to the financial reports for the last few months," Kat said.

A half hour later, they'd found more. Expenditures in other line items, supplies, programs, and communications, increased beyond projections. Operational expenses had reached eighty-five percent by the most recent month, with four months to go before the end of the fiscal year. But no mention or concern was made of the potential problem until two months ago, when Paul Schwimmer raised the question. Even then, he simply asked, he didn't accuse. But Seiler Corporation continued to receive payments each month in increasing amounts, the most recent being ten thousand three hundred. In all, the Seiler payments totaled twenty-nine thousand eight hundred. The group also identified two other entities that were receiving payments well beyond the budgeted amounts.

"If we add these three together, figuring they're all questionable, we've got well over fifty thousand dollars," Kat said.

"That should be enough to spark the sheriff's interest," Sydney said.

"Now what do we do?" Micki asked.

The four exchanged glances. Marianne shrugged.

Sydney took the lead. "Find more suspects. Except before I agreed to help Olivia, I committed my time to Trip tonight and tomorrow. To help with his follies."

"Follies? Is that what he's calling it now?" Marianne asked.

Sydney made a face. "No. That's my name. Or attitude. I don't know why this latest project is getting under my skin, since it's keeping him occupied and happy. He's even been whistling lately. It just seems so unlike my husband to produce such a big extravaganza."

Kat studied her. "Has he asked you to do anything yet? Sing, dance, costumes, whatever?"

"Other than act as his personal assistant, which I'm resisting, no."

"He, uh, approached me yesterday about singing," Kat said.

That was news. But then, it shouldn't surprise her. Everyone in town knew about Kat's voice.

"Uh, he asked me to be part of a dance ensemble," Micki added. "He wanted me to direct the group, but I begged off."

The involvement of her friends was starting to get serious. Sydney turned to Marianne.

Marianne raised her hands, palms out. "Don't look at me."

Sydney shrugged it off. "He knows I'd say no to any kind of performing."

"Really?" Micki asked. "Didn't you learn how to tap dance last winter?"

"Not with three lessons. But don't worry about me. If I know my husband, there'll be some crisis I'll have to handle before the show opens. Meanwhile, this case is more than enough for me to get my arms around."

Marianne shot her a tolerant smile. "Case? You're now calling it that, like we're real investigators?"

Sydney waved away the comment. "First word that came to mind."

"I rather like it," Kat said.

Chapter Nine

Marianne's occasional bout of tendonitis in her foot chose the day of the funeral to reappear. She hated how vulnerable it made her, but she wasn't about to stay home. With the help of Beau's arm, painkillers and an ankle wrap, she made it through the service, although she stayed in their car for the trip to the cemetery. At the reception, she hobbled to a seat and stayed there the rest of the time, gathering information solely from passersby and observation.

Olivia's daughter, Lilith, had called Sydney at the last minute and asked her to serve at the reception, because one of the family friends had come down with a bad cold.

"The family really appreciates your doing this," Lilith said as she assigned Sydney to the chair where coffee was poured. "Here's an apron to protect your skirt, but be careful you don't splash your blouse. I love that color of blue."

"If I do, I'll have to get the name of the dry cleaner you and your mother went to the other day."

Lilith looked confused. "Excuse me? You must have heard wrong. We didn't stop at a dry cleaner. Maybe

Mother went on her own, although she's hardly left the house except to visit the funeral home."

Olivia had lied to her. It didn't mean she was guilty, but Sydney's faith in the woman slipped. "I guess like you suggested, I heard wrong."

Since Sydney was occupied at the beverage table and Marianne was temporarily disabled, Kat and Micki had to do reconnaissance, like they had the night before at the visitation. Fortunately, that worked well. Kat was a great listener, once she got people talking, which was the key. Micki was great at asking questions but had difficulty remembering everything she heard. Together, they were dynamite; separate, not so much.

Kat was seated alone at a table when the sheriff joined her. Her hands began to perspire. What was with that? Was she afraid he knew about their investigative efforts...or was something else afoot? "Sad day," she said, unable to think of anything else to say.

"Yes. Very sad," the sheriff answered.

"Did you know the family?"

"Not well. I don't play golf. Occasionally the local water board asks me to appear. He was on that, since this land originally belonged to his family."

Kat arrived in Serendipity Springs long after the Schwimmer family had sold some of their land to the developer, but occasionally she'd come upon a reference to the long-ago transfer of ownership. "That's right. I'd forgotten. This town used to be an orange grove, right?"

"Family still owns land nearby. Where the springs are located. Although they don't control the water rights, they hold a lot of clout on the water board."

"I don't know much about that group. What do they do?" she asked, at the risk of appearing too interested.

He leaned his head to the side, took several bites of his

finger sandwich and returned his gaze to her. "Haven't heard you sing much lately. When's your next gig?"

In other words, he wasn't about to share any more info. Wait. He knew about her musical career. Had he been in the audience? She didn't recall seeing him, but then, she didn't pay much attention to who was in the room. If she did, she'd lose focus. "As a matter of fact, I'll be appearing this Saturday night at the hotel downtown. And I'm also part of the show Trip Bonner is producing for the Men's Club. Are you part of that venture, Sheriff?"

"Rick. No, I can't sing or dance. But if he needs someone for security, I'll help. That is, if we've got this Schwimmer thing wrapped by then." Once again, he cocked his head. "Speaking of which, I probably should be getting back to work. I came as a private citizen to show my respect, but the best thing I can do for the family right now is find out who killed Paul."

"How's that coming?" She couldn't resist asking.

He pulled a blank expression. "Can't say much. Mainly gathering intel at the moment. How 'bout you?"

She struggled to keep her expression neutral. Was he on to them already? "Me?"

"Right. By your presence at the family home the other day, I thought you were a close friend of the Schwimmers. Should I be interviewing you?"

She released her breath slowly. "I play mah jongg with Olivia. That's all. I'm here to support her. I hardly knew Paul."

"Had to ask." He rose to leave. "I'll try to be there Saturday night."

"Oh. Great." News flash. He seemed to be genuinely interested in her music. Go figure. She studied his lengthy stride as he made his way across the room and out the door. Too bad his jacket covered his butt. How old was he, anyhow? His salt and pepper hair and weathered face and hands suggested he was closer to her age than she had thought. Maybe sixty? Perhaps the internet would provide a bio.

Across the room, Micki faced her own salt and pepper situation, as she fought not to cough after a bite of what she thought was coleslaw.

"Micki, are you okay?" Bitsy Melzer from mah jongg stuck a glass of water in front of her. "Here, drink this. I haven't touched it."

Micki did as directed, took a few cautious sips.

Bitsy leaned in. "You sampled some of Candy Carruthers' coleslaw, didn't you?"

Though still reviving, Micki attempted speech. "Bite." Candy Carruthers? As in wife of Hanes Carruthers, the rancher?

"That's all it takes. Sorry, somehow the dish got past me. It's taken care of now, but I wasn't sure who all took some before its, uh, removal."

Micki sipped more water. "This isn't the first time?"

"Oh, no. Candy means well. She lives out on their ranch and doesn't get into town much, but to support her husband, she attends events like this every so often. This is her *signature* dish. I got to know who she was when I nearly choked a while back, so I've made it my business to get rid of the contents before her food ever hits the serving table. I don't want her to be embarrassed, but I don't want her to unintentionally kill someone either."

"Why don't you just tell her not to bring the concoction?"

"Probably should, but I don't want to risk offending her husband." Bitsy sent a quick glance over her shoulder. "Word has it Paul and Hanes went to school together before Serendipity Springs existed. Their families barely got along, because Paul's were into growing oranges and the Hanes people ranched. Even though the springs were located on the Schwimmer property, Hanes' grandfather somehow managed to finagle water rights for a period that's about to end in a few years."

Micki silently thanked the salt- and pepper-wielding Candy for inadvertently sending Bitsy and her font of knowledge in her direction. She'd heard about Hanes Carruthers' powerful reputation but had never met the man.

They reconvened at Sydney's house after the reception. Kat and Micki helped Marianne make her way from the car to Sydney's house while Syd ran ahead to open the door. To her surprise, they were not alone. Trip stood in the middle of the living room holding a flimsy paper pamphlet.

"Just in time," he said. "We could use someone else's interpretation of these instructions."

The "we" referred to himself and Beau. At least, that's who Sydney thought the body encased in the box was. "Is that what I think it is, the old saw-the-woman-in-half trick? Only in this case the woman is Beau, and he still appears to be in one piece, although it's hard to tell with his legs and arms dangling like that."

"Beau? What are you doing in there?" Marianne asked as Micki and Kat helped her into the room.

"Yeah, it's me. Remind me never to agree to help this guy with his stupid magic tricks again."

Sydney retrieved the slender book from her husband's

hands. A manual. She read the title. "Since when have you been dabbling in magic, Trip? Is this for your follies?"

"Is that your word for it now? Not bad. It appears the town's various organizations are taking their own sweet time deciding they want to be part of our program. Thought I should find a backup."

"Magic?" Marianne asked, her voice going well beyond its normal alto range. "You couldn't just tell jokes or show a movie or something?"

Trip clapped his hands together. "Tell jokes. Great idea, Marianne. Wish that had occurred to me before I rented this contraption."

"I wish you'd thought of it before you convinced me to get into it," Beau replied. "Get me out of here before I get claustrophobic."

"You can't get claustrophobic if your head and limbs aren't confined," Trip said.

Even though she was temporarily disabled, Marianne didn't wait for Trip's help before she grabbed what appeared to be a door on the upper half of the apparatus and yanked. "It's stuck. How do we open this, Trip?"

Sydney's spouse took a few steps back and avoided the others' stares.

"Trip? Answer her," Sydney said. "Wait, is that the problem? It's stuck?"

Her husband still didn't answer but instead grabbed the manual from her hands and flipped through several pages.

Sensing her man would be no help until he found something in the book, Sydney checked with the others. "Any of you ever operated one of these?" She felt around underneath the edge of the door, seeking a release of some sort, but came up short.

Micki joined her. "I was once in Beau's position for my

sorority's talent night, but all I had to do was lie there and smile. And not panic."

"Did you get stuck?" Marianne asked.

"Uh, no. Now I wish I'd volunteered to be his assistant rather than the victim, uh, participant. I might have learned how the trick worked."

While this discussion had been going on, Kat was on her phone. "I've been searching the internet for how this works. It says there's usually a latch somewhere near the top, so the magician can easily access it."

"Found it," Sydney said. Within seconds, the top door sprung open.

Micki located another latch near the bottom with a similar result. "Uh, Beau? Why did you stick your feet through these holes down here?"

By now, Beau, who was almost as tall as Trip and twenty pounds heavier, had sat up inside the box and was attempting to remove said feet. "That's where they go."

"Uh, no," Kat said. "According to this article, as soon as the participant gets inside the box, they stick a fake pair of feet out, and their feet go down under the top part of the box."

"I saw that opening, but there's no way the bottom part of my body would fit there."

"That's because this box is intended for a female," Sydney said, reading a label inside the box.

By now, with Micki's assistance, Beau was making his way out of the device, albeit with little grace. "Are you kidding me? Trip, you could've killed me if you'd attempted to saw me in half with my actual legs sticking out. You so owe me." He glanced around. No Trip. "Where is he anyhow?"

"As soon as that bottom door flipped open, he was out of here," Micki said.

"After cajoling and begging me to do this for him?" Beau was incredulous. He barreled toward the door. "Excuse me, ladies. I have to see a man about a debt he owes me. Big time." Then he remembered Marianne. "You okay, hon?"

Marianne gave him a tolerant nod from the chair where she had gone to sit. "I'm fine. I'll catch a ride home from someone here. Go settle things with Trip."

As soon as they heard the backdoor slamming, Kat looked at Sydney. "What do you make of that? Do we have the beginnings of a raging feud on our hands?"

"With those two?" Sydney shook her head, offered a rueful smile. "I doubt it. Once Beau has vented, Trip will apologize, take him out for drinks and, before Beau knows it, he'll have agreed to an even crazier scheme for the follies. That sound about right, Marianne?"

Marianne scrunched up her forehead, considering. "I don't know. It was bad enough to get stuck in a box never intended for a man his size, but for all four of us to witness his humiliation, it might cost Trip a little more to make things right."

"Like two drinks?" Micki suggested.

Marianne offered a sly smile. "Maybe, but I'm thinking there may be a new putter in my husband's future."

Syd led them to the kitchen, where she plated a box of cookies and started the coffeemaker. She didn't know about the others, but she had been too busy serving at the reception to eat.

Once they were all seated, Micki was the first to report. "Attending last night's visitation was a good idea. Something's going on with the son, Donovan. At least he didn't behave like his father had been killed."

"How did he act?" Marianne asked. Kat answered for Micki as she selected a cookie. "For one thing, he stood apart from his mother, sister and the other relatives at the visitation."

"Was his wife with him?" Sydney asked.

"Not that we could tell. Probably stayed at Olivia's house with the kids," Kat responded.

"He spent his time joking with a bunch of other guys who looked to be his age. Like this was some sort of reunion rather than a visitation."

"Maybe that's how he's processing his grief," Marianne suggested.

"Some grief," Micki said. "I wouldn't be surprised if they were sneaking hooch from a hidden flask. Or sharing a joint, although I didn't see anything pass between them. They were laughing, slapping each other on the back. Stuff like that."

Sydney put down her half-eaten second cookie. "Were you able to talk to him?"

"Just because we knew you'd ask," Kat said, "yes, we did. We introduced ourselves as mah jongg friends of his mother, then offered our sympathies. He broke away from his buddies long enough to thank us for coming. Just as Micki and I decided he'd said about as much as we'd get from him, he asked if we'd seen much of his mother lately. Before we could respond, he inquired whether we'd noticed anything strange about her behavior."

"We played dumb. Told him we hadn't noticed anything except her competitiveness," Micki supplied.

"He didn't need to know how competitive," Kat added.

"How did he react?" Marianne asked.

"Surprised," Kat answered. "But he didn't push it."

"Probably wanted to get back to his friends," Marianne surmised.

Micki scrunched up her eyes. "Not immediately. He started to say something, I'm guessing to challenge our response, but stopped. Like what we'd said fit some private thought he kept to himself, because he didn't pursue his question. Merely thanked us again for coming and gave us a look that said we could now leave him alone."

Marianne waved a hand in front of Sydney. "You're staring into space. What are you thinking?"

"I'm trying to remember how long Olivia has been playing with us. More than a year but not quite two."

"I'm guessing around eighteen months. Does it matter?" Kat asked.

"Maybe. Maybe not," Sydney replied. "Olivia's been competitive ever since she joined us. But if that description didn't wash with her son, something changed in the last two years or so. I'm guessing her son has picked up on it. If not the competitiveness, something different in her personality."

"Keep talking like that, Syd, and Olivia will land exactly where she's trying to avoid, topping the list of suspects," Micki said.

That's what concerned Sydney. Olivia's explanation of the "blood" on her sleeve was a little too pat, but she couldn't accept that Olivia would want the four of them sticking their noses into her private life if she really had killed her husband. Sydney finished her third cookie, not the least bit ashamed of her sudden gluttony. "What you've reported seems to suggest a major change in Olivia's life in recent years. The most likely cause would be her relationship with Paul."

When they'd exhausted the topic of Donovan Schwimmer, Micki moved on to her next discovery. "I may have come across another suspect, quite by accident." She related her experience nearly choking on Candy Carruthers' dish. "Ironic," she mused, "Bitsy came to my aid with a glass of water, and water seems to have been a point of contention between Paul Schwimmer and the rancher."

"Paul sat on the area water board," Kat said. "I haven't had time yet to research what all they do, but it seems to be a pretty important body."

"How did you happen upon that tidbit?" Marianne asked.

"The sheriff joined me at my table and told me."

"You learned all this from Sheriff Formero?" Sydney asked, amazed the law enforcement officer had been willing to share anything about the victim.

Kat pursed her lips, stared at her hands. "Uh, yes. From Rick. Sheriff Rick Formero."

"You're on a first-name basis with the man?" Marianne's voice rose.

"He was there in a suit, not his uniform," Kat said, her tone defensive. "As a private citizen, he goes by his first name. That's all."

"That's all?" Micki asked. "Without trying, you've gotten us an in."

"I did?" Kat gazed from Sydney to Marianne to Micki, seeking explanation. Then her unwitting accomplishment sank in. "I did, didn't I?" She chuckled, then relayed the rest of her conversation with the peace officer. "He likes my singing. Can you believe it?"

The other three exchanged glances. "You're a great songstress, Kat. Even sheriffs recognize talent."

Marianne glanced up from her notes. "It appears we have at least three more areas to research. Who are Hanes and Candy Carruthers? What's with their water rights agreement? And what has been going on with the water board?"

Who knew when they agreed to help Olivia their efforts would involve so much time on the internet?

Chapter Ten

They met for breakfast at the coffee shop to exchange their findings. It was the first time Sydney had been there since the day of Paul's death, but with their current task in mind, she was able to get past that.

Syd drove Marianne, who was still limping but had shed the ankle wrap.

Micki tore in at the last minute, fanning herself before she sipped the hot coffee Sydney had waiting for her. "Thanks," she said, after a couple of gulps. "I need this. I think I struck pay dirt."

"With the Carruthers?" Marianne asked.

"With Hanes Carruthers, anyhow. Bottom line? If he loses his water rights, he'll have to haul in water from elsewhere, a very expensive proposition for a man who's already overextended. That last part is the reason why I was late. I called one of the contacts I use for the financial op-ed pieces I freelance. She didn't want to talk on the phone or email. Had to meet in person for breakfast."

"She confirmed Carruthers's business problems?" Sydney asked.

"Not exactly. She was speculating based on a few items she's heard from various sources. For instance, he's selling off a few hundred acres of the ranch. Not prime land for cattle-raising purposes but near the state highway. Also, some of Candy's jewelry has made its way to a private broker. Just a few pieces, but as a whole, worth almost a quarter of a million."

Kat considered. "Interesting. Not enough to confirm, but it certainly suggests they have financial problems to a certain degree."

"How does Paul's death help Carruthers with his water rights? Won't he still have to deal with whoever takes over the reins of the family business?" Sydney asked. "There's still no guarantee, with Paul out of the way, his replacement would be kinder."

"That makes sense, logically," Micki said. "But Paul's death wasn't planned. It has all the appearance of being spur of the moment, like you suggested with Don Martin, Syd. Whoever killed Paul Schwimmer must have approached him out on that trail, and Paul's lack of empathy incensed them so much they struck out without thinking."

"A possibility," Marianne said. "A template we should apply to everyone else on our list as well."

Sydney considered. "I can see Cole McGraw or Don Martin or now, Hanes Carruthers pursuing him around the lake path, confronting him over whatever issues they had with him and arguing. But letting their anger get out of hand so much they struck him and left him for dead, I don't know. They may all be volatile types, but irresponsibly violent?"

Kat advanced another theory. "I suppose either of his kids, for reasons we've yet to uncover, could have picked a fight with him away from the house. But kill their own father? Even if they had words with him, would they run away? That's horrible. Guess we need to dig deeper there, just to find motives."

"That leaves Olivia," Marianne said. "From what we know at the moment, she had the strongest reason for killing him, although there's the mistress. If she even exists."

"Which is why she wants us to prove she didn't kill him," Sydney said.

Micki rubbed her jaw. "At least we have a framework to share with her."

"You think we should tell her about everything we've learned so far?" Kat asked.

Sydney finished off the last of her sweet roll. "Still debating. I'd rather we question her more than reveal too much of what we've discovered."

"Because she could actually be the murderer?" Marianne asked.

"More like I prefer we not plant any suggestions. Any information we draw from her should be based on her firsthand knowledge."

Micki used the tip of her index finger to pick up muffin crumbs on her plate. "Plus, we can't just come right out and ask if she thinks either of her kids has a motive for wanting their father dead."

"Good point, Mick," Kat said. "So how do we find out more about the kids?"

"We may have lost our chance with both children, if they already returned home after the funeral," Sydney said. "Hopefully, one or both have remained in town for a few days, so she won't be alone. If that isn't the case, perhaps her cronies at mah jongg have learned a few things about the kids over the past months."

"You know what I think?" Kat didn't wait for a

response. "We take the rest of the day off and let our brains chill. Then tomorrow we play mah jongg."

"That's right. I've lost track of time. Can you believe this has all happened in just the last week?" Marianne asked.

"Do you think Olivia will be there?" Micki asked.

"Surely she won't venture out socially this soon," Sydney said.

Micki touched Sydney's forearm. "But if she's not there, maybe the others will loosen up and talk."

"You mean gossip?" Sydney interpreted.

Micki nodded. "Exactly. Just what we need. Maybe someone knows something about an affair."

<hr>

As anticipated, Olivia did not show up for mah jongg the next day. By prior agreement, the four amateur sleuths did not play together but instead filled in at other tables, including the table with the three women with whom Olivia typically played. With Olivia absent and Paul's death and funeral so recent, his passing was bound to be the topic du jour, so the four of them decided to take advantage of the situation.

Sydney drew Olivia's tablemates. "Thanks for making us a foursome, Sydney," Julie Poindexter said. "We certainly understand why Olivia didn't feel it appropriate to be here today, but playing with four is so much more fun than with three."

"I called her last night and ran this idea by her," Sydney replied. She'd also told Olivia why, and the widow had suggested who might be best to tap for information.

"Good idea," said the second woman, Clarissa White.

"Olivia's a great player, but she's somewhat particular."

The third woman, Bitsy Melzer, laughed. "Sorry. We're really quite fond of Olivia, despite her rather particular ways. If you know what I mean?"

Sydney didn't want to disparage Olivia, but she also wanted to glean as much information about her *client* as she could. She only had a few hours to do so. "She is a bit of a stickler for the rules when it comes to this game, but Paul's death has hit her hard. She hardly seemed like the same person at the funeral."

Clarissa angled her head, apparently digesting Sydney's remark. "I noticed the same, which now that you mention it, seems strange, considering how she felt about her husband."

Careful. Don't show too much interest. "Oh? What do you mean?" Sydney attempted to keep her tone as innocent as possible.

The other three women lowered their heads and began setting up the tiles.

Damn. She'd already gone too far. "Did I say something to offend you?" Sydney asked, dialing up her tone to her sweetest level.

"No, of course not, Sydney," Julie said. "It's just that, well, we don't really know what to say about Olivia and Paul's marriage. Amongst the three of us, we think things had cooled between them."

"Oh. Sorry to hear that."

"Not that she ever said so," Bitsy added. "As much as she can dish out the advice about mah jongg, Olivia has been tight-lipped about her marriage. But every so often, she'd receive a call from him canceling one plan or another. She put on a brave face afterward, but it was evident to us how disappointed she was."

Clarissa leaned in. "Or she'd try calling him without

getting through. She'd excuse it as his being in a meeting and having turned off his phone. But every time?"

Okay, they'd opened up. Sydney took a deep breath and plunged ahead. "Was there, uh, another woman?"

Once again, the trio turned their attention to the tile walls they were building. Julie glanced up first, followed by Clarissa and finally Bitsy. "We think so, although Olivia never said. And we never asked," Julie said.

Bitsy threw the dice and got a five. "Paul had a bit of a reputation around town as a skirt chaser. Whether he ever followed through with any particular woman or women, we can't say."

Sydney's dice came up eight. "Or won't say, if she lives here in town."

Julie rolled her dice, then Clarissa. Julie rolled a high of nine, so she was East, or "in charge," for the first game. No one spoke until each had her hand of thirteen tiles and Clarissa fourteen. "Though it may not appear to be the case," Julie said before starting the game, "we don't like to gossip. We probably shouldn't have told you as much as we did. But to speculate further doesn't feel right."

"I understand." Sydney said it quickly, so they'd get that she didn't feel right about asking either.

Bitsy inclined her head to the side. "What realty company did you use when you bought your house here, Sydney?"

"Bitsy!" Clarissa said a little too fast. Julie simply bit a lip.

Interesting question. The responses of the other two women even more interesting. "Uh, why do you ask?" Sydney replied, puzzled.

"No particular reason. Just curious. Thought you might have dealt with Golden Home Realty, that's all."

Golden Home Realty. Where had she heard that name recently? Then she remembered. Johnny Bayliss and the gossip he'd shared at coupon clipping last week had Periwinkle "Peri" Dawson of Golden Home Realty involved with a local man.

"From that smile on your face, I'd say you have a pretty good hand," Bitsy surmised.

Huh? Actually, it wasn't too bad, since she'd picked up two jokers. More than that, though, if Bitsy's hint rang true, the gang now had another suspect.

Though they each drove separate cars—Marianne's foot was almost back to normal—the four met up at the coffeehouse to compare notes. "Do you think we should be meeting in public like this?" Kat asked. "Won't someone suspect we're up to something?"

Micki smirked. "Someone like *Rick, uh, Sheriff* Formero?"

"We're just here celebrating our wins at mah jongg, if anyone asks," Sydney said. She lowered her voice. "Speaking of wins. I think I struck it rich as far as a suspect goes. The woman he was having an affair with."

"I got the same info," Micki said.

Marianne's eyes went wide. "No kidding? Who?"

"Peri Dawson of Golden Home Realty," Sydney said in a whisper.

Micki frowned. "Not the name I uncovered. Nor the realty connection. Carmen Trudeau said her daughter saw Paul about a month ago. Her daughter and Lilith Schwimmer were friends in high school, which is how she recognized Paul. He was in the parking lot of the hotel, that new fancy suite place up in Ocala just off I-75, where the daughter works. He was talking to a young woman in a car. It wouldn't have registered, except he leaned down and kissed the car's occupant."

"It could've been a friend or a relative," Marianne said.

Micki's face registered one of her trademark you've-got-to-be-kidding-me expressions. "Don't think so. Apparently the lady's hands were wrapped around his neck, and it lasted well over a minute."

Kat twiddled the cardboard cover on her paper cup of hot tea. "It could've been Peri. I can't imagine their sticking around town for their trysts, unless neither cared who saw them, so she could've potentially met him up there."

"In an older model compact car?" Micki said. "Even if Peri used a car other than her own, I can't picture her demeaning herself in an old car."

Sydney stirred her cup of coffee. "Let's table that one for now, since we have so little to go on. But a mistress gives us a whole new motive. All we have to do is get more evidence that mistress was Peri Dawson."

Marianne rolled her eyes. "All. How do you suggest we do that? If she did kill Paul, she's been busy for over a week burying any link to their relationship."

"We could start with Johnny Bayliss," Micki said. She described how she and Sydney had first heard of the Dawson woman's affair. "At the time, the rest of us discouraged him from spreading gossip like that, so I don't know how much more he might know and be willing to share."

Kat finished off her tea. "I might be the most likely one to establish a direct link to the Dawson woman. I could say I'm looking into investment options for my lottery money. The only problem is I'm not very good at that kind of undercover work, playacting. It's been one thing to ask questions and listen to people but taking on a role, not so much."

"Maybe Marianne should go with you, and I'll go with Syd," Micki said. "I'm not so hot in the people skills department, either."

Since it was already late afternoon, they agreed to put the next step of the investigation in place the following day. Kat called ahead to make an appointment, ensuring Peri Dawson would be the one to assist her.

As soon as they arrived the next morning, Kat and Marianne were immediately ushered into Dawson's private office. Dawson stood, came around her desk and offered her hand to Kat. "Katrina Faulkner, I'm Peri. I think we've met at some social event or another, but it's nice to see you again."

Kat shook hands, then introduced Marianne, with whom Dawson also had passing familiarity. "She's my second set of eyes and ears."

"Wonderful. Maybe you'll see something you like as well as we get into this discussion?"

Marianne kept her response ambivalent. "You never know." Smile, smile.

"So, Katrina…"

"Call me Kat. Everyone else does."

"So, Kat, I understand you're looking for an investment property here in town?"

"That's right. I already own a home in Mangrove Estates, but I have some funds that have been tied up in CDs I need to convert to a more lucrative investment. I'm considering putting them into property, residential property that I'd rent."

Dawson immediately began nodding her head, as if she was already reading Kat's mind. "Uh-huh. Very wise decision. Residential property in Serendipity Springs has been increasing in value at a respectable pace the past several years. Are you thinking about a house, condo or townhouse?"

"I'm not sure," Kat replied. "Does one type have a better return on investment than the others?"

"That usually depends on location, but in this town, there's a demand for all three types."

The plan was for Kat to be undecided at this first meeting, necessitating further meetings with the real estate agent, during which time the two sleuths hoped to engage her in personal conversation. Not that Dawson would slip up and admit outright to having been Schwimmer's mistress, but she might drop a few conversational tidbits that would suggest she'd been playing around.

"I've got about an hour before my next appointment. How about we go for a drive around town and I'll show you some properties that are on the market? We won't tour the interiors today, just get a feel for what you're seeking."

"I like the way you think," Kat replied. "Ready, Marianne?"

Marianne stood, but rather than pivoting to leave, she stopped and examined a framed photo on a nearby bookcase. "Nice picture. Who's the guy with you?"

"Him? That's my brother, Chuck. We were vacationing in Cancun a few years back. He owns a deli over in Shasta."

"He's good-looking, like you."

"Thanks."

"If I recall, aren't you a former Miss Florida?"

"Runner-up. I used to have pictures posted here in my office, but my reputation as a former beauty queen outdistanced my credibility as a real estate agent, so down they came."

Kat took her turn buttering up Dawson. "That's too bad. I'd think being a former beauty queen would only add to your professional profile."

"It gets old, believe me." Dawson grabbed her purse and car keys from somewhere under her desk and herded them toward the door.

Marianne waited until they were ensconced in Dawson's luxury sedan before she followed up on the woman's statement. "What about being a beauty queen gets old?"

"Former beauty queen. People expect you to continue to act the part years later. Heaven forbid I be seen around town in sweats."

Seated in the passenger seat, Kat offered a sympathetic expression. "That must be a strain."

"I'll say it is. I like nice clothes as much as any woman, but my wardrobe bill is embarrassing."

"But that's understandable," Marianne said from the back seat. "You have to look good for clients day after day."

"True, but it's the formal wear that's been killing me. For social things as well as my private life, although that's more or less died off."

Had they struck gold? Kat attempted to remain casual in her response. "Oh? Did you recently break up with someone?"

Dawson's back stiffened and her hands seemed to grip the steering wheel tighter. "Uh, no. I didn't mean to give that impression. Several of my friends leave town for the summer months to avoid the heat, so I don't go out as much."

"Ah, I see," Kat said. Plausible reason, although summer was long over. Had the woman actually slipped? Whatever, the Realtor most likely would watch what she said the rest of this junket. On the other hand, maybe they could learn more from pumping her about her wardrobe. "Your clothes are really quite nice. Would you mind telling me where you shop? I need to upgrade my wardrobe." That made a certain amount of sense, coming from a recent lottery winner.

"I buy my fancier things at a boutique in Naples. Yvonne's. Feel free to mention my name if you go there."

So she could receive a nice discount for her referral. Marianne was impressed. The woman didn't miss a trick when it came to making a dollar. Nonetheless, maybe a road trip shopping venture would appeal to the others. Some shop owners weren't above talking about their clients to obtain new clients.

"Thanks. I'll make a note of the place," Kat said.

Dawson retreated behind a wall of realty information the rest of the trip, pointing out properties currently on the market and a few she suspected soon would be available. Kat and Marianne remained noncommittal, nodding while doing their best to appear interested.

An hour later, they pulled up in front of the realty office. "I'll put together a list of places we can tour in the next few days. Were there any you'd definitely like me to include?"

"That condo over on Blue Heron Way caught my attention," Kat replied. "Also, the townhouse on Hibiscus Lane."

Kat and Marianne shook hands with Dawson, and then she hurried back into the building while they remained on the sidewalk. "Let's get out of here," Marianne said. "That whole experience gave me the creeps."

Kat waited until they were back in Marianne's car to reply. "She is a bit of a diva, isn't she?"

"She's quite a contrast from Olivia. I can sort of see why Schwimmer might have been attracted to her."

Chapter Eleven

Sydney and Micki faced an even more daunting challenge tracking down information from Johnny Bayliss. Fortunately, it was the day for coupon clipping again. Sydney hadn't planned to go this week, preferring to put it off for investigative efforts. But it proved the perfect chance to pin down their informant.

Sydney attempted nonchalance when she inquired if he'd heard any more about Peri Dawson and her boyfriend. She and Johnny were seated at the end of the long work table. She kept her voice low, hoping not to attract the attention of the others. Micki did her part keeping them distracted with her chatter.

"Two weeks ago, you told me to back off the gossip. Why are you asking about her now?"

"That was before a friend of mine took her business to Peri's firm. It was a done deal before I could warn her. I'm trying to find out if Dawson's business has been or might be compromised by her uh, dalliances."

Johnny stopped cutting and gazed at her. "Guess that's as good an excuse as any to share information, but 'fraid I can't help you. My friend has met with her twice since that time I told you about, and nothing happened to suggest she was still seeing whoever it was. The only weird thing was she had to cancel one meeting unexpectedly."

"Why was that weird? Things change all the time for real estate agents."

He nodded. "Sure, sure. I know that. But this was like at the very last minute. He'd already arrived and was in her office talking to her when she got this call and went running."

"Some emergency?"

"Maybe. But whatever it was, unless she was going north, she woulda had a hard time getting wherever she was headed, because sheriff's cars and EMTs blocked the south end."

Was it possible? "Did he say what day that was, Johnny?"

"Don't remember the date, but it was the same day that big shot orange grove owner got hisself killed."

"Paul Schwimmer?"

"Yeah, that was his name."

Sydney gripped the sides of her legs under the table to keep herself from reacting to this news. Johnny couldn't know he'd just supplied her with a gem.

As it turned out, Marla Trudeau, the daughter of their mah jongg partner, Carmen, was the day manager at the new suites hotel in Ocala and happened to be working that day when Sydney and Micki arrived.

Once they were seated in Trudeau's office and introduced themselves, Sydney got right to the point. "We play mah jongg with your mother. As you probably know, one of our other mah jongg players, Olivia Schwimmer, recently lost her husband, Paul."

"He was murdered, I've heard," Marla replied, her attention focused on straightening several stacks of paper on her desk.

Micki took her turn. "You know about that? Good, we can skip the pleasantries. Your mother mentioned you saw Paul Schwimmer in the parking lot here at the hotel about a month ago with some woman. We hoped you might help us figure out who it was."

That got Trudeau's attention. She jerked in her seat and eyed Micki directly. "My mother never should've said that. It's not good for the hotel's reputation, especially since we're so new. We don't need gossip like that floating around."

"Let me assure you," Sydney said, "we're not here to spread gossip. We want to protect the widow from that very thing. If we can shed any light on the identity of that woman, we can hopefully put those rumors to rest, if she was a family friend or relative…"

"Or prepare Mrs. Schwimmer for whatever might come of such gossip," Micki added.

Trudeau sprang from her seat. "The only way such 'gossip' might go anywhere is if supposed 'friends' like yourselves go out of your way, literally, to keep it alive. I don't have anything further to say."

Sydney's stomach flipped over. She hated being seen in such light by the younger woman. But they'd had so little to go on, this story was the best she and Micki had been able to manufacture. "I realize the two of us must look like two out-of-control gossipmongers, but we truly are here to help Olivia Schwimmer. You can call her, if you want."

"I was in a hurry to get to my car. I didn't get a very good view of the woman because he was standing by her door, blocking her from view. My impression was that she was much younger than him, maybe early thirties. I also got the feeling she'd just gotten into the car and was about to drive off, and he was saying goodbye...with his lips."

Since that seemed to be all they were going to get from the young woman, Sydney rose too, Micki following suit. "That's not much to go on, but thank you."

"Wait. The car was a beat-up older model sedan. Dark. Navy or maybe black. But there was some kind of sign on the door. I don't remember what it said exactly, but there was this big pink flower that was part of the logo, like she might work for a florist."

"How did you see it, if he was standing in front of the driver's door?" Micki asked.

Trudeau squinted, as if trying to remember. "You're right. I think the writing was on both the driver's door and the passenger door behind it. That's why I don't remember the name, just the flower. It must have been on the far right."

"That's a start," Sydney replied.

She and Micki both echoed their thanks and scooted for the car.

"Just so you know," Trudeau called, "I'm going to call Mrs. Schwimmer. And my mother."

"Please, do that," Micki replied.

They drove off and headed down the street to a coffee shop where they could digest their latest finding.

"Do you think whoever was in that car was local?" Micki asked after taking a sip of her vanilla latte.

"Local or close by, unless she was the owner. Then she could have driven here from anywhere without alerting her boss."

Micki pulled out her phone and did a quick internet search of local florists. "There are four in town. None with any kind of flower in the name. We'll have to take them one by one."

To avoid another trip, they started tracking them down right then. The first was quite small and appeared to focus mainly on green plants. The proprietors weren't able to talk to them immediately. One was busy with a customer and the other, the husband, seemed preoccupied with an order he was preparing in the back of the store. As it turned out, they were a "retired" couple who now spent their days here in this shop. They employed a couple of high school kids part-time, but neither was working today. Micki came up with a big fat zero when she asked if they owned a car with a flower logo on both doors.

The second florist used two vans. Yes, both sported logos, but they didn't include flowers.

They struck gold, of sorts, at the third shop. Though he used a van for large deliveries, the owner also drove a dark sedan with a pink flower logo on both the driver and passenger sides. Yes, he had a small staff. His wife came in once a week to do the bookkeeping. She was in her fifties. Their thirty-three-year-old daughter, Wanda, who worked afternoons, joined them after she finished checking in an order. Everything seemed to fit, except she was overweight with complexion problems and wore glasses. A possibility but probably not.

Micki and Sydney were turning to leave when the wife asked the husband when someone called Shelly was due back from her vacation. The duo turned in their tracks. "Shelly?" Sydney asked. "Who's that?"

The wife eyed the husband, as if asking him whether to proceed. "Shelly Ludwig is a floater. We call her in for overflow days like Valentine's. Right now, we're in our low season, so she's off somewhere on a cruise," the owner replied.

"Such a life," the wife added. "She works a few days a year and can afford to go off on cruises whenever she feels like it. We, on the other hand, are stuck here week after week. Our vacations are spent attending florists' conventions."

"When was the last time she worked?" Micki asked.

The man scratched his head. "Right before Memorial Day? We do a lot of wreaths for graves then."

"That was over three months ago," Sydney said. "Are you sure she hasn't worked since?"

The daughter had entered the front part of the store during the latter part of this discussion. "Don't you remember, Dad? She filled in for me those three days when I had my wisdom teeth removed."

"Forgot about that," her father responded.

"When did she fill in for you?" Micki asked.

The daughter pursed her lips. "My surgery was in late July. That was about five weeks ago?"

Sydney forced herself not to steal a peek at Micki, but little bells were going off in her head. "Would she have, uh, driven your car?" she asked the owner.

He shrugged. "Maybe. She sometimes makes deliveries. Depends on what I have going on here."

Micki edged a little closer. "You say she's on a cruise right now. Do you know when she'll be back in town or when she'll work next?"

The owner squared his shoulders. "Why the interest? Are you with the police?"

Minor problem. They hadn't developed a cover story. Now they had to punt. "No, we're not with law enforcement," Sydney said, attempting to sound natural and in charge. "A friend of ours was involved in a minor collision in a hotel parking lot about five weeks ago. She thought she got all the information she needed from the driver of the other car, but that has proven to be false. Our friend thinks she remembers seeing a woman matching your description of Shelly about that same time, who might have witnessed the accident. We're attempting to find that woman."

Sydney took a deep breath. Her explanation had been a mouthful.

The man narrowed his eyes. "How do we know Shelly wasn't the one involved in the accident?"

Now it was Micki's turn to get creative. "The other car suffered minor but noticeable damage to the front fender. Did you notice anything like that with your vehicle?"

"Well, no. But Shelly's always been a good worker. I don't want to say anything that would get her in trouble."

Sydney did her best to appear understanding. "Of course. We understand."

"What do you want us to do?" the wife asked. "Call you when we hear from her?"

"That won't be necessary," Micki said. "If you could just give us her contact information."

After exchanging several looks, the wife jotted something on the back of one of their business cards. "All I've got is an email address."

"Thanks. We'll start there." Sydney quickly stuffed the card in her pocket, and she and Micki got out of there as soon as they could.

They waited a full five minutes before they felt safe enough to talk. "Congratulations, my friend. We've solved the mystery of the woman in the flower-marked car," Micki said. "I'd high-five you, but I prefer not to disturb your steering."

Sydney held up her right hand. "I can steer with one

hand. At least long enough to celebrate our discovery." They touched hands, then Sydney went back to two hands on the wheel.

"Do you think she's a suspect?" Micki asked.

"Maybe. Or she could be one of many women Paul was seeing. But she's still one more name on our list."

They drove a few miles while each contemplated their achievement. "What do you suppose Kat and Marianne are doing?" Micki asked.

"Surely they couldn't have unearthed a detail as juicy as ours."

Chapter Twelve

The next night, Kat performed at a hotel downtown, and the other three plus the two spouses went to support her. The Bonners and Putnams found a table while Micki checked on Kat in her small dressing room.

"So, Trip, how's your show coming along?" Marianne asked.

Sydney rolled her eyes. Wrong subject.

Trip nodded, although he didn't smile. "Still a few kinks to straighten out, but we're almost there."

"No more magic, though," Beau reminded him.

"Hey, it would've worked fine with a woman. You just jumped the gun, then got stuck in a case that was too small for you."

"I jumped the gun? I beg to differ."

"Maybe it was my idea," Trip admitted. "I've lost track. Anyway, Marianne, we still need one or two acts to round out the program."

"Got any leads?" Marianne pushed.

"Why don't you guys get us some drinks from the bar?" Sydney suggested.

Beau started to rise, but Trip held out a hand. "My

wife is trying to change the subject, because she thinks we're doomed to failure."

"No, I don't, Trip. I just hear so much about the show at home, I'd hoped we could find a different topic tonight."

"Like what the two of you and your two cohorts have been up to lately?" Trip replied. "Don't think Beau and I haven't noticed how often you've found excuses to have coffee or lunch or whatever. We haven't asked, because we were afraid to know."

"And we've been too busy with your follies, Trip," Beau added.

"We've been consoling Olivia Schwimmer. Her husband's death has been very difficult for her."

"Didn't think you two were big fans of hers," Beau stated. He turned to Marianne. "You're always coming home from your mah jongg sessions complaining about her."

Marianne flipped out her hair. "That's just girl talk. When it comes down to the important things in life, we stick together. I'm sure if something that horrible happened to you, the whole mah jongg group would be there for me."

"I know I would," Sydney said.

Micki joined them before Trip pushed to know more about their recent activities. "It still amazes me how Kat can be two persons, the one we know and love but have to push to be assertive and then her stage presence. The latter has taken over backstage. I was no longer needed as cheerleader."

"I need to find myself a new pastime," Sydney remarked, "so I can assume a new personality."

Trip placed a hand on her shoulder. "Like you need to become any more assertive."

She returned a fond smile. "Thanks, but that's not what I meant."

"Let's hit the bar, Beau, before Kat starts her show," Trip said.

"You want something from the bar, too, Micki?" Beau asked.

"White wine. Thanks."

While the men were busy at the bar, the three compared notes about their discoveries the previous day. "I thought they'd never leave," Marianne said. "Kat and I have established a foothold with Peri Dawson, but despite coming across so chatty and open, she keeps her personal life to herself. Other than a picture of her brother we noticed in her office. She said he owns a deli in Shasta, so unexpectedly running into him on purpose is next on our list."

Micki updated Marianne on the mysterious flower deliverywoman, Shelly. "We'll have to wait until she's back from her trip to speak to her, if we decide it's warranted. In the meantime, though, we can poke around and see what we can find out about her."

"In other words," Sydney summarized, "more working behind the scenes for all of us. I wonder if the sheriff and his crew are even looking beyond Olivia."

Micki, who'd been surveying the room while they talked, suddenly turned to them. "Tonight might be our chance to find out. Don't look, but guess who's sitting near the back."

"Tell us, if we can't look," Sydney ordered.

"None other than Sheriff Formero." Micki pronounced the name like the man was Public Enemy Number One instead of the man who caught criminals.

Sydney clasped her hands together. "That's right. Kat said something about his mentioning her singing.

He must be here as a private citizen. A fan."

"Maybe so," Micki kept her voice down, "but he's never totally without his badge."

"Do Trip and I even want to know who you're gabbing about?" Beau asked as he and Trip delivered the drinks.

"Sheriff Formero is here. In civilian clothes. Apparently to hear Kat," Marianne explained.

"We were just wondering how much progress he's made on the Schwimmer case," Micki added.

"Now's your chance to ask him," Beau said. Before any of the women could react, he swiveled, caught the sheriff's eye and gestured for him to join them. "We've got an extra seat."

Sydney eyed the other two women but couldn't do anything fast enough to keep the sheriff at bay.

"Evenin', folks," the sheriff greeted them as he pulled out the chair between Micki and Marianne.

"Sheriff," Trip said.

"Rick, for tonight."

Trip and Beau took turns shaking the newcomer's hand. The women simply nodded and stared at their own hands.

Fortunately, the lights dimmed and the emcee introduced Kat. Her backup trio started to play the intro to a recent classic. Within seconds, Kat floated in and stepped onto the tiny stage. The change in persona Micki had referenced became apparent to all of them. Kat surveyed her audience like she owned the world. Her shoulders dipped and swayed to the beat. Even her face was different, like her skin had been pulled back.

But it was the voice that made them believe someone else had taken over Kat's body. A tantalizing mix of sultry and sweet. The kind of voice that made one put down their drink and concentrate entirely on the vision singing the adult contemporary, Southern blues and neo soul of female songstresses like Adele, Kelly Clarkson and Alicia Keys.

Sydney shot a covert glance at the sheriff, who also seemed to have transformed. He sat back in his chair, one hand draped on the table. His head nodded to the beat of the song. His eyes never left the stage.

Sydney exchanged looks with Marianne, who also seemed to have noticed the man's interest.

Kat exited the stage once the set ended and soon appeared at their table. "Well, how was it? Oh, uh, hello… Sheriff."

"Rick. Can you join us for a few minutes, or would you rather go back to your dressing room?"

Kat quickly surveyed the table, seeking a sign from one of her friends. "Uh, sure."

"You were fabulous," Micki said, hugging her. "I never fail to be amazed by that voice of yours."

"Oh, good. I enjoyed myself up there, but that didn't mean I sounded okay."

"You have nothing to worry about," Rick reassured her. "Your voice is so distinct."

"Thanks. Up there, you can't hear yourself clearly. You have to go with what you think is working."

When Trip offered to get her a drink, she refused, saying she needed a few minutes to herself before her next set. "You're staying, I hope?"

"Wouldn't dream of leaving," Sydney said.

Once it was just the six of them again, Trip took the initiative at grilling the sheriff. "So, Rick, uh, Sheriff Formero, how's the investigation of Paul Schwimmer's murder going? The ladies here have been worried about his wife, their friend."

Formero slid forward, sat straighter, like a cat eyeing a bird. "Shoot. I'd hoped I could enjoy just one evening as a civilian."

"We can appreciate that, as I'm sure you can also appreciate these ladies' concern." Beau, bless his heart, was also intervening on their behalf.

Formero settled back a few inches. "Sure. But you all have to understand why I can't say much until we have an arrest."

"But are you looking beyond his wife?" Sydney pushed.

Formero gave Sydney his full attention. "Why do you think I'm looking at his wife?"

Oh, he was good. "Isn't that what they always say? Look first to the spouse?"

"That will probably work in my situation," Trip said, attempting to defuse the situation. He didn't look at Syd. "My retirement activities could easily push her to the limit." Now he did gaze at her, shooting her the kind of smile only the happily-marrieds shared.

"Something tells me you know more about my investigation than I realized," the sheriff said.

"Me? Just because I don't believe the wife did it?"

"If you know anything, Mrs. Bonner, I hope you'll come to me with it." His tone wasn't threatening. In fact, it was actually friendly. Strike that. Encouraging.

"I'll, uh, keep that in mind." She kept her eyes on her hands, not daring to check out her two friends' expressions.

Fortunately, the lights began to fade. Time to support Kat again.

Kat had changed to a different cocktail dress, just as shapeless as the last. The four of them really needed to check out that dress shop in Naples and introduce Kat to sexy.

Normally, Sydney or Marianne would have invited the group to one of their homes afterward for coffee and dessert, but the sheriff's presence put a damper on that idea. They exchanged goodbyes, while Rick cornered Kat. "If you're not ready to collapse, how about the two of us get some coffee."

He could have invited the rest of them, but he didn't. Could he be any plainer with his interest in their friend?

What would Kat do? What did they want her to do?

"Can you wait while I change?" Her eyes were only on him.

Had they lost their friend to the enemy?

Chapter Thirteen

Sydney waited until Trip left for the golf course the next morning before texting her friends to come over. "Our husbands are getting suspicious of our investigative activities," she said, once Marianne and Micki arrived.

"At least Beau went golfing with Trip, or I'm not sure I could've found an excuse to leave," Marianne replied.

"Where's Kat?" Micki asked.

"She's here," Kat replied, dragging through the door. "This had better be good. I'm drained from last night."

Three sets of lifted brows greeted her.

"No! That's not what I meant. I was home within an hour. We just had coffee, that's all."

"Did he grill you about what the four of us have been doing?" Sydney asked.

"Why would he do that?" Realization dawned. "Oh, no. What did you all say to him when I wasn't there?"

"Actually, it was my dear husband who wanted to know about the investigation," Sydney replied.

"Because he didn't want you doing it," Marianne returned. "Let's face it, Syd. Our guys are on to us."

"If so, they haven't told us to stop. Yet."

"Then we have to wrap this up fast before they do," Micki warned.

"Kat, we did a short status update last night while the men visited the bar," Marianne said. "I briefed these two on our business with Peri Dawson and mentioned that we might do better gleaning information from her brother. Syd and Micki think they've figured out who the woman was that was seen kissing Paul in the parking lot of the motel in Ocala, except she's currently on a vacation or something and out of the country."

Sydney folded her hands and smiled at Marianne. "Nice summary. Our work is cut out for us the next few days.

Micki checked her watch. "I have a hair appointment in half an hour. Here's what I suggest. We can't do much today, since it's Sunday, other than come up with a list of questions and see what we can glean from the internet. But tomorrow we get serious."

"Uh, thanks for sketching out a plan, Mick. Let's you and I get together for coffee tomorrow morning and take it from there," Sydney said.

Sydney spent the rest of the day attempting to research Shelly Ludwig. There wasn't much to find. She and Micki would have to get creative.

Micki had come to the same conclusion when they met the next day. "We need to go back to that florist and get more information."

"Won't they get suspicious?" Sydney returned. "I can't believe they told us as much as they did with the skimpy excuse of seeking a witness to a parking lot collision."

"If the man is there, we simply thank him for his help and buy a plant in appreciation. But if we get lucky, maybe it will only be his daughter staffing the shop. They said she worked afternoons, so I'm hoping she relieves her dad around noon while he takes off for lunch."

"He looked the type who'd bring his lunch to work."

"Be optimistic. He might also go home over the noon hour to be with the wife."

They timed their arrival for ten minutes after twelve. No one answered at first. But they were patient. At length, they were rewarded with the appearance of the daughter.

"Hello, Wanda," Micki greeted her. "We were here the other day. Maybe you remember us?"

"Sorta. You were looking for Shelly, or at least that's the part I remember."

Sydney entered the conversation. "That's right. We think she might have witnessed an accident involving the car of our friend."

"Why isn't your friend here with you?"

Good question. They should have anticipated it and now had to improvise. Sydney took the lead. "Our friend is very shy. She didn't want to make waves and was prepared to pay for the repairs herself, even though she wasn't at fault."

"We're not as shy," Micki added.

So far, the woman seemed to buy their story. "Why are you back? We told you Shelly is out of town."

Micki attempted to appear embarrassed. "We should've asked when you expected her back in town and for her address."

Sydney jumped on board the embarrassed angle. "We may be less shy than Lucy, but we're not very good detectives."

"That's personal information I'm not at liberty to share."

"We were afraid of that. But she's not listed in the

phone book, so we hoped you might relax your rules this once." She didn't give the woman a chance to respond before she pointed to a plant on display a few feet away. "Oh, look, Grace. Isn't that exactly the kind of alocasia you've been seeking? The kind they call the elephant ear."

Not terribly thrilled with her cohort saddling her with the purchase of a plant, Sydney, or Grace for these purposes, feigned excitement. "You're right, Daisy." She ambled over to the plant and made a show of examining it. Then she turned back to the woman. "This is beautiful. Do you have your own greenhouse, or do you get your plants from a distributor?"

"We have a small greenhouse where we grow most of our plants. For the more exotic, we bring in a distributor."

Sydney shook her head slightly. "I really like this one, but it's a little pricey." She left it there, hoping the woman would take the bait.

"I overheard my mom say Shelly would be back in town on Friday. I don't know her address, but she lives in a small apartment complex over on the far east end of Carmody Street. I dropped her off once and remember it's a blue building."

"Thanks," Micki replied. "I recall your mother wondering how someone like Shelly could afford such a trip."

Wanda snorted. "That's Shelly. She's always going on a trip or showing up with new jewelry. How she pays for them, one can only speculate." Her tone made it obvious Shelly Ludwig was not a close friend.

"Does she have another job?" Sydney asked.

"Beats me. She once mentioned picking up a side job here and there, whatever that means. I wouldn't be surprised if she was into some sort of escort business, because she'd show up at times with the remains of a fancy hair style and a fairly new manicure."

"Is she, uh, attractive?" Micki asked. Sydney cringed at her friend's audacity, but it was worth asking.

"Compared to me, you mean? Don't worry, I'm not offended. As you can see, I'm not into appearances. I'm in charge of the greenhouse. As long as my plants love me, I'm okay. But yeah, Shelly's a looker. Medium height, built and blond. The type a lot of men would die for."

Micki shot Sydney an unobtrusive look. Had that been the case with Paul? Sydney picked up the plant. "You know, it may be a little more than I'd like to pay, but I can't resist this alocasia." The woman deserved something for her information.

They were walking out of the shop as quickly as they could without jumping up and down when Wanda offered a parting comment. "You know, it's strange about her cruise. It seemed to come up mighty fast. She hadn't mentioned it when she worked here the week before. It was like she was in town one day and out of here the next."

Sydney and Micki couldn't get back on the road fast enough. "What do you think?" Micki asked.

"I think we got lucky. Even though it cost me a pretty penny for a plant I don't need."

"You're the one who thought of the bribe first."

"You pay next time, then. Did you bring a map of the town?"

Micki pulled a folded sheet of paper from her purse. "It doesn't have every street on it, but, ah, here's Carmody. Looks like we have to go south a few blocks, then turn east."

It wasn't difficult to find the small apartment complex. Like Wanda had said, it was blue. Very blue. A fourplex. But the mailboxes did not include names. Their only choice was to knock on doors.

"Hello," Micki gushed when a woman of about eighty opened the door at the first apartment they tried. "My friend and I are looking for Shelly Ludwig's place. We were told it was in this building."

"Shelly? No one here by that name." She started to close the door.

"Uh, wait. Maybe if I described her? She's blond and quite good-looking."

"You must mean Miranda. Don't know her last name. She lives above me."

"Do you know if she's been around lately?"

"Funny you should ask. I was just telling my home health aide this morning that I wondered where she was this time."

"This time?" Sydney asked. "Does she go away often?"

The older woman narrowed her eyes. "You bill collectors? Sure a better-looking class of people, if you are."

"No, we're nothing like that," Micki supplied. "We think she witnessed an accident involving our friend, and we need to hear her side of the story."

The woman didn't invite them in, but she didn't make any moves to close the door. "Sure she didn't cause it? That's more likely."

"You don't sound like you're much of a fan," Micki pushed.

"You picked up on that, huh? It's bad enough with all the men who show up, usually just park their fancy cars outside and honk, but the noise coming from her place when they do come in gets to me. And I'm hard of hearing!"

"Different men, you say," Sydney repeated. "Any particular type?"

Now the woman turned her gaze on Syd. "You're awfully curious just to be tracking down a witness. You want to leave your names and numbers for me to give her when she does show up?"

"Actually, now that we're sure this is where she lives, we'll just send her a note. Thank you for your help," Micki said.

"One more question," Sydney added. "Did you see her leave this last time? If you did, was she with a man?"

"As a matter of fact, I did. I was just waking up from my nap when the honking began. Maybe it woke me, who knows? Anyway, when I went to the window to check, it was a taxicab. Miranda hustled out the door with her own luggage, got in and took off. I didn't see any man other than the driver."

They thanked her once again and sped off to the car.

"Are you thinking what I'm thinking?" Micki said as soon as they were under way.

"I think we have a bona fide suspect, although it's still not clear why she'd want to murder Schwimmer."

"The way Paul Schwimmer was killed suggests a fit of passion. Why not a love affair gone wrong?"

"Maybe. But there's more to it than that, if she's the one."

"More than we can probably piece together."

"But we now know one thing we only suspected before. If Paul had something going with Peri Dawson, he was also seeing at least one other woman. That might have been enough to turn either woman against him."

Chapter Fourteen

*M*arianne and Kat were as anxious to check Chuck Dawson's deli as they were to question the owner.

"Thanks for driving," Marianne said. "My foot is pretty much back in shape, but I prefer being the passenger at least one more day."

"Glad you're doing better. As for this trip, how do we introduce the subject of Peri?" Kat asked.

"I think we should stick as close to the truth as we can by telling him we saw his picture in her office when we were there. You can tell him all about your search for investment property, even ask about possibilities in Shasta."

"Okay, I'm tracking that far, but how do we go from 'we saw your picture' to 'was your sister having an affair with Paul Schwimmer'?"

Marianne checked the address for the deli she'd noted in her phone. "At the moment, I haven't a clue. I was hoping to pounce on whatever he says and redirect it toward Peri."

"That's not much to go on. I prefer a little more structure in my investigations."

"You come up with something then. I'm watching for the turnoff to Shasta."

Kat scanned the road signs they were passing. "I wasn't criticizing, just warning you I might not be much help if I don't have more of a script."

"You want to stop for coffee or something first, so we can plot this out for you?"

"Okay. Then we can go over everything we know about him and build on that."

They hadn't been able to learn much about Chuck Dawson from their internet search. He was Peri's older brother by five years. They'd both grown up in Florida. Before she was working her way up through the beauty pageant circuit to becoming runner-up Miss Florida, he'd been playing football at the University of Florida. But he hadn't gone on to the pros. Instead, he'd taken culinary training and for several years had been a chef in several top restaurants in the area. In just the last few years, he'd purchased a small store in Shasta, named it Fromage and created a boutique deli.

"Somehow, we have to go from talking about cheese to his cheesy sister," Kat said.

"Okay, I'll take the lead, although I have no idea at the moment what that will be. But you need to follow up. Okay?"

"Okay." Kat's reply came out anything but assured.

"Hey. Where's the woman who just two nights ago overpowered the room with her singing?"

Kat made a face. "That's different."

"Not really. You take on a different personality when you're up on stage. Just do the same thing when we're talking to him."

"You should've been in sales instead of pharmacy."

"I never could've survived that career style. I think in black and white. I had to when mixing medicines or filling scripts. But thanks for the vote of confidence."

They approached Fromage somewhat more sure of themselves than when they arrived in town. "Hello," Marianne said as they came through the door. "We've been hearing good things about this place over in Serendipity Springs. We came to check it out for ourselves."

"Hello, yourself." A tall, muscular man in a knit sports shirt, khakis and a white chef's apron came around the counter and held out his hand. "I'm Charles Dawson, the owner. But call me Chuck."

"I'm Marianne Putnam, Chuck. And this is my friend Katrina Faulkner."

"*The* Katrina Faulkner?" he said as he extended his hand to Kat.

"I guess you could say that. How do you know about me? My voice or…my lottery win?"

"Both. One of my earlier customers raved about hearing you sing the other night. Recommended I get myself over to Serendipity Springs the next time you've got a gig."

"Thanks. That's nice to hear." This was going much better for Kat than she'd imagined.

"But I also heard from my sister that she's working with a lottery winner to locate an investment property. Hope that's not betraying a confidence."

It probably was, but it was the perfect lead-in to asking about Peri. "If it is, you're forgiven," Kat returned, a bit of the flirt slipping into her tone. "Although I've just started looking at properties recently. I haven't found anything yet, as helpful as your sister has been."

"She'll be happy to hear that."

"For any particular reason?" Marianne asked. "She seemed somewhat preoccupied the day we met with her."

"She has seemed not quite herself lately. I hope her

mood didn't affect your faith in her. She's a great real estate agent. That's pretty much all she lives for."

"She's also quite active in many civic and charitable activities," Kat put in.

He nodded. "True, although a lot of that comes from needing to get her name out there. You know she was once runner-up Miss Florida? Of course, you do. You couldn't have spent any time with her without coming away with that tidbit."

"Uh, since you brought it up, yes, she told us, although we knew already," Kat replied.

"That was the highlight of her life and, in my opinion, her worst nemesis. For years, she couldn't get past it and didn't understand why others didn't remember as well." He seemed to be speaking more to himself than to them. After all, until a few minutes ago, they'd been total strangers.

"I hadn't realized it affected her so deeply," Marianne said. She'd gotten the impression from Peri that she was trying to live down her beauty pageant fame. "Is that why she never married? Never mind, that's too personal."

"It is, but it's good to talk about it. I've carried a lot of my concerns about her inside for too long."

"You still have them?" Kat asked.

He drew in his lips, then eyed the rest of the store. "Want some coffee? You could review a new type of coffee cake I'm offering." He led them to a small table off to the side of the display counters and returned shortly with a tray laden with his offerings.

Marianne and Kat barely sipped the coffee, since they'd just imbibed elsewhere. As for his concerns about his sister, they didn't push but let him take his time framing his answer. Meanwhile, they feasted on delicious coffee cake.

"There was a guy in her life several years ago. They made plans to marry. She was working in another realty office at the time, but she'd already made a name for herself and was earning some hefty commissions. Then he took off with all her liquid assets. Just disappeared. Left her in shock at first, which later became a terrible distrust of men."

"Understandable," Marianne replied, unaware of this part of Peri's story.

"Maybe, but my optimistic, fun-loving sister was gone. Eventually, she started seeing men again, but mainly for what she could get from them."

He stopped. Marianne and Kat glanced at each other but remained silent.

"Not a very flattering portrayal, but a truth I've had to accept over time. I like to think besides promoting herself through her charitable activities, she's also finding some sort of balance against her private life."

"Has she been seeing someone lately?" Marianne asked, keeping her voice even. She didn't dare look at Kat for fear her friend would be frowning. She held her breath, praying she hadn't gone too far.

He sipped his coffee but didn't touch the coffee cake. "Peri and I haven't seen much of each other in recent years. I don't want to speak ill of her, but I told her the person she was seeing was all wrong for her. She'd told me about this guy in confidence and felt I'd turned on her. Just the opposite. I was worried for her. But after that, she stopped calling and wasn't available when I wanted to get together."

"I'm so sorry, Chuck," Kat said. She started to reach for his hand but quickly withdrew.

He raised his head her direction. "Thanks. Maybe one of these days she'll feel the need for a brother again."

Marianne bit a lip. He seemed so open. Nice. Did they dare push him? Uh, yes. That's what they were here for. At least she was. Kat, she wasn't so sure about. "Do you think she's still seeing him, which is why she's remained distant?"

He blinked, appeared to come out of a fog. "Now? Like I said, I've hardly seen her lately, except at public events where we just exchange pleasantries." He picked up his mug, then set it down. "Wait. She did contact me. A little over a week ago. Just an email and just a 'how're you doing' kind of communication. I wrote back, but there hasn't been a response."

This time, Kat did take his hand. "Hang in there. One of these days she'll realize how precious family is. I was an only child, but I had a mother until a few years ago. I look back on those years with her as a privilege."

His hand still in hers, he seemed to change moods. "I, uh, should be getting back to my inventory."

"And we have other errands to run," Marianne filled in. She and Kat, who'd now removed her hand from his, reluctantly jumped up. Before they left, though, they each made a purchase—Marianne, a pound of gruyere, and Kat, a blueberry coffee cake and some Kona coffee.

"That may or may not have been the information we've been seeking," Marianne began once they were on their way back to town. "We now know she was seeing someone her brother didn't approve of. We don't know if the reason was because the guy was married. Nor if she's still involved with the guy."

"Don't forget her recent email, right around the same time as Paul's murder. It had to mean something that she'd contact him out of the blue."

"Very little hard evidence for your boyfriend to be impressed."

"My boyfriend? Don't get carried away. Sheriff Formero likes my singing, not necessarily me."

"I like the way you qualified that statement. What do you think he'd do if he knew you were holding another man's hand today?"

Kat let out a huff. "I was not! Well, okay, I was, but purely to comfort him. He's several years my junior."

"Comfort him, right. As for him being younger, times are changing, girl. You'd be right in style if you started seeing him. But for now, you're right. You probably should keep your distance until we know if his sister is a murderer or not."

"Marianne! I can't believe you can be so cavalier about something so serious."

Several beats went by before Marianne replied. "You're right. I'm sorry. He seemed very nice, and as nice as Paul Schwimmer wasn't, I shouldn't minimize what happened to him."

"So, what's the plan from here? We can't very well approach Peri and tell her we know she was, is, dating a married man."

Marianne played with her purse strap, her way of thinking. "Didn't Peri say something about a shop she frequents in Naples? Yvonne's? Maybe it's time to check it out? For Sydney and my purposes, we need to set the guys' minds at rest about all the time we're spending together. They'll buy a shopping trip."

"I like that idea. You've all been dying to change up my wardrobe. This will be your chance."

"I think we've found something about our investigative activities Sheriff Rick would actually like."

Chapter Fifteen

"This is our best idea yet," Micki said as the four headed south in Sydney's SUV the next day.

"Other than this infernal I-75 traffic," Sydney complained. "You guys talk amongst yourselves, while I get through Tampa. Once we're farther south, we can compare notes on our findings."

Kat reached into a paper bag she'd brought. "I brought the coffee cake I purchased yesterday at the deli. Syd, I'll save yours until we're out of the heavy traffic."

"Thanks," Syd called over her shoulder. "All I netted from my investigative activities was a new plant."

"Hey! That's one beautiful alocasia," Micki told her.

Marianne turned around from the passenger seat up front. "We have a second mission today, besides pumping this Yvonne woman for information. Kat has given us permission to do a makeover."

Micki turned toward her companion. "Really? We've been begging you for months to let us help you spend all that lovely money." She paused briefly to consider the announcement. "This wouldn't be because you have someone you want to impress?"

"What makes you say that?" Kat returned an innocent smile.

"Oh, no reason, other than the admirer who joined us at our table Saturday night. The very man the rest of us have been trying to avoid until we have some hard evidence to hand him."

"As I told Marianne yesterday, Rick and I just went out for coffee after my second set. I was home within an hour."

"Rick, huh?" Micki said.

"That's his name. At least when he's off-duty."

"Ask her about Chuck," Marianne said.

"Who's Chuck?" Sydney wanted to know.

"He's Peri's brother. The one we're not supposed to talk about until the road is clear."

"Oh, all right. I'm curious now. So, tell us about Chuck."

Kat and Marianne described their meeting with Charles Dawson. "In other words," Marianne finished, "we're pretty sure Peri was seeing a married man a while back, but we don't know if she still is or was at the time of Schwimmer's death, nor do we have any proof he was the man."

"No matter who she's seeing or was seeing, he's worried about her," Kat added. "They've hardly been in touch." She mentioned the recent email. "He didn't seem like Peri at all. You know, flashy, self-involved, that type."

"And our Kat here felt moved to hold his hand after he expressed his concerns."

"You did?" Micki gushed. "Good grief, girl, that makes two men panting after you. Could you spare one for me? Although I'm not into the straight arrow types like Formero, so I guess it would have to be this Dawson guy."

"I did for him what I'd do for anyone I felt needed a little human sympathy, although he was kinda cute."

"Hmmm. I feel a need for boutique cheese in my future," Micki replied.

"Careful, Kat," Marianne warned. "Sounds like she's on the prowl."

"If he's as much a catch as you're not saying, I'm surprised there aren't more Serendipity Springs singles over there satisfying their *deli* needs," Micki added.

"Okay, traffic has thinned. Let's get back to the subject of our respective trips yesterday," Sydney cut in. "Why don't you update them about our time in Ocala, Mick?"

Micki finished her piece of coffee cake and handed the wrapping to Kat for the paper trash bag. "First, you both should know that Syd and I used aliases, for future reference. She's Grace and I'm Daisy. It was a spur of the moment decision, so if the woman at the flower shop called to check on us or mentioned us later to Shelly Ludwig, she'd get nowhere."

"At least you didn't come up with Thelma and Louise, although I'm surprised you decided on Grace instead of Rose or Violet around all that greenery," Kat said.

"Anyhow," Sydney continued, "we didn't learn anything specific either, although we now have a better picture of Shelly. She appears to be living way beyond her means, mainly through her men friends."

"You mean she's a..." Marianne asked.

"Not that we know. We don't even know if she's on this cruise with a man, since she left her apartment in a taxi by herself," Sydney returned.

"At least we now know where she lives," Micki added. "And we have a rough idea of her description. Blond and built. Oh, and she goes by the name Miranda at her apartment building. At least that's what her neighbor called her. That's a red flag right there."

Sydney pulled into another lane. "I have a feeling we could have pried more information from the woman at the flower shop, if we'd been more creative with our questions. As it was, we had to do more tap dancing than we anticipated when she asked why our friend wasn't with us, since it was her car that was hit. I said our friend was shy and didn't want to push to get it repaired."

"It was clear she didn't like Shelly, though," Micki went on. "Could be simply envy, since Shelly's supposedly so good-looking and this woman isn't, but her antipathy seemed to go deeper. Like Shelly wasn't a very good person."

"And you didn't get anything from the neighbor?" Kat asked.

Micki fished in the paper bag for another piece of cake. "Not more than what we already told you."

"So, who do we have here?" Sydney asked. "A woman who goes by one name at work and another where she lives. She doesn't appear to have a steady job or other means of income, yet she takes off on at least one cruise. Or that's what she told her boss. So, let's say she did murder Paul. Why would she suddenly go on a cruise?"

"It gets her out of the country for the first week of the investigation," Kat volunteered.

"But she has to come back sometime," Sydney pursued. "Unless she really didn't go on the cruise. Maybe she took off for parts unknown."

"Without taking any more of her possessions than a suitcase? And leaving in a taxi?"

"Maybe that was for show, for her neighbor," Micki said, playing along.

"Weird," Sydney continued. "Oh, well, one more question to file away for future follow-up."

Micki leaned into the front seat. "You mean we have to go back to Ocala? Who else would we talk to except directly to Shelly or Miranda or whoever she is?"

"Sounds more like a job for Rick, uh, Sheriff Formero, if we can ever convince him Shelly might be a suspect," Kat threw in.

They continued to discuss their respective reconnaissance trips plus other aspects of the case as the car made its way farther south. "Maybe it's time to revisit the three men on our list," Marianne suggested. "Perhaps talk directly to them. Or their wives."

"Sounds like a plan," Micki replied. "Unless we unearth something big about Peri today."

"We'll soon find out," Sydney announced. "That was the first exit to Naples. Check the GPS, Marianne. I think we have to go farther to reach the old downtown."

Twenty minutes later, they entered Yvonne's Boutique, located a few streets away from the fancier shops in Old Naples. It was graciously appointed with a silver blue carpet, ecru walls and stainless-steel clothes racks.

"Hello, ladies. Welcome to Yvonne's." The speaker was a thin woman with a platinum bob.

"We've come from Serendipity Springs on a shopping expedition," Sydney told her, taking the lead while the other three fanned out to explore the various clothing items.

"I'm delighted you chose to spend some of your time here. I'm Yvonne."

Sydney shook the proprietor's hand. "One of our acquaintances back in town, Periwinkle Dawson, mentioned your shop and suggested we stop by the next time we were in Naples."

The woman offered a studied smile. "Ah, Peri. How do you know her? Did she find you your homes?"

"Actually, we know her more from other civic connections, although my friend over there, the one with the gray hair, is currently one of Peri's clients. She's the one Peri told about your place."

The owner glanced toward Kat, who had worn a beige knit pullover with her navy slacks. "Yes, I see." She excused herself and made her way over to Kat. "Are you looking for something in particular?"

Before Kat could respond, Micki was there beside her. "She's here to refresh her wardrobe. She recently came into a small inheritance, and we've convinced her to put part of it toward new clothes. Your gain, if we can find some things here we like."

Yvonne's eyes took on a glow. "How exciting. Are we interested in casual things, business or more formal?"

"A little of each," Micki said.

"Then let's start with formal." Probably the most expensive, but who could fault the woman? Her goal was to make money. "Have you ever had your colors done, dear? Although they probably call it something different these days. You look like a winter with that fair skin and blue eyes."

"I, uh, have no idea what colors I should wear," Kat responded.

"Amen," Micki said more to herself than the others.

"For what kind of events would you need formal clothes?" Yvonne asked.

"Kat's a lounge singer. That wardrobe could use a real boost," Micki said.

Yvonne raised a pointed index finger. "Ah! I have just the things." Without even asking Kat's size, she disappeared into a back room.

"You're having too much fun, Mick," Kat chided her friend.

"I have so been waiting for this opportunity, I can't help myself."

Yvonne returned shortly with a pile of dresses, which she hung nearby. One was black, one navy, another magenta, and the last one was a beaded silver. "Which would you like to try first?"

While Kat disappeared into a dressing room with the black one, Micki used her absence to quiz the owner. "Peri told Kat she purchased a lot of her formalwear here."

"She has, although I haven't seen her much lately."

"She told Kat she typically needs less for summer months."

Yvonne patted her perfect coiffure. "Oh. That might explain it, although I suspect that her social life may have altered a bit as well. A year or so ago, her shopping expeditions seemed more upbeat, like she was not only excited about the clothes but also the reason why they were needed. I suspected a man. A very special man."

"Oh, good for her. I didn't know. Did she, uh, say who the man was?"

Yvonne waved away the question. "Heavens no! Peri's too discreet for that. Although I think he may have been with her here in Naples on a few of her trips. She kept checking her watch, like she needed to get to an important appointment. She wasn't wearing the kind of look you get when you have a dental appointment." She offered a knowing smile.

"You never saw him?"

"No, although he may have waited outside in a car."

"Did she ever mention him by name?"

Yvonne took a step back, her eyes suddenly wary. "You're asking a lot of questions about a mere acquaintance."

Micki laughed it off. "Sorry. I've been told my curiosity sometimes gets out of control. I was just passing time while we waited for Kat to change. Oh, here she is now."

Kat had emerged from the dressing room wearing a one-shoulder, black crepe number that ended just under the knees. "It's kinda snug but very sophisticated."

"It's supposed to fit like that," Micki reassured her. "Who knew you had that figure?"

"It's okay?" Kat's voice had grown tentative.

"More than, dear," Yvonne said. "Why don't we put that one in the yes pile while you try on the next?"

"Uh, okay." Kat pivoted and trudged through the royal blue velvet curtains.

"She isn't really into clothes, is she?" Yvonne said.

"Until recently, she lived on a shoestring budget. Much of her earnings went toward supporting her ailing mother. Since she's received her, uh, *inheritance*, she's had no idea what to do with it."

Yvonne studied Micki, her eyes gleaming. "Lucky for her she has you to help her learn."

Micki sloughed off the comment. "That's my job! Although I may just spring for something for myself also."

"What can I help you find?"

"I'd like to see some skinny pants."

As soon as the woman moved away, Sydney and Marianne joined Micki.

"So?" Marianne asked, keeping her voice low. "Pick up anything?"

"Not much," Micki grumbled. "There appears to have

been a man with Peri on several occasions, but Yvonne never saw him. So she says."

"That's it?" Sydney asked, deflated.

"Might as well do some shopping for all we've uncovered here. Better yet, we could stop at the outlet mall up the road. Why reward her?"

Yvonne reappeared carrying several pairs of slacks. "You look like a summer to me and one who isn't afraid of color." She hung them on another rack a few feet away from Kat's items. Coral, turquoise, tan, and lavender.

"They look great, Yvonne. I just hope they aren't too pricey. Kat's the one with the inheritance, not me."

Yvonne followed her back to the dressing room, apparently determined to make the sale with Micki. "I remembered one more thing. Several months ago, Peri confided that down the road she might have to change up her style somewhat, look more matronly. When I asked why, she got this sparkle in her eyes and said something about orange blossoms in her future, once a few minor details had been addressed. I presumed she was talking about a married man."

At least that confirmed their suspicions. "Thanks. This pair is starting to appeal to me." She hadn't meant to hint the sale was linked to gaining more information but was delighted her hesitation had brought that result.

"That day, she spent a great deal of time going through sterling silver money clips and bought one. An 'S.' When I appeared puzzled, she smiled mysteriously and said it was for the future."

Bingo. Not exactly the full name, but it certainly was the closest connection they'd found yet between Peri and Paul Schwimmer.

They spent another half hour waiting for Kat to decide on her purchases. In the end, she bought the black, the navy and, thanks to Micki's pleas, the silver dresses.

Sydney found a gorgeous emerald green silk blouse.

Marianne walked out with a belt.

And Micki wound up with the coral slacks.

A very productive trip, both for them and Yvonne.

Chapter Sixteen

he four were a half hour away from town when Sydney's phone rang. Marianne answered it for her.

"It's Olivia Schwimmer, Marianne. I need to talk to Sydney." She spoke quickly, sounded desperate.

"She can't come to the phone right now. She's driving. Can you tell me what's on your mind?"

"You have to come to my house immediately. All four of you, if you're together."

"Okay? What's up?"

"Sheriff Formero is here. I'm his chief suspect. Maybe his only suspect, for all I know."

"Okay, Olivia. Take a breath. All four of us are in the car. I'm going to put you on speaker, so we can all hear about what's happening." She played with Sydney's phone and switched the audio so it came through the vehicle's speaker system. "Okay, go ahead."

"I have to make this quick. I said I had to go to the bathroom, but that was so I could call and warn you. He's been going through all the files and records and what-not he claimed as evidence and found my diary. I haven't entered anything in weeks and must have forgotten it was even there."

The car's occupants exchanged looks. Why hadn't Olivia told them about the diary? "Go on," Sydney said.

"There were a few entries about my suspicions that Paul was being unfaithful. I wrote things when I was angry, like I wanted him dead. But I didn't mean it."

"Did you call your attorney? You shouldn't have to answer anything without your attorney present," Micki counseled.

"I, uh, no, not yet."

Three sets of eyes rolled. How could she expect them to get her off the hook when she did dumb things like this? "Go out there now and tell him you won't be answering any further questions until your attorney gets there." Sydney attempted to keep her voice even and not let her anger seep through.

Olivia hung up only to call again a minute later. "The sheriff wants to speak to you," she said, her tone terse.

"I want to talk to the four of you, so drop whatever you're doing and head to the Schwimmer house." His voice was flat, authoritative in a way that would brook no refusal.

Once more, they exchanged looks. This time, their expressions held panic.

Sydney attempted to keep her fear out of her voice. "Uh, Sheriff, as much as we'd like to accommodate your request, we are currently out of town. We went to Naples to shop."

"When will you be back?"

"Uh, hard to say. We're on our way home but hard to predict interstate traffic."

"Where are you now?"

He wasn't about to let them off the hook, and Sydney didn't make it a practice to lie to the authorities. She named the town they'd just passed.

"In other words, about thirty minutes away. Come straight here when you reach town." He hung up.

Sydney gripped the steering wheel tighter. "Formero wouldn't want to see us unless he knows about our involvement. Olivia must have told him."

"The reality of actually being suspected of her husband's death must have hit her so hard, she told him there were others with more reason to kill him than her," Kat surmised.

"Okay, let's think this through in the time we have remaining," Syd said. "Bottom line, we haven't done anything wrong or broken any laws. All we've done is ask a few questions and listen to people."

"We also have the church board records," Marianne reminded her.

"Hopefully, Olivia hasn't mentioned that," Micki replied.

"I nominate Kat as our spokeswoman," Marianne suggested.

"No! I'm just getting to know the guy personally."

"Exactly," Marianne returned.

Sydney held up a hand. "I'll take the lead. First, what do we tell him? How much do we tell him?"

"I vote for telling him everything and letting him decide what to do about it," Kat said.

"But what if it's not enough to convince him to look elsewhere?" Marianne asked. "Don't we need a Plan B?"

Sydney huffed. "We need a Plan A first. What if we just give him the names of the men we've looked into? There's not much follow-up we can do with them anyhow."

"Okay, I like that," Marianne replied.

"Thank God we haven't told Olivia about the two women yet," Micki said.

"Will Olivia have mentioned the mistress?" Marianne asked.

Marianne rubbed her chin. "Even if she hasn't, the one thing we do know is that the sheriff found her diary entry mentioning her belief there were other women. He won't let that drop if all we produce are three male names."

"Maybe that's Plan B, then," Sydney said. "Reluctantly turning over at least one name."

"How much do you think Olivia has told her attorney about us?" Kat asked.

"My guess, nothing," Syd replied. "I'll bet she's been telling herself this day would never come."

"The lawyer will probably arrive before we do," Marianne said. "Let's call Olivia back and suggest they meet privately as long as possible. In that time, she can tell the attorney about us, so whoever she's hired can help us deflect whatever the sheriff throws at us." With the others' agreement, she made the call. When she hung up, she had more to report. "She didn't sound like herself. Not the woman who's always in control. It's like she's in shock."

Sydney shook her head. "I hope the lawyer gets there in time. There's no telling what else Olivia has revealed."

Fifteen minutes later, they pulled up to the Schwimmer house. "Ready?" Marianne asked.

"You're kidding, right?" Micki responded.

"Think good thoughts, ladies," Syd directed. "And I repeat, we've done nothing illegal. Our goal all along has been to help find the real killer."

When they entered the house, Olivia and another woman were seated side by side on the sofa. Olivia identified the other woman as Colette Brownley, her attorney.

The sheriff was planted near a window, gazing out.

Sydney strode in, the other three behind her. They didn't sit; instead, they asked to see Olivia and Brownley in private.

"Sorry, ladies. Mrs. Schwimmer was allowed to speak with Ms. Brownley without me present, but you don't have that right. In fact, you don't have any rights in this case at all. Please be seated."

Sydney forced a tight smile. "First, we want to know that our friend is okay. She hasn't sounded like herself on the phone."

"I only know these women tangentially, Sheriff," Brownley interjected. "I'd at least like to meet them." She rose and came over to them. "I'm Colette Brownley," she said, holding out her hand.

"I'm Micki Demetrius." The others followed suit.

"You were wise to suggest Olivia bring in counsel before answering any more of the sheriff's questions." She pivoted slightly in Formero's direction. "I'm surprised the sheriff didn't advise her of such."

Formero didn't reply to her comment, apparently accustomed to attorneys' ploys to weaken his role. "Okay, if all the introductions are finished, I'd like to get on with this."

"This?" Sydney repeated. "What exactly is *this*?"

"First, please sit down." He waited until each of the six women was on a chair or the sofa. He remained standing. "Now then, I understand from Mrs. Schwimmer that she has enlisted your help investigating her husband's case. Is that correct?" His hard stare went from Sydney to the other three, barely resting on Kat.

As already agreed, Sydney handled the response. "I don't know if those are your words or Mrs. Schwimmer's, but that's not exactly the case. Because we're quite active in the community and Mrs. Schwimmer is still in shock over her husband's sudden death, she asked us to keep our eyes and ears open to be on the lookout for the person who might actually have done this terrible deed to her husband."

"Uh-huh. How exactly have you done this?"

Sydney kept her voice even and clear. "Like I said, we're active in the community. We've listened to speculation, and, uh, gossip, as the people in Serendipity Springs have reacted to Paul's death." She kept her answer short and truthful.

"Do any of you have any training in law enforcement techniques, especially how to investigate a murder?"

"Like I said," Sydney replied sweetly, "we weren't investigating. That's your job, Sheriff. But to answer your question, no."

"Have any of you ever worked in a law enforcement agency?"

"No."

"Then why do you think you can do a better job at figuring out who murdered her husband than I or my department?"

"With all due respect, Sheriff Formero," Colette Brownley interjected, "why are you harassing these women?"

He switched his attention to the attorney. "We both know these women have been interfering with my case. I want to know right now what they've learned."

"Then I suggest you allow them to tell you in their own words without hassling them."

Though his nostrils flared, he took a deep breath and then exhaled slowly. "All right, counselor, I'll give it a try." He turned back to Sydney. "Please tell me what you've learned."

Marianne took over. "Shortly before Mr. Schwimmer's

death, my husband and I, as well as Mrs. Bonner and her husband, attended a dinner of our social group, the Serendipity Springers, along with the Schwimmers. A comment made by Don Martin, a member of the same church the Schwimmers attend, elicited a sharp confrontation between the two men with Martin telling Paul they needed to talk soon about church finances. Shortly after that, Paul dragged Olivia away."

Sydney took over. "On their way out, Paul ran into and confronted another acquaintance, Cole McGraw. Both men came to mind, a few days later, when we learned about Paul's death."

The sheriff placed his hands on his hips. "So, the guy wasn't the most liked person in town. That's no reason to see every one of his detractors as a potential murderer."

Marianne tried again. "Don and Paul's church is facing a major shortfall in its treasury. Paul questioned several checks written by Don."

"How did you learn this?"

"From some things Paul shared with Olivia. I assume you already have Paul's board minutes and reports in your possession?" Marianne answered. No need to tell him they'd also seen the board's records.

Marianne wasn't finished. "Cole McGraw has developed a reputation for skimming his scores with his golf partners. When others started finding excuses to exclude him from their foursomes, Paul wound up with him as a partner. Per Olivia, Paul was considering turning him in to the club oversight committee."

"That wouldn't have been enough reason to kill the man."

"You don't play much golf, do you? Of course, you don't, you put in too many hours safeguarding our community," Sydney said. "If you did, though, you'd have some idea of the brotherhood that exists in golf clubs. Men are hesitant to report their friends, but when someone continuously shaves his score, that's a different matter. It would be tremendously humiliating for McGraw to lose his membership."

"That it?"

Kat, who'd been huddled in a chair farthest from the sheriff, stepped up to the plate, since the next one was her story. "There's one more. Paul's family owns an orange grove outside of town, which borders Hanes Carruthers's ranch. A long-term water rights agreement is about to expire, and if Carruthers couldn't convince Paul to extend it, hauling in water would be an expensive proposition."

Formero raised a brow. "Had Schwimmer actually refused to extend?"

"I think he'd been hinting but hadn't actually refused. Also, word has it Carruthers has been having financial problems. I guess he recently sold off some land."

"And you got all this information where?"

"I'm not at liberty to say, just that I came by it through legitimate means." Kat steeled herself for his reaction, since she was in essence refusing to cooperate.

Formero pursed his lips. He looked like he wanted to pursue this one but was restraining himself. Instead, he paced past the group once, then returned. "Okay, my staff and I will look into these possibilities."

The four returned tentative smiles.

"Now, that's the end of your *investigating* or whatever you've chosen to call it. Do I make myself clear?"

The four smiles faded, but no one spoke.

"Ladies?"

Three sets of eyes turned toward Sydney. "Yes, Sheriff. We hear you. We won't seek any further information about these three individuals."

"Unless something falls in our lap," Micki added. "Then, we'll pass whatever we learn right on to you."

"There's a murderer still out there. If they were to learn what you've been up to, there's no telling how they might react. You could be in danger." He gazed directly at Kat. "I'm concerned for your welfare. So, please, take me seriously."

"Does that mean Olivia, Mrs. Schwimmer, isn't a suspect?" Micki pursued.

"Not completely. From what we discovered, she apparently had a strong motive to want her husband out of the way. That doesn't necessarily mean she would have killed him."

Colette Brownley rose. "Does that cover what you needed to say to my client as well as her friends?"

Formero paused, as if loath to leave. "For now. But remember what I told you."

Colette followed him to the door and stood there staring out the window until he took off in his car. She turned back to them. "He's right, you know. What the four of you have been up to could be dangerous."

"I asked for their help," Olivia said. "They were quite hesitant to get involved, but I was sure what would happen was exactly what happened today. Although I was also sure he'd arrest me."

"He doesn't have enough evidence yet, or he would have," the attorney replied. "Your diary entries weren't very helpful, but they were your private thoughts. I suspect he's been talking to people around town and has learned something about your marriage. You and I need to sit down and you tell me everything that's been going on between you and your husband. I'm already sensing there's more to this than any of you have let on so far. I called an acquaintance here in town and asked if she knew you or your husband. She knew his reputation, and it wasn't good."

Olivia stared at her hands. "Yes, I'm aware of that, although I don't think I know the half of it. That's why I asked my friends to look into Paul's dealings, business, social and...otherwise."

"Let me guess," Colette added, turning her attention to the other four. "You've all been more successful than she dreamed."

"I suspect we've just begun to unearth the extent of Paul's secret life," Sydney admitted. "We've not reported much of this to you, Olivia, for fear of hurting you as well as, well, we weren't sure what you'd do with the information."

Olivia's eyes widened. "What? You were afraid I'd confront the woman and make myself more of a suspect?"

"You've had enough on your mind with the funeral and settling the estate," Marianne said. "We didn't know how you'd react. We were prepared to tell you, once we had more to go on."

"So? Did you find someone?" Olivia asked.

"It's okay," Colette added. "Spill. I've already surmised you came up with more than those three men. You gave the sheriff enough to chew on for now."

The four of them spent the next half hour reviewing everything they'd learned about Peri Dawson and Shelly Ludwig.

"Wow, you've been busy," Colette said when they finished.

"It doesn't prove a thing," Marianne said when they were done. "Other than the man got around. Sorry, Olivia."

"Don't worry about sparing my feelings. I've known for some time he was unfaithful."

Colette put a hand on Olivia's forearm. "You can tell us that, but keep it to yourself unless asked directly, okay? Foreknowledge makes a case for premeditation."

"True," Sydney put in, "but given what we've been told about Paul's injuries, they seem to have been spur of the moment, either an act of passion or anger. Which fits all five of the suspects we've identified."

"You're right, of course, but I'll take it from here. As Olivia's attorney, I have a legitimate reason to look into all those people. And find additional suspects, if it comes to that. If I have more questions, I'll call you. But in the meantime…"

"We know," Micki replied. "Stay out of it."

"I agree with the sheriff and Colette," Olivia added. "I am so grateful that you believe in my innocence and have gone to such lengths to prove it."

They hugged and said their goodbyes. Then the four headed for Sydney's car.

Marianne was the first to speak. "Well, that's that, I guess."

"Back to normal life," Micki added. "Kat and I can finish her makeover."

"Are you okay, Kat?" Sydney asked. "The sheriff didn't appear too pleased to discover you'd been part of our so-called investigation."

"I chose to be part. If there's something there between us, he'll have to get past this."

"And if he doesn't?" Micki probed.

Kat cocked her head and offered a mysterious smile. "Then I guess I'll be taking another trip to Shasta to check out cheeses."

Chapter Seventeen

*S*ydney arrived home to discover Trip at the dining room table moving items around what appeared to be a checkerboard. He was so engrossed, he didn't notice her until she was right there next to him.

"What's all this?"

"My version of a diorama of the community center stage."

She leaned in closer, placed a hand on his shoulder. "Figuring out if you've got enough stage for all your acts?"

"Sorta. I lost my director. His daughter's expecting at the same time as our show, so he and his wife are going north for a few weeks. First grandchild."

"I thought you were serving as your own director anyhow?"

"I was, at first. But given the number of complicated acts I've recruited, I decided I needed to be managing things backstage."

Did she really want to pursue this? What the heck, she was out of business as an investigator, so she had the time. "Complicated?"

"I've lined up several groups. Dressing rooms at the

community center are virtually nonexistent. There's one small room backstage. There's a few other meeting rooms, a small office and the bathrooms. I've got to figure out where to put everyone before they go on, where they get dressed and how to get them to the stage."

"You are totally up to it, Trip. What do you want for dinner?"

"I need to run over to the community center to review my assumptions. They're open for some meeting tonight, so this is my opportunity."

"Should I order out and let you pick it up on your way home?"

"Why don't you call one of the girls and go out for fast food? I'll catch something on the way home or make myself a sandwich here."

Was this his way of begging her to volunteer to help? She didn't want to find out. "Great idea." She grabbed her purse and headed for the door. "See ya." Too late, she realized there was a trill in her voice.

Since she'd been with the other three all day, dinner by herself appealed. Fortunately, her e-reader was in her purse, so after picking up her burger and fries at the diner, she made her way to a corner booth and read.

"I hope you're not waiting for your three cronies," a female voice said.

Syd looked up to find Colette Brownley. "Actually, we all went our separate ways after our dressing down by the sheriff. I'm here because my husband is off planning his follies event tonight, and I escaped before it occurred to him he could use an assistant."

"Mind if I join you?"

What could she say? "Please do. I can't seem to get into this book anyhow."

"Could it be you're still too involved with the Schwimmer case?" She took a sip of her soft drink while she waited for a response.

"Have to admit, I do feel a little lost. I've been spending a lot of time gathering information lately."

"For what it's worth, you and your pals did a good job. The sheriff wouldn't, or couldn't, admit as much, but the fact that he didn't chew you out any more than he did attests to that."

"Olivia told you it was all her idea, I hope? We advised her to let you know."

"Yes, she did, although I still don't understand what drove her to ask for your help."

"For pretty much the same reason she gave. She was afraid the sheriff would stop looking once he learned she and Paul had been having problems. This is the first time I can recall a murder happening in Serendipity Springs. She wasn't sure how much experience the sheriff and his people had solving murder cases and thought they might stop at the first likely suspect."

"How close are you all?"

"The four of us are all close. We play mah jongg with Olivia."

"But the five of you aren't close?"

Where was Olivia's attorney going with this? "We all know each other socially."

"Not quite what I asked. But that's okay. I got my answer. I was wondering why Olivia turned to you four in the first place, if you aren't all best buds. Why didn't she hire her own investigator?"

"That's a stumper. She certainly can afford it. When she first asked us to consider helping her, she said it was because we knew so many people in town, we could observe and listen and yes, ask questions, without being as obvious as a professional."

"Although a professional would have been familiar with the techniques of information gathering."

"They still would have stuck out in Serendipity Springs."

Colette sipped more soda. "True."

"Did we hurt her case?"

"Remains to be seen. Right now, I'm thinking you helped. The sheriff will never let on that he's been in over his head. You most likely gave him some new directions to go. Plus, you probably couldn't have dug much deeper into any of those three men's dealings without access you didn't have unless you broke the law. He has that access."

"What about the two women, Dawson and Ludwig? How do we steer him their way?"

"You could have told Sheriff Formero about them also. Why did you hold back?"

Syd took more time to chew her burger. "We didn't realize he'd go so far as prohibiting us from further inves—information gathering. We weren't sure what else we could do, but we held back, thinking some new idea would come to us."

"Olivia needs you to share with the sheriff what you learned about those two women. She realizes you were attempting to spare her feelings as long as you could unless and until you had some real evidence, but now she needs for it all to come out. It's very likely given what I've been hearing about this guy, there are other women who could have killed him."

"We told you all we know. Can't you take this to the sheriff?"

"I could, but I think it will carry more weight coming from the four of you."

Sydney's stomach dropped, and not from the burger

and fries. How were they going to tell the sheriff they'd come up with two other suspects? "You're right. Can it wait until tomorrow, though? The four of us have done enough for one day."

Rather than wait, Sydney called an impromptu meeting of the four at the diner once Brownley left. Marianne had to cut short dinner out with Beau. "Fortunately, Beau was ready to leave anyhow. There's some game he wanted to see on TV. What's up?"

Micki and Kat were just entering the restaurant. "Wait a sec, until the other two are seated."

"This had better be good," Micki said. "I was in the middle of my yoga class. The instructor doesn't look fondly on those who rush out in the middle. Something about the vibes not being closed properly."

"I've been trying on my new wardrobe," Kat confessed. "I can't believe I let you talk me into all three, Micki."

"But you liked what you saw, didn't you?" Micki chided.

Kat offered a shy smile. "Couldn't believe it was me."

"Wait till you see yourself once we get that hair cut off and styled."

Kat returned a frightened look, then turned to Sydney. "Enough about my makeover. Why the summons, Syd?"

"Colette Brownley was here earlier. Could've been coincidence, or maybe she tracked me down. Doesn't matter. The message would've been the same. She wants us to come clean with the sheriff about the two women suspects. I couldn't come up with a very good rationale why we shouldn't. We've already agreed we're at a standstill with both."

"Actually, that's no longer the case with Peri Dawson," Kat said. "She called after I got home. She's found a property for me and wants to stop by tomorrow."

"Is that good or bad?" Marianne asked.

"Could just be Peri wanting to snoop around your place. Establishing a foothold, in case you ever decide to sell," replied Micki, the pessimist.

"What do you think, Syd?" Kat asked.

"I think this changes things, at least for the time being. While we have the opportunity, we should attempt to learn more from the woman. But you shouldn't do this alone. Marianne, can you be there as backup? You went with her the first time."

"Tomorrow? I'm supposed to drive the lady next door to her doctor appointment."

"I'll do that," Micki volunteered. "So you can sit in, Marianne."

"I'll be nearby," Sydney added, "in case you need me."

Kat greeted Peri Dawson at the door the next day. "You remember Marianne, don't you? Marianne Putnam, my friend? She accompanied me when we took a quick tour of properties around town."

"Oh, right," Dawson said as she followed Kat through the large entryway into the formal living room. She made a show of scanning the surroundings. "I've admired your home from afar, but I've never been inside. This is beautiful, Kat. How long have you lived here?"

"Just a few years." No need to tell her about her lottery

win. Peri Dawson had probably done her homework and already knew.

"Is it, uh, just you who lives here?"

"Seems almost self-serving, doesn't it?" Kat said easily, although she'd long ago made peace with the idea. She'd lived so frugally for so long to care for her mother, for at least a little while, this home was just what she needed. She offered a seat on the light blue leather couch. Marianne had already made herself at home in a nearby easy chair. "I'm anxious to hear about the property you found."

The Realtor didn't bother to open her notebook computer. Instead, she settled back and crossed her legs. "I don't have anything in writing. Yet. This just came to my attention, and I wanted to make you aware of it before word got around. This is prime development property near town. Ten acres. Enough for a small complex of condos or even luxury homes."

"Oh, my. That seems a tad more ambitious than I was considering. I must say I'm surprised. I thought most of the land around town had either been sold or was tied up in trusts for several years."

Dawson licked her lips. "That's why this opportunity is so promising. But like I said, if you're interested, we need to act quickly."

"Do you have a prospectus or any information she can review?" Marianne asked.

For the first time since her arrival, Dawson seemed to close up, become less personable. "The specifics are still developing. It's that new."

"You expect Kat to make an offer on a rumor? Where is this property? Who owns it?"

Dawson bit a lip. "I can't really divulge that information. If I tell you more and you decide not to participate, Kat, who's to say you won't tell someone else who isn't represented by me and I lose the fee?"

Years of coaxing her mother to take her medicine and calming her moods swung into play for Kat. "That's understandable, Peri, but you can also see my friend's point. I don't want to invest my money in something I hardly know. Can't you tell us anything? Like why this land has suddenly come on the market? Or, better yet, who owns it?"

Dawson appeared to consider Kat's concerns. But she didn't speak.

"Wait! I heard something recently about a large landholder selling off some of his property in a very hush-hush transaction. Few people around town know about it. This wouldn't be Hanes Carruthers selling off more land?" Marianne wasn't sure how Micki would react to her sharing that nugget of information, but since the sheriff already knew, it shouldn't matter.

Dawson opened her mouth, then closed it.

"You're not answering because I'm right, or you don't want my erroneous supposition to force you to correct me?"

"Where did hear that, Mrs. Putnam? Have you been sharing it with others?"

"It's Marianne. And I'd rather not say except that it came from someone in the know." She wasn't done cross-examining the Realtor. "If you don't have anything in writing yet, that must mean you've heard about the sale through a trusted source. Surely it wouldn't be Candy Carruthers. She doesn't get to town much. Was it Hanes himself?"

Dawson blinked. Once. Then she pulled her notebook toward her. "It would appear you're not interested in development opportunities. I won't take up more of your time, but I'll stay on the lookout for apartments or condos." She rose and fled, not even taking in the rest of the house as she went.

"So much for that," Marianne asked once it was just the two of them again.

"You were really pushing the idea of it being Carruthers. We still don't know if Dawson's hot prospect was his land or not. In fact, did we learn anything new?"

"We learned someone has land to sell but wants to keep the transaction quiet. However, Peri knows about it. How? I know real estate agents only succeed if they have confidential sources, but if hers is Carruthers himself, then we've connected two of the dots. Also, if it is Carruthers who has the land to sell, then his financial situation is becoming increasingly more dire, which might have made him desperate enough to kill Paul."

Kat studied her friend. "That was brilliant. I think you've been hanging out with Syd too much."

"Let's see what she thinks."

Sydney arrived ten minutes after they called, with Micki not far behind, the woman she was chauffeuring having gotten into the doctor's office faster than usual.

Kat summarized her meeting with Peri Dawson, and Marianne went over the same conclusions she'd shared with Kat.

"So?" Micki asked. "Now what?"

Sydney planted her chin on her folded hands. "Is there anything more we can learn on our own that will take the sheriff longer to uncover?"

"One thing would be if there's a direct connection between Peri and Carruthers," Marianne offered. "Let's say it is his land. Is he one of Peri's *men* or simply a client or even a potential client if she's still trying to get the deal, which could be why she didn't have anything in writing."

Micki took up the trail. "But say the two of them do have something going, how does that relate to Paul Schwimmer?"

"If he was having an affair with Peri and he learned that she was seeing Carruthers as well, he could've broken things off with Peri and denied Carruthers his water rights," Sydney speculated.

"Which brings us back to Carruthers finding him on the trail and putting him away, either in the heat of the moment or deliberately, thinking Olivia, as his heir, would be more amenable," Micki said.

"Can we learn any of that if we continue this farce with Dawson?" Sydney asked.

"Give us a day," Micki said. "Kat should show up at Peri's office tomorrow without warning and say she's reconsidered, at least enough that she'd like to know more about the property, like actually see it."

"I'll give it a try, but I don't think I'll get any further with her than we did today."

Marianne agreed to go with her again. Luck was with them in that the receptionist had stepped away from her desk, so they could pop in on Dawson unannounced. The door was slightly ajar, and as they approached, they could hear a woman crying. Peri?

Kat turned to leave, but Marianne stood in her way. "She's vulnerable. We can't pass up this opportunity. Go in there and do your sympathy thing."

Kat grimaced but switched direction. "Peri? Is everything okay?" She kept her voice low, understanding.

The woman who gazed up at her was a different Peri. This one's eyes were red-rimmed, her face blotchy. "Kat! You caught me at a bad time. Can I call you later?"

Kat advanced. Marianne remained in the hall. "I came by to tell you I'd reconsidered the offer you brought me.

At least I would like to hear more about it. You can call me about that later, but I don't feel right leaving you on your own like this."

Peri waved her away. "I'm okay. I just have some personal issues to deal with."

"Perhaps if you talked to someone? I'd be happy to listen. Or I could call someone for you? Your brother, maybe?"

"No, no! I don't want Chuck involved in this."

Kat continued toward Peri's desk. "Okay. But I'm here, and I'm almost a perfect stranger, the best kind of counselor when you need to get something off your chest."

Peri appeared to consider Kat's offer briefly but then shook her head. "No, thank you. This is something I have to face alone."

"If it's something you did that you don't think others will understand, you're selling your friends short."

Peri's eyes narrowed. The tears stopped. "Why do you think I did something?"

"I don't. I was just trying to get you to talk. Maybe someone did something to you?"

The other woman seemed to jerk in her seat. "Why would you think that?"

"Just a lucky guess. If you didn't do something you regret, then you regret what they did to you. A man. Right? Because if it is, you have a major leap to make. You can't change the past, you can only move on."

"Are you a psychologist or something? Where do you get that mumbo jumbo?"

"A long time ago, I went through my own heartbreak. I waited too long to say yes to the man I loved and missed out on what could have been the best years of my life. If my case sounds familiar, don't let that happen to you."

"You have no idea what or who I am, Katrina. I'm sure you never took up with a married man."

Kat couldn't believe her ears. She was so close. "He promised to leave his wife?"

"Hinted at it. I wasn't in a rush, except I didn't like having to keep things on the down low. My professional reputation could be ruined if it became public." Peri noticed Kat's reaction to her last statement. "Why am I telling you, you wonder. Because you caught me at my most vulnerable moment. It's over, and like you said, all I can do is move on. But first, I have to mourn my loss."

She'd almost mentioned Paul. Kat just had to hang on a bit longer. "Mourn?"

Peri seemed to snap out of her reverie. "Uh, yes. The loss of our relationship."

"Oh. I thought you meant he'd, uh, passed."

Peri didn't answer. Instead, she grabbed a couple tissues and dabbed her eyes. I'll... I'll be fine. As soon as I have a chance to cry this out. Thank you for listening, but now I need to be alone. I'll call you as soon as I can."

Kat could recognize a dismissal when she heard one. "Uh, sure. Please take care." She backed out of the room, closing the door as she left.

Marianne was several feet away. Kat put her index finger to her mouth and fast-walked to the exit.

"May I help you?" The receptionist had now returned from wherever.

Marianne took the lead on this one. "There was no one here when we arrived, so we went on back. Peri asked us to tell you she'd like to be alone for a while."

"Do we need to make another appointment for you?"

"Thanks, but that won't be necessary," Kat called as the two of them sailed out the door.

Chapter Eighteen

While Kat listened to Peri Dawson's problems, Sydney had a problem of her own: her husband's over-ambitious plans as follies director. The fact that he'd fixed waffles for her breakfast was her first clue. He only did that when they had company or he wanted something. To her amazement, he never realized she was on to him, and like any smart wife, she wasn't about to tell him.

"How were the waffles?" he asked, hovering nearby. "Not too hard, not too soft?"

"Very good. I like the blueberry sauce. Nice touch."

"Nothing's too good for my lovely spouse." He dropped a kiss on the top of her head.

"No golf today?"

"Uh, no. Needed to work on the show." No golf? Second clue something was coming. "How about you? You've been spending a lot of time with the girls lately. Taking today off?"

She didn't want him to think she had free time to spare. "Not sure. I'm waiting to hear from Kat."

He slid into the seat opposite her at the breakfast table. "While you're waiting for her, I sure could use your advice."

Advice? New ploy. "Oh? What's up?"

"I checked the logistics at the community center, and I was right. There's just no way I can direct up front and keep everything moving on schedule backstage. I need a stage manager. But the thing is, it's getting so close to the night of the show, everyone I've talked to is already booked. Any ideas who else I could tap?" His voice had taken on a soft, coaxing tone.

They both knew who he had in mind, but before Sydney succumbed to her husband's charm, actually his current predicament, she did a mental inventory of how much time this new task would take. At least the night of their run-through and the actual performance as well as studying the entire script, if there was one. Kat and Micki were already involved in this production. Maybe she could talk Marianne into helping her. Then they could convince Sheriff Formero they really had put their investigation days behind them.

"Would you like me to volunteer?" She kept her tone innocent.

"Oh, gosh, Syd, would you? You'd be the perfect person to do this. You have all the requisite skills for managing backstage."

She pretended to consider, although she'd already made up her mind. "I guess my participation could be bought. For the right price."

"Uh-oh. Is there some fancy new outfit involved?"

"No. I already bought a new blouse yesterday in Naples. The girls and I have a project we're working on. That's why I've been involved with them a little more than usual recently. It's really hush-hush. So, if you're willing to put your curiosity aside about what we're doing and will agree to convince Beau to do the same, I'll take the job."

He studied her for a few beats. "I've noticed that the girls' club has convened more than usual lately and have been wondering if I should be worried. But you've got me over a barrel, so okay to your terms. As long as you're not doing anything dangerous."

Sydney paid a little more attention to cutting the second half of her waffle than necessary. "Dangerous? Heavens no. We're just a bunch of retired ladies who play mah jongg and enjoy lunching with each other."

Trip went to the counter and returned with several sheets of paper stapled together. "Here. Probably not as pretty as you'd like, but these are my notes on the acts in the order in which they'll appear. Your job will be to have the next act waiting in the wings at the same time the first act goes on stage and have the act after that nearby. If anything goes wrong in the course of the show, you need to be the first one there to do damage control."

"Sounds critical. What will you be doing?"

"I'll be out front with the accompanists giving them their cues."

"Will I be able to see you?"

He shook his head. "Only if you come out on stage, which we want to avoid."

"So, I'm on my own?"

"That's the beauty of the dress rehearsal. We'll work out all the kinks then."

Sounded rather risky to her. "Are you auditioning these acts before all this?"

He turned his chair around and straddled it, clasping his hands together. "You're not sounding very confident about all this. Tell me what's on your mind."

"I wasn't sure you were ready to hear. You've been so high on this project, I don't want you to think I'm trying to undermine this show. But, yes, I do have a couple concerns."

"Okay, shoot."

"First, just from skimming the lineup you've given me, you seem to have placed all the groups in the latter part of the show. There may be a very good reason for that, but it also means there will be a lot of people wandering around backstage before they appear."

"They're near the end because many of these folks have jobs and can't get there until after the show starts."

"Will they be able to be there the night before for the dress rehearsal?"

He cocked his head, as if thinking through their various schedules. "Most. The ones who can't make it will be filled in by their group members."

She couldn't very well offset her concern by requiring the stragglers be there on time. "Do you know who all those latecomers are?"

"Uh, not specifically. Their leaders are the ones who are on top of that."

"This is just a suggestion. Get a list from each group leader. Let them worry about the stragglers, but you still need to know exactly what to expect."

He nodded his head, apparently considering.

"Another thing. Have you seen each of these groups perform?"

"Not all. Well, only one. The others have all been wrapped up in their own rehearsals."

"If it were me, I wouldn't trust that all is well. I'd want to see them perform now, before the dress rehearsal."

Sighing, Trip rose and poured himself a glass of water. "These are all volunteers, Syd. If I demand to see them ahead of time, they'll think I don't trust them."

She shrugged. "Suit yourself, although I bet you could

come up with creative reasons for dropping in on them in the time before the show. Maybe to thank them personally for appearing, maybe to wish them luck."

He took a few sips. "I suppose I could do something like that."

She had one more concern. It was a doozy. "You need to keep us in communication with headsets, so we don't have to send messengers back and forth."

"Headsets? But those are expensive. We don't have that kind of money."

"But you have community backers. Ask them to loan you communication devices."

Trip didn't say anything. He finished his water, set down the glass. He came over to her and pulled her out of the chair into an embrace. "You are fantastic."

"You don't mind my suggestions?"

"Well, yeah, but they make good sense. I knew I was missing some things but couldn't put my finger on them."

"See if you can get at least four headsets, one for you, one for me, and one each for Marianne and Beau. I'm going to ask her to help me, and I'm guessing you've already corralled Beau, so he won't have to perform."

"In other words, although we now know Peri had a thing going with a married man that has come to an end, we still haven't confirmed it was Paul Schwimmer." Micki summarized after Kat and Marianne related their trip to visit the Realtor earlier in the day.

"We couldn't have expected her to provide the name," Syd said. "It surprises me she said as much as she did."

"I caught her when she was vulnerable," Kat replied.

Marianne patted her friend on the back. "You guys should have heard our girl. She kept probing as far as she dared go, even though it was obvious Peri wanted to be alone."

"She seemed to want to talk until she realized she'd probably said too much," Kat added.

This afternoon they were meeting at Micki's condo. She didn't offer to be hostess often, because by her own admission she was a bit of a slob, but her cleaning person had just been there the day before, and the place was still in good shape. "But she didn't say how it ended?"

Kat shook her head. "She did say she needed time to *mourn*. But when I followed up on that word, she said she meant mourn the end of the relationship. That's when she decided it was time to get rid of me."

Sydney stirred her coffee absentmindedly. "It sounds to me like we've run out of items to check. Is it time to talk to the sheriff again?"

"Peri is supposed to call Kat," Marianne reminded them. "But my guess is she'll be so embarrassed to have revealed so much, she'll be all business if Kat meets her again."

"Then let's do it," Sydney said.

The sheriff agreed to meet them at Micki's. He arrived about a half hour later. "I hope I'm here because you've *remembered* something else and haven't been snooping again?"

Micki sat up straighter. "We never said we were snooping."

He returned a tolerant expression. "Uh, sure. So why am I here?"

"We have another name to give you," Sydney said. "We had a chance to learn a little more before we said anything, which is why we refrained from saying anything about this person the other day."

The sheriff shifted position, folded his hands as if restraining himself from speaking.

"As you know, it was rumored that Paul Schwimmer was seeing other women. Several women around town have commented on how he came on to them, but no one had actually seen him out with someone besides his wife. We'd heard a rumor about a local real estate agent we've been trying to confirm," Sydney continued.

"Real estate agent, huh? There are several female agents in town."

"True," Sydney replied, "but we'd heard of one in particular. Peri Dawson. We learned from her personally that she's been seeing a married man until recently when the relationship ended."

Though he sat forward, he narrowed his eyes. "She came right out and told you?"

"Actually, yes," Kat said, deciding it was time for her to enter the discussion. "I've, uh, been looking into investment property and had gone to talk to her about it yesterday. When I got there, I found her in tears, and when I tried to comfort her, she broke down and told me that much."

"Investment property, huh?" The man who repeated her words did not sound like the one who'd raved about her voice just days ago.

"I, uh, was lucky enough to win some money in the lottery a while back. You probably know that. I've taken my time deciding how to handle this windfall."

"You just happened to pursue this interest recently?"

Of course he was on to them. But they'd already agreed to admit only as much as necessary. "Yes." She didn't look at him directly but instead stared at a point over his left shoulder.

"What am I supposed to do? Ask her point-blank who she was sleeping with?"

Sydney stepped in for Kat. "We don't expect you to do anything, other than realize we're attempting to tell you who we've come across as potential suspects."

"Okay. Thanks." Then a thought occurred to him. "Anyone else you haven't told me about?"

All three women looked to Sydney. "There's one. We didn't mention her before because, like Dawson, we don't have much to go on. Her name is Shelly Ludwig, although we think she also goes by the name Miranda." She told him how they'd learned Schwimmer had been seen kissing a woman in a car in a parking lot in Ocala and how they tracked that car to a local florist.

"How did you…" His voice rose.

"We've given you a name. Isn't that enough?" Sydney challenged.

He blew out a breath. "For now. Since you said he was seen kissing her, that's enough for me to look into her."

"She may or may not be back in town," Micki said. She explained about Shelly's cruise. "It's possible he was going with her before his death prevented it. You should be able to learn if he was also registered, although he may have put his reservation under another name."

"I'll do that." He made ready to leave. "Like I said before but mean more than ever now, no more investigating, ladies." He turned to Kat. No smile. "If this Dawson woman contacts you again, let me know."

Kat screwed up her face. "Why, if you don't want us poking our noses into police business?"

"We might be able to get a little more from her, if it's done under the guise of business. But only if I'm aware of what you're doing and can be nearby."

The likelihood of Peri Dawson calling her again seemed low, so Kat agreed.

That settled, Sydney reclaimed the floor. "You'll be happy to know all four of us are now involved in the community follies my husband is producing. Are you one of the acts?"

"Me? No," the sheriff said.

"Oh, well, in that case, I hope you'll buy a ticket."

"I'm doing volunteer security detail."

"Even better," Marianne added. "It promises to be quite a night."

Chapter Nineteen

*C*ontrary to Kat's expectations, Peri Dawson called her the day after Kat's visit. Kat told her she'd reconsidered and definitely was not interested in this particular deal. Apparently, Dawson wasn't ready to give up. She called Kat a week later with a new possibility, a home in her part of town, and wanted to show it that afternoon. Unfortunately, Marianne wasn't available. Nor were Sydney nor Micki. Sydney and Marianne were over at the community center helping Trip block out the follies, and Micki was getting her hair done. But Dawson was in a hurry. Kat got the address and agreed to meet her there.

Then she called the sheriff. "Since your friends aren't available, I'll hang around the neighborhood. If things start to get suspicious, get yourself out of there and call me immediately."

"This just came on the market," Peri said in greeting once Kat arrived. "I thought of you as soon as I read the blurb."

Kat stepped inside a large entryway, now devoid of furnishings. "It's a totally different style than my own place." Her voice echoed as she spoke.

"Spanish. Yours is more Italianate. I, uh, looked it up on the internet."

They made their way into what must be the formal living room. "Where's your friend today?"

"Working on the follies with my other friend, Sydney. Are you performing?"

"Me? Heavens, no. My talent is selling real estate. How about you? I've heard you're making a name for yourself as a cabaret singer."

"Yes, they talked me into singing a few tunes. But I won't be needed until the dress rehearsal later in the week."

Dawson kept moving farther into the house. This next room was a den. It could be an office or a small sitting room."

"Are there many people who want to rent houses like this?"

"More than buyers at times. A lot of executives are transferred to this area for two- and three-year stints and don't want to risk having to turn around and sell the house after just a few years."

"Do you handle renters?"

"No, I send them to a friend who specializes in rentals."

They were well inside the house when Dawson twisted around. "I wasn't sure you'd show up today."

Kat lifted a brow. "Oh? Why not? I said I'd come."

"You also said you'd consider the property I told you about."

"Which I did. I came to your office last week to ask for more information. That was the day you, uh, weren't able to talk to me."

Peri tilted her head to the side. "The day you found me in tears."

"Uh, yes." Kat was surprised she would bring it up again.

"I told you things that day I should have kept to myself."

Kat remained quiet. Did the woman expect her to agree or what? She couldn't very well reassure Dawson that those things would remain confidential. "We all have days like that, though maybe not for the same reason. I hope you're doing better."

"I didn't want you to get the wrong impression. As your real estate agent, I want you to view me in only the most professional of terms."

"I get that, but I wouldn't have shown up today if I didn't see you as the consummate professional."

"Thank you. My reputation is my stock in trade. I'd hate to see it slip a notch."

Was there a hidden message or appeal in that statement? The woman was staring at her pointedly. She might as well pursue it. "Like taking up with a married man?"

Her question seemed to crystallize and hang between them. Peri's eyes flickered. "You're right. I've been with a lot of men in my life, but I've shielded my professional life from my private interests. I was a bit reckless this time, but I couldn't help myself."

Since all furniture had been removed from the house, Kat found herself standing just a few feet away from Peri. Maybe the woman would talk more if they were both more comfortable. "I'd like to see the patio."

"Oh, sure."

Outside on the screened-in patio that surrounded the pool, a wall cut off the deck from a landscaped section. Kat settled onto it. "Join me." Dawson seemed to hesitate, then came over. "You're a beautiful woman, Peri, with a great business going. I don't mean to sound judgmental, but if, like you said, you had plenty of men to choose from, what was there about this man with a wedding ring you couldn't resist?"

Peri wrung her hands, then turned mournful eyes toward Kat. "Haven't you ever done something you never would have thought you'd do?"

"Sure. I didn't have money before. I never thought I'd be treating myself to a few luxuries now or considering rental property. But my experience with men is more limited. The one serious relationship in my life was with a man who died too soon in a car crash."

"I'm sorry. You mentioned something about him before, but you didn't say he'd been killed. We seem to have that in common." It was stated simply, like two strangers who suddenly found themselves sharing the same past, but it was a major admission.

This was her chance to confirm the man was Paul Schwimmer. Kat had to handle this right to get there, and Peri may have said all she was going to say. "I, uh, didn't realize you'd lost your man to death. Was it a car crash also?" She held her breath. She wouldn't have a better chance.

Peri seemed to stare off to the other side of the patio. "No. I think you know what happened. Isn't that why you've developed a sudden interest in rental property? To gain my confidence so I'd tell you about him?"

Though seated, Kat felt her stomach plummet. Peri was on to her. Why go to this elaborate ruse to get her here, if she already knew what Kat wanted? Why bring her to this empty house? Time to end this. *Rick, I hope you're close by.* Slowly, she came to her feet. "This wasn't a good idea." She started for the door, but Peri caught up with her and grabbed her arm.

"Oh, c'mon, you're not giving up now? You're almost there. Stick around a bit longer and find out for sure."

"Let go of my arm, Peri."

"So you can run to your friends and report what I told you? Fine. But you haven't quite confirmed your suspicions, have you?"

Might as well go for it. "That the man you lost was Paul Schwimmer?"

Peri smiled wickedly. "Why are you so interested? He never mentioned you."

Possibly half the truth would suffice. "Olivia Schwimmer is a friend of mine. She believes he was involved with another woman. I thought I could bring her peace if I could either confirm or deny it."

"What good will it do for her to know the truth now?"

Concede and get out of here. "You're right. I told her I'd find out, so she wouldn't investigate on her own and probably make things worse for herself. Now I can tell her she was imagining things." She hoped that made more sense to Peri than it did to her.

Peri released her arm. "I knew what he was, you know? Before we hooked up, I'd seen him in action. A philanderer, although to the best of my knowledge, he didn't push himself on other women. I knew the chances of his being faithful to me were slim, but I kept telling myself I was different. I was the one who'd stop him in his tracks. Foolish, yes, but I saw him as a challenge. For a while, keeping a low profile was all the excitement I needed."

Peri's willingness to talk was a surprise. Maybe she'd been holding things in so long, now that she'd started to talk, she couldn't stop. "You said he promised to leave his wife. What changed?"

"Paul thought someone had seen us together a couple times recently, even though we were out of town. He was

167

afraid his wife was having him followed so she could divorce him and get all the money. So, he figured he'd split with Olivia before she had the chance. She may be your friend, but everything points to her as his murderer. She must have confronted him about me and killed him in a fit of anger."

Was this an act or did Peri really believe Olivia killed Paul? Best to let that supposition go and back up. "Did you ever see who was supposedly following you?"

"Once I saw what looked like a woman retreating into the bushes at the motel where we were staying. At least I saw shapely bare legs that didn't look like a man's. But I dismissed it. In my mind, women don't do that kind of work. In the movies, it's always some scumbag guy."

"Where was the motel located? Near town?"

"No. Paul didn't want to chance running into anyone else he knew. Apparently more than one man in Serendipity Springs cheats. Imagine. We were just off the Interstate, about an hour away."

"North of town?"

Peri screwed up her eyes. "Yes. How did you know?"

"Just a guess."

Neither said anything for a bit. Kat sensed her opportunity to escape. "I should go. I'm sorry I took up your time." She didn't wait to shake hands or for Peri to accompany her to the door but instead strode as fast as she could without actually running.

"Tell her I truly loved him," Peri called behind her.

Kat nearly ran to her car, drove a couple of blocks, turned and went a little farther before calling the sheriff. "It was Paul."

"You don't sound good. Did she threaten you?"

"I was afraid she might. She caught my arm as I was trying to leave. But no."

"Meet me at your house. Give me a few minutes. I'll park a block away, so anyone passing won't see I'm there."

Kat did as instructed, fixed herself a cup of hot tea while she waited. She was nearly in tears by the time he arrived.

"Are you okay? Stupid question. Of course, you aren't. C'mere." He pulled her into his arms and simply let her calm her breathing. "Just relax, hon. You did great."

She heard what he called her but didn't react. She was just happy to be out of there.

He steered her into her living room, helped her to a chair and placed an afghan from a nearby chair around her shoulders. He brought her the cup of tea she'd prepared but refused any for himself. While she sipped, he stood several feet away and waited.

"Have a seat, Rick. You're making me nervous standing there like that."

He did as asked but still stayed at least five feet away from her.

Finally, she was ready. "I'm not sure what her original plan was in getting me alone in that empty house, but by the time I left, I no longer felt threatened, although I didn't stick around to see if her mood changed again." She related as much of Peri Dawson's "confession" as she could recall.

"She just *offered* it?"

"Strange, right? I asked a few pointed questions, which she answered."

"Did she say how she got on to you?"

"Not really, although she didn't push when she wanted to know how I got on to her either. She seemed more interested in revealing details about their relationship."

"That happens sometimes when people are ready to talk. They just keep going."

Kat removed the afghan. "Unless she's a terrific actress, she doesn't know that there was at least one other woman besides Olivia in Paul's life." She told him how Peri thought she had seen a woman disappearing into the bushes, but had dismissed her as only a private detective hired by Olivia. "If that's the case, she would've had no reason for killing him, unless he suddenly called things off or she learned he wasn't serious about leaving his wife."

"Plausible." He stroked his chin. "But let's not write her off just yet."

She gave him a funny look.

"On second thought, I'll amend that statement to 'I won't write her off yet.'"

"Thanks for being nearby and coming here to talk me down. She gave me the willies."

He gave her a mock salute. "Just part of the personal service offered by my department. Plus, I actually encouraged you to go there. I probably shouldn't have done that, now that we realize it could have been more dangerous than we thought. I'm sorry. I asked you to do the very thing I told you and your friends not to do."

She waved away his apology. "I'm not used to putting myself in the center of things, other than when I'm singing. That's why Marianne Putnam went with me the other three times."

He raised a brow. "Three times? I only recall you mentioning two."

"Uh, right. On the first visit we commented on one of the photos in her office. Turns out it was her brother. He owns a boutique deli over in Shasta. Marianne and I, uh, decided to check out his establishment. I bought some wonderful Kona coffee and a coffee cake."

"You haven't mentioned any of this."

"It didn't seem necessary, since we didn't consider him a suspect. He was just collateral information."

"Katrina! You had no idea if he knew about his sister and Schwimmer, and if he did, if he wasn't happy with the guy leading her on. For all you know, he could've driven here to Serendipity Springs and tracked him down on the path."

To her chagrin, he had a point. "Fortunately, he was the only one tending his store. If he'd been the murderer and the least bit suspicious of us, he couldn't have done anything about it."

That sent him to his feet. "You're kidding. No deli counter would prevent him from doing something dire to you if he wanted. If he was by himself, he could've easily put a 'closed' sign on the door and hurt both of you. Or driven back here at any time and done who knows what to you. From what you've said, he could still be a suspect."

She frowned. "I, uh, hadn't thought of that."

"Well, start thinking of it. See what happens when civilians start nosing around police cases? Unintended consequences." His tone wasn't scolding. Instead, he sounded genuinely concerned.

Kat wasn't sure how to take his mood. If she had to guess, she'd say it bordered on the personal. If that was the case, how did she want to handle it?

Suddenly, the air in the room seemed too tight. She bounced up. "You've never been here. How would you like a tour?"

"Uh, sure."

"It's too much house for me, but I went a little crazy with my newfound wealth when I first moved here and decided I wanted it anyhow. I hardly use some of the rooms, but I've grown to like having all this space. Does that seem selfish?"

He examined several of the books on a nearby shelf. "Selfish? No, although one of these days you may change your mind, decide to downsize." He turned, offered a shy smile. "Or bring in more people to enjoy this."

"I suppose either is possible. For now, though, I'm just enjoying the change in my lifestyle after years of much more stringent spending. The next room is the library."

"You mean this isn't it with all these books on the walls?"

"One thing I allowed myself over the years was books. The library was already pretty well stocked when I moved in, so these are my books in here."

"I checked out a few of those titles. Quite a wide variety of interests."

"You're welcome to borrow anything that strikes your fancy."

He returned the oddest look. Stared at her a bit, then his expression relaxed. "Uh, thanks. I'll keep that in mind."

Uh-oh, had she suggested more than she intended? "The same goes for the library," she said as they entered that room. She pointed toward the desk. "I don't know how anyone could study or do business with that massive thing. I prefer the kitchen tabletop or the small secretary in my bedroom whenever I'm writing something."

"You mind?" She nodded, and he slipped around the mahogany desk, lowered himself into the chair. "Nice. I could get used to something like this back at the office. Gives a guy a real feeling of power."

"Don't you already have that with your badge?"

He angled his head. "Do I come across like that?" The notion seemed to bother him.

"Aren't you supposed to?"

He scratched his head. "Yeah, I guess so. It's just when I hear it stated like that, it makes me feel like I'm too big for my britches, as my mom used to say when I'd get too arrogant about a football play."

"You don't strike me as the arrogant type, Sheriff."

They left the library and checked out the dining room. "How often do you use this room?"

She wandered around the table. "Once for a formal dinner party. A couple times, I've entertained our mah jongg group and used this room to set out food." She fingered one of the dark blue damask placemats. "It's not me."

"Perhaps a redo so you can use it more?"

"Lighten it up?" She took in the heavy toile wallpaper and the dark ceiling. "That's a thought. If I ever decide to entertain more."

"Or, the other way around, you might decide to entertain more with a dining room more to your liking." He smiled again. Was it her imagination or was there some hidden message there?

"Moving on. This is my informal living room," she said, leading the way. "I spend the bulk of my time here." She quickly shoved a pile of magazines together.

He made himself at home on the sofa. "Much nicer than what I've seen so far. This looks more like you. By the way, you were all correct about Don Martin. He was embezzling church funds."

Kat stopped in her tracks. "Uh, okay. Did he admit it?"

"Through his attorney, yes. Seems Schwimmer did confront Martin about taking the church's money. According to Martin, he denied it at first, hoped he could convince Schwimmer there was no problem, but

Schwimmer persisted, showed him incontrovertible evidence of his misdeeds."

Without realizing what she was doing, she plopped down next to him, her body touching his. "And that's when he killed Schwimmer."

"Uh, no. The deceased gave Martin a couple days to lawyer up before meeting with the church council, at which time Martin agreed to resign and pay back the money over time. He had no reason to kill Schwimmer after that."

She attempted to absorb the new information. "Not even out of spite?"

"I suppose it might seem that way, but Martin was truly sorry for what he'd done and, in a way, welcomed Schwimmer's accusation. Plus, and here's the clincher, he and his attorney were meeting with Martin's banker about restitution at the time Schwimmer was killed."

"Oh."

"You and your friends couldn't have known that part. I probably could've discovered Martin's money problems, if Mrs. Schwimmer had shared her suspicions with me instead of you and your three cohorts. But she was so worried about looking guilty in my eyes, she turned to all of you instead."

"Would you have really looked beyond her? The words in her diary and Paul's reputation were damning. Murder cases don't come your way very often, thank goodness. One can understand why you'd be anxious to wrap it up as soon as you could."

He rocketed off the couch and turned on her. "You really think I would've zeroed in on that woman just to supposedly solve the case?"

She'd stepped on his toes in her attempt just to be honest with him. "I didn't know you then as well as I'm starting to know you, Rick. Have you ever been in charge of a murder case before?" She kept her voice low, non-challenging.

"There've been a few in the county, and I worked several cases as a deputy sheriff in Orlando. That was the first thing they taught us in the academy: Never assume until you've got all the facts."

"A good watchword for my friends and me as well. We should have given you more credit."

"You do realize, Katrina, Mrs. Schwimmer is still a suspect, especially since we've eliminated one of the people on your list."

"I guess there are certain things that make her look suspicious, but I, we, my friends and I, believe her. Besides, you still have the other names we gave you. What about them?"

"Still checking out those leads. Which I should get back to. You'll be okay here by yourself, right, in this gated community?"

She nodded. "State-of-the-art security system also."

Kat walked him to the door. "Thanks for seeing me home. And for the update."

He took her hand. "Stay safe."

Chapter Twenty

When mah jongg day rolled around, the four decided once again to play at different tables to maximize their chances of picking up on current gossip. They'd already met for lunch so Kat could update them on Peri Dawson's latest investment proposition.

"How did she know you weren't serious?" Marianne asked. "I was there with you both times before. You came across spot-on as a bona fide investor. Was there a slip-up when it was just the two of you?"

"She didn't say. All I can come up with is either how much I listened to her confession when we went to her office or even my coming back, saying I was reconsidering. In either case, she may have wondered why at the time and later concluded I was there for another purpose."

"You think we should eliminate her as a suspect based on what she told you?" Sydney asked.

"I thought we were out of the suspect identification and investigation business," Kat said.

"How much time did you spend with the sheriff after your run-in with Dawson?" Micki asked, her brow going up.

Kat returned an innocent expression. "What are you suggesting?"

"Like you don't know. The guy's got you under his spell."

"Don't forget, he did update me about Don Martin."

"His thank you for giving him five suspects he didn't have before we got involved."

"We don't know that, Micki."

"He certainly got busy checking out Martin pretty fast once we gave him the name," Micki reminded her.

"What are you saying, Mick?" Sydney asked. "Do you want us to keep investigating? We've gone about as far as we can."

Micki rubbed her hands together, as if the action would crystallize her thoughts. "Martin was one of the most likely culprits. Cole McGraw just cheats on his golf scores. Not nice, but would he really be foolish enough to kill Paul to keep others from knowing?"

"What about Hanes Carruthers? And Shelly Ludwig?" Marianne asked.

Sydney sipped her coffee. "Whether Carruthers killed Paul or not, he's now in a better position to retain his water rights with Paul out of the picture. Let the sheriff poke into Carruthers's financial affairs to determine just how bad things are for him. Olivia is still the point person."

"And Shelly Ludwig?" Marianne asked. "What about her?"

"We leave her to the sheriff. He can check her passport and determine her location better than us. There's nothing more we can do there until and unless she returns to Ocala," Micki replied.

Sydney set down her coffee cup. "Eat up, my friends. It would seem besides helping my husband survive his follies, the only thing we can do for now is pick up what we can at mah jongg this afternoon."

Carmen Trudeau was the first to approach them as they arrived at the game room at the community center. She pulled Sydney aside. "My daughter told me about your visit to her office. When I mentioned what she'd told me about seeing Olivia's husband in the parking lot where she works, I had no idea you'd actually drive up there and question her."

"Did she tell you why we were there?"

"Something about protecting Olivia's reputation, a train that has apparently already left the station."

Sydney's face crinkled up. "What do you mean? What have you heard?"

"Oh, c'mon, Syd. The sheriff can't spend all afternoon at Olivia's house without word spreading that he was doing more than comforting the widow. Especially when you four all showed up en masse later."

So now the four of them were objects of gossip as well. Probably should have expected it sooner or later. If their involvement in the Schwimmer case was now community knowledge, their chances of gleaning more information had dramatically decreased.

"What are people saying?" She knew she shouldn't have asked, but she needed to know just how much others knew about their investigative efforts.

"That you guys are doing whatever you can to deflect attention from Olivia as a suspect in her husband's murder. I don't get it. Since when have you all become such good buddies? Olivia has grown on your nerves just as much as she has with the rest of us."

Sydney attempted to put their reasoning into words. "She asked for our help and seemed so lost, so overcome by his death, we didn't have much choice."

"Help with what? The funeral? Settling his affairs?"

"That's kind of personal. I'd rather not go into it."

Carmen raised a hand. "It has something to do with Paul's extracurricular activities, doesn't it? Not everyone in town knows about Paul's interest in other women, but enough people do, including, I suspect, Olivia."

How could she reply without giving away too much inside information? "Think about it, Carmen. Have you ever seen Olivia cheat at mah jongg?" She didn't give the other woman time to answer. "No, of course, not. Olivia is the original rule follower. She's not a murderer. If anything, she would have collected enough evidence of his peccadilloes and sued the pants off him."

Carmen appeared to think through Syd's words. "You all believe she's innocent?"

"Yes. She probably should have confronted him long ago, but who can judge another woman's marriage?" Although she answered Carmen without hesitation, Sydney was only ninety-nine percent sure of Olivia's innocence. There was still that spot of blood, or jam, according to Olivia, on the jacket sleeve and Olivia's lie about taking it to the dry cleaner. Sydney hadn't shared that piece of information with the others. It could be nothing. Perhaps Olivia had still been in shock when she tried to explain the location of the garment.

Carmen offered a tentative smile. "I'll reserve judgement, then. When she returns to this group, I'll do my best to welcome her back."

"Thanks."

Marianne sat in with the group Olivia usually joined. Julie Poindexter finished laying out her tiles and set her case aside. "You're welcome to sit in with us, but why aren't the four of you playing together? This is the second time you've sat apart. Not getting along these days?"

Marianne laughed it off. "Good grief, no. We've been spending more time with each other than usual lately, what with helping Syd's husband with the follies and all, so we thought we'd split up today."

"Word has it you've been spending more time with Olivia too," Clarissa White added.

"We've stopped in from time to time. Just to check on her."

Bitsy Melzer stacked the last two tiles in her wall. "I thought her daughter was still staying with her. Now that her father is gone, she has no reason to stay away."

Marianne tilted her head. "Didn't she and Paul get along?"

The other three checked each other. "Sometimes Olivia received calls from her daughter while we were playing. We always knew it was her by the ring tone," Julie said.

Bitsy leaned in. "She seemed to call at least once each session, sometimes twice, even though she knew her mother was occupied. Unlike the rest of us, who either let our calls go to voicemail or quickly tell the caller we'd get back to them, she usually stopped the game, excused herself and would leave the table to talk to her. Typically, she'd return to the table frowning or distracted."

"Did she ever share with you what her daughter had said?"

Once again, the trio glanced at each other before anyone responded. Clarissa took the lead. "All Olivia would say was that Lilith and Paul had argued to the point where Lilith didn't come home more often than necessary, even though she lives nearby."

"Frequently, the calls were to determine if Paul was home or on the road," Julie replied.

"But you never learned the reason?" Marianne asked.

"She never came right out and said, and we didn't ask, but she'd make comments from time to time about her daughter's concerns about the amount of time Paul was on the road."

"You mean she was worried about Olivia being left alone so much? For security reasons?"

"We should probably start the game," Bitsy said. With that, she threw the dice, then the others followed suit to determine who would start the game.

Kat's experience went a slightly different direction. "Heard your song night at the hotel was a big success," one of the women at her table said.

"I was happy with how things went."

A second woman studied her card of mah jongg hands. "I heard there was a special audience member. Sheriff Formero."

"A lot of people were there besides the sheriff."

"But he also joined your friends' table," the third woman said.

"You're just jealous," the first woman replied, coming to Kat's defense. "Our sheriff is quite the catch."

Kat didn't reply, but the second woman did. "I heard he's a widower. His wife died several years ago, before he moved to town."

"Cancer, I heard," the first woman added.

Kat studied her tiles, not just because it was time to pick three to pass right but also because she didn't dare appear too interested, even though this was news to her.

"I'm surprised he found time to hear you sing when he's got his hands full finding out who killed Paul Schwimmer." The second woman said this while passing her own three tiles.

"The man can't work 24/7," the third woman put in. "That would dull his brain."

"Did he share any of his findings with you?" the first woman asked.

Kat wasn't about to tell them what Rick had told her the day before, but some response was required. "It's still an ongoing investigation, and they're looking into all possibilities."

The first woman huffed as she drew a tile. "I could tell you that much."

"He wouldn't tell her who his chief suspect is," the third woman added, "even if they were dating."

"We're not..." She stopped. They were baiting her. "That's all I'm going to say. I want to win a game for once."

Meanwhile, Micki pulled the serious group, the ones who were there to play and not socialize. Nonetheless, she made a valiant effort to enliven things. After the first game, she noted the winner writing on her card. "You check off new hands as you make them?"

"Yes," the woman replied. "Don't you?"

"No, I never have."

"Oh. Suit yourself." She went back to mixing up the tiles and making a new wall.

Silly topic, but it was all Micki could think of at the moment. "Why do you do it?"

The woman blinked, like Micki's question brought her out of a fog. "My goal is to win at every hand on the card before the new one comes along. Mastering the card is like a graduation of sorts."

"Doesn't that eventually make it more difficult to win?" Now she was on a roll. She couldn't stop herself.

The woman across the table from Micki answered for her friend. "Yes, that's the idea, isn't it? Meeting the challenge of the card?"

Not for her. All she wanted to do was win as many

games as she could. If that meant playing the same hand over and over because those were the tiles she'd been dealt, that's what she did. But if she was going to survive the next three hours with this group, no need to stir the pot. She needed to stay noncommittal. "Interesting idea." Just to fit in and loosen their tongues if at all possible, she made a check mark on the card by the hand she won in the next game.

"You probably don't want to do it like that," the first woman offered.

"Huh? Why not?"

"A check mark is too easy for the others at the table to see. If they know you're attempting to fill out the entire card and can see which hands have been checked off, they may surmise which hands you're still going for. I make a small dot in pencil which only I can see. Good defense."

Wow. This group really took this game to heart. She and the other three enjoyed it immensely, too, but they didn't go to these extremes. "I'll, uh, keep that in mind, if I win another game."

For the next half hour, they played in silence, except to announce what tile they were discarding. She sure hoped the other three were doing better at uncovering intel. Then, during the brief break they took when two of the women excused themselves to use the restroom, the third woman in the group leaned in closer. "I heard you and your friends have been playing amateur detective."

Micki jerked. "What?"

The third woman kept her voice low. "My brother works in the sheriff's office. He overheard the sheriff talking about your efforts with his closest confidante."

"What did he hear?"

"That the four of you have been trying to find Paul Schwimmer's murderer. That even though Olivia appears to be the most logical suspect, you've been trying to find others who might have wanted him dead."

"Did he also hear that the sheriff put the kibosh on our doing any further investigation?"

"Yes, but I know you four. I couldn't believe you'd go along with his edict."

"He's the law. We can't very well defy him."

The woman looked her in the eye. "If that's the party line, I'll go along with it. But I'm rooting for you, whatever you're doing. Olivia may not always be the most congenial person, but she didn't deserve any of this."

"Thanks. It concerns me that so many seem to know about our involvement, so if you wouldn't mind keeping what you know to yourself, we'd appreciate it."

"That's why I waited until the other two left the table, so you'd know I'm doing exactly that. I can't tell you about any leads the sheriff's office is following, because my brother won't share anything like that. But I personally know the sheriff is upset with some of his staff, because you all appear to have uncovered more than they had."

That news was alarming, since the four of them had barely unearthed anything substantial. Just names and possibilities. "If you hear anything more you feel you can share with us, please let us know."

The woman started to reply, but then the other two players returned. So much for today's fact-finding.

Chapter Twenty-one

*A*s the day of the follies drew near, Trip became increasingly more hassled. One of the acts had come down with a cold and had withdrawn from the show. Since he'd overbooked, the cancellation actually worked to his benefit, except now he needed to move a few acts around so he didn't have three singers in a row. Then the programs came back with two misprints, even though he and Beau had proofed them twice. Fortunately, there was still time to print an entire new set, providing they didn't find any more errors.

Trip was on the phone constantly, checking in with his acts, with the merchant sponsors and the community center crew.

Sydney decided she'd had enough when he chided her for making tea for breakfast instead of coffee. "Why don't you take a break from all this and go have your coffee downtown?" She tried to keep her voice sweet, although if she was honest with herself, a tad bit of sarcasm may have slipped into her tone.

"I don't have time to indulge myself at the moment. I'm not like you and your friends, dashing off to the coffeehouse whenever one of you has a splinter. The least you could be doing to support me when I'm under so much pressure is to brew me some Kona."

"Sure, Trip. I'd be happy to do that much for you." Which she did. And as soon as she'd set the steamy hot mug in front of him, she took off for the same coffeehouse she suggested he try.

"I'm here in your hour of need," Marianne told her as soon as she arrived. "Trip summoned Beau right after you left. Something about you not understanding how much stress he's facing."

Sydney rolled her eyes. "Three more days. If I can get through them, we'll come out on the other side and get our lives back. Until he comes up with his next *project*."

"Are the other two coming?"

"No. Kat's at the spa."

"Oh, right, Micki's been crowing for days about finally convincing Kat to get that makeover. But I thought she wasn't going for two days, the day of the follies."

"Today is the consultation. They'll go over hair styles and colors and determine what other services to provide."

Sydney couldn't help but chuckle. "If Kat didn't have all that money she hardly spends, I'd worry about her getting taken. But she deserves to pamper herself occasionally, and Micki has been salivating for days at the prospect."

"I hope they don't go overboard. I like Kat just the way she is."

"Me, too. And Kat seems happy with herself."

Marianne's name was called for her latte. When she returned to the table, she studied her friend. "Are you okay? I know how Trip gets as each of his big event days approaches."

Sydney patted her friend's hand. "Your understanding is mostly what I needed. That, and caffeine. I deliberately made tea at home, thinking it would help calm my husband. He took my gesture as a personal offense. Funny, huh, here I am guzzling the coffee I denied him."

"Sure you're not getting even?"

"Of course, I'm getting even. He has no idea how his projects always drag me in, one way or another. Thank goodness I've got you to drag in also this time to help."

"Actually, being the remote stage manager sounds like fun. But do you think I'll have enough time tomorrow night at dress rehearsal to catch on?"

Sydney took another gulp of the much-needed coffee before replying. "We could check out the community center on our own now, if you've got time?"

"Sure. But only after we've both infused our bodies with this fuel."

Several groups were meeting at the community center when they arrived. Fortunately, one of the two rooms where Marianne would be overseeing the troops was open. "About all we can do today is get the layout in your head and start a list of questions," Sydney said as they opened the door to the vacant room.

"It's not like I don't know this place. I'm here at least once a week for mah jongg, but I need to see and feel it from the perspective of the follies. Will all these tables and chairs be in here both nights? Do we need them? Do we need more?"

"Hold on. I'll get out my notebook."

Marianne strolled about the room, her eyes narrowed as if picturing the groups that would populate the room the next two nights. "Who all will be in here? How many? What acts? Who will need to change in here, and who will arrive in costume?"

"Slow down. I know you're on a roll, but my handwriting isn't."

"Since you're writing and not replying, I assume you don't know either. When will we both find out?"

"Depends on the mood Trip is in when I finally go home. If he's calmed down, I'll lay these on him. If not, I'll suggest a nap and hit him up afterwards."

Marianne stared at her. "You've almost got this down to a science."

Syd chuckled. "I've had enough practice."

Marianne wasn't finished with her questions. Syd continued to jot them down until her friend finally ran out of steam. "Let's see if the other room is open yet," Syd suggested.

"Wait. First I want to get a feel for where the people who are in this room go to get to the stage and you."

They stepped off the route, essentially a straight line from the room to the backstage entrance, then discussed how Beau would do similar wrangling from the second room, a little farther away, where spillover would be located.

"What's Trip doing? Sounds like the three of us will be handling the bulk of the work," Marianne observed.

"He'll be flitting around from place to place checking on everything until a few minutes before the show starts. Then he'll be up front directing."

Marianne scratched her head. "This is sounding more and more confusing, especially since the four of us will be spread all over the place."

"That was one of my first concerns. Trip got us each a headset so we can stay in communication with each other."

"Headsets?" Marianne's voice rose an octave. "I can't do that. I'm fine with computers but other devices, not so much. A headset will make me crazy."

"Not as much as running back and forth to backstage or depending on messengers would be. They're really easy to operate. You're listening all the time, unless you shut that part off. There are more controls on your car, and you don't complain about them."

"Just sayin'. Don't blame me if you've got static in your ear during the show and can't hear a thing."

"Trust me, okay? One of the local big box stores gave them to Trip as their donation. He plans to use them later for a raffle."

"Later? As in another *event*?"

"I pretended not to catch that part. Maybe we can use them instead for a women's club fundraiser."

"You may complain about Trip's various schemes, but you never let them get to you."

"You could say the same for yourself and Beau. He also gets caught up in Trip's crazy ideas."

Marianne nudged her. "You're right. In fact, I should be more worried about him. He just follows along."

"I'm glad they're good friends like that."

"But not as good as us." Marianne hugged her.

"You know, I think I can return to the house now without killing him." Pause. "Oops. If I've learned anything with this Paul Schwimmer thing, it's not to take that expression lightly. Forget I said it."

Marianne followed her home, ostensibly to extract her own husband from the activities but also to serve as buffer, if one was still needed. They found both men in the living room with an unexpected visitor. Candy Carruthers?

"Sydney and Marianne, do you know Mrs. Carruthers?" Trip asked.

Sydney walked over and shook her hand. "Candy, right? I'm Syd. We met at Paul Schwimmer's funeral reception."

A smile of recognition seized Candy's face. "That's

right. I knew you looked familiar. I get into town so rarely these days, I don't know that many people."

"This is my friend Marianne Putnam, the wife of Beau there. She was also at the reception but confined to a chair."

Marianne shook hands with Candy also. "I've got this thing with my feet. Every so often I get these sharp pains that make walking difficult."

"I'm sorry to hear that, as well as sorry I didn't have the pleasure of meeting you that day. I'm not very good at things like that and wanted to get out of there as soon as it was socially acceptable. I didn't even know the man, but his family and my husband's family are neighbors, and Hanes felt we should make an appearance."

Introductions addressed, Trip stepped forward. "Mrs. Carruthers just offered her act for the follies."

"Call me Candy. Like I said, I apologize for not contacting you sooner, but I just heard about your little show yesterday. I thought about it overnight and decided I owed it to the town to make my contribution."

"Thanks for stopping by. Dress rehearsal starts at six tomorrow night at the community center. Will you be able to make it?"

"Oh. That's a problem. Hanes and I are due in Tallahassee tomorrow for a meeting with the state water board. Hanes has been working with the local board to extend our water rights, and now they're sending him to the state body. There's no way we can miss it. I don't need any rehearsal time. I've done this many times before. And I have my own props and costume. You just need to point me toward the stage at the right time, and I'll take it from there."

Syd knew that expression on her husband's face. He was torn between turning down the woman's offer and risking a potential problem because he'd never seen her act.

"You don't by any chance have a video of your act, Candy?" she asked. "That would give us some idea how to fit you into the program."

Candy shook her head, her platinum-blond curls bobbing. "That would have been a good idea, but I'm afraid I don't. Just mark me down for five minutes." She leaned over to retrieve her purse, revealing a view of her ample bosom, and scuttled to the front door. "Thanks again for seeing me," she called over her shoulder.

Ever the good host, Trip sailed after her just in time to catch the door for her.

Syd waited for him to return and comment before she reacted.

"I don't know whether to be relieved or worried," Trip said, once back in the living room. "It should be okay, don't you all think?"

Syd tried not to think about the dull ache in her stomach, warning the addition of Candy to the show without their ever having seen her act could mean trouble. On the other hand, the opportunity to gain more information about Candy's husband and his dealings with Paul Schwimmer was too much to pass up. Besides, it was a done deal, and Trip needed reassurance. "Sure, we'll make it work." She went to him and placed her hand on his shoulder.

"What exactly is her act?" Marianne asked. "We came in too late to hear."

Beau screwed up his mouth. "She sings. Right, Trip?"

"Yeah, that's right. But she also said she did a little dancing too. With a tad bit of audience participation."

"That's all you know about it?" Marianne reflected Sydney's skepticism since Sydney was still attempting to appear supportive of Trip. "What kind of music does she sing? What kind of accompaniment will she need?"

Trip rubbed his chin. "Pop with a touch of jazz, she said. She'll bring her own music. All we'll have to do is plug it into the sound system."

"She also has her own costumes," Beau added.

"Costumes?" Marianne repeated, emphasis on the last syllable. "Plural? And five minutes to both sing and dance and interact with the audience?"

"It'll be okay," Trip said. "We'll put the comedian right after her. He can be spontaneous with his jokes. If there's a problem with Mrs. Carruthers' act, he can make light of it and set the audience at ease."

"Why don't we adjourn to the kitchen, Marianne. I'll, uh, pull up that recipe you wanted to see." The two of them fled.

Sydney put a finger to her mouth to keep Marianne from exploding. "I know what you're going to say, and I agree, but let me explain first why I didn't protest." Sydney kept her voice low, so the men wouldn't overhear. Trip's hearing these days wasn't what it used to be, but she wasn't sure about Beau.

"Okay, I'm listening," Marianne whispered.

"I'm very leery about putting that woman in the show without knowing any more than we do about her act. But it's a chance for us to find out more about Hanes Carruthers from someone very close to him."

Marianne cocked her head and gave her a *you've-got-to-be-kidding-me* look. "That part makes a certain amount of sense, but when do you propose to chat with her since she'll only be there one night, and it's going to be crazy enough the way it is without working in a bit of questioning?"

"Especially since I have to be backstage."

"Is anyone else going to use that room behind the stage?"

"I was saving it for Kat, thinking it would help her relax before her numbers. You think I should put Candy in there instead?"

Marianne gave her a wicked smile. "What if you put both of them in there? Let Kat do the sleuthing. She did a great job with Peri Dawson."

"Then she'll feel obligated to tell the sheriff."

"Let her. Afterwards, once she's gotten her information."

Sydney returned Marianne's conspiratorial look. "Are you vying for my job as chief strategist, my friend? That was brilliant."

Kat wasn't quite as effusive in her praise when they met later that afternoon at her place. Micki came limping in from rehearsals for the dance number Trip had roped her into.

"Are you sure you want me in this fancy room in my sweaty gym clothes?" Micki asked as she gingerly lowered herself onto one of the dining room chairs.

"You're fine," Kat said. "I may be changing the fabric on these chairs soon anyway. What do you all think? This room could use a makeover, just like me."

"Speaking of which," Marianne said, "how'd the consult go?"

"Don't ask," Kat returned, placing a tray of coffee cups and a plate of sugar cookies on the table where a carafe already rested.

Micki grabbed a cookie immediately. "Sustenance," she told the others. "I've had a demanding day, first convincing Kat here to cut her hair and then trying to keep up with the other seven women in my dance troupe."

"What do you two think? Should I go short or just take off an inch?"

"We played with computer images. The hairdresser threw in a couple more extreme styles just for fun, and she looked absolutely fabulous in one, a pixie," Micki said.

Kat poured coffee for each of them. "I'll think about it and go with whatever I'm feeling when those scissors take aim. But enough about me. Why did you call us together, Syd?"

Sydney shot a glance at Marianne, who shrugged.

"It's your husband's follies," Marianne said.

"But your idea."

Marianne released a sigh. "Okay. Here's the deal." She went on to describe their recent encounter with Candy Carruthers. "We'd like to put her in your dressing room along with you, Kat, if you don't think her presence would get on your nerves?"

"Something tells me I don't want to know why."

Syd wiped her lips with one of the cloth napkins Kat had provided. "We all agree this is a terrific opportunity that just fell in our laps. We have to take advantage of it, but I will be tied up backstage, and Marianne's in one of the staging rooms. Micki will be off with her fellow dancers getting ready."

"And I won't be? How can I stay focused on my own act, if I'm preoccupied interrogating this woman I don't know while she's trying to focus on her act?"

"That's the beauty of it," Marianne told her. "You're singing a few songs from your own act. Nothing new to worry about. You'll have just had your makeover, so you'll feel on top of the world. This Carruthers woman will be so into her own thoughts, she won't notice how the conversation she's having with her friendly roommate centers around her husband as a suspect in a murder case."

Micki reached for a third cookie. "They're right, Kat. You've been our point person all along. Look how well you did squeezing information from Peri Dawson. Then there's the sheriff. Who knows how hard he would've come down on us if he wasn't sweet on you. He certainly wouldn't have told any of us what he learned about Don Martin."

"Okay, okay, I'll do it. But only if you guys write down the questions I'm supposed to ask her."

"We can do that," Sydney replied, "but we can't anticipate her responses, so you'll have to take things from there. If she reveals anything about her husband's business or financial problems or his relationship with Schwimmer, you need to dig deeper with whatever questions that occur to you."

Kat closed her eyes, considering. "Fine. So now that I've agreed to do this, let's deal with the important question. Should I redo this room?"

Chapter Twenty-two

*D*ress rehearsal did not get off to a good start. Beau was in a minor accident on his way to the community center. He was about to head through an intersection after stopping when another car collided with the front passenger side of his car. He wasn't hurt, nor was the driver of the other vehicle. But his front fender was a loss, and he had to be towed to the repair shop.

That meant Trip was on his own to oversee the run-through. He had to be out front at the same time he was lining up acts backstage and in the hallways. As it turned out, since both Sydney and Marianne got more of a workout than they'd anticipated, it was a great though exhausting run-through. However, Marianne was a basket case until Beau finally showed up.

"Are you sure you're okay?" she asked when he trudged up to her, a tiny bandage covering his high forehead.

He planted a chaste kiss on top of her head. "Nothing a few painkillers and a good night's sleep can't handle. How's it going?"

"Much better, now that you're here, although you should go home and get that rest now."

"And give Trip one more thing to worry about? Nah, I'll survive. Where is he anyhow? I looked in the auditorium, and he was nowhere to be seen."

"I haven't seen him for a while. If I could remember how to turn this thing on, like Syd showed me, I'd call him."

"Here, let me try. Hey, these are cool. Trip said the four of us would be broadcasting on our very own frequency." He hit a tiny switch on the side of her headset. "Syd? Trip? This is Beau. Where are you, Trip?"

"I'm in the first staging room," Trip's voice replied in her earphone. "Tell him to come find me. I could, uh, use some help."

Beau relayed the message to Marianne, and they both rushed off, since Beau wasn't sure where to go. They found Trip on his knees, looking under a desk, a group of ten or twelve other follies participants gathered together near the door. Trip got to his feet, dusted off his hands. "Things were going so well until one of the maintenance crew informed me a mother of a kid who'd been here this afternoon had forgotten to bring his pet's cage home with him. When the maintenance guy went to retrieve it, the door was open, the *pet* gone. We could probably have gone on with dress rehearsal with no problems, but too many people overheard and refused to go on until we located the escapee."

"Okay, we'll help look," Marianne volunteered. "What are we seeking?"

Trip said something, but his voice was so low, neither Marianne nor Beau could hear. "What?" they said in unison.

"Snake. It's a snake."

The group clustered in the room's entrance scooted in unison closer to the door.

"What kind of snake?" Beau asked. "Small, I hope?"

"Common garter snake, I was told. Harmless. But things are at a standstill until I can reassure everyone the creature has been found and returned to his cage. Don't tell Syd. That woman's a rock about everything except snakes. I don't want her to panic."

"I heard that," Syd said into her husband's and Marianne's earpieces. "Glad I suggested these headsets. They really do keep us in touch."

"Sorry, Syd," Trip replied. "Forgot I had this thing on. I take it you're hiding backstage, or have you left the building entirely?"

"I'm still here. I'm on a table I dragged to the middle of the stage so I can see in all directions whatever is coming toward me. Find it fast, Trip. I'm not the only one around here who's freaking out."

"We're on it, hon." He turned off the send button. "She's fine for now, until someone points out snakes can climb and slither across high branches, like the overhead supports above the stage."

The room was an all-purpose type of meeting room. Just chairs, table, the desk, a podium, whiteboard along one side—nowhere for a snake to hide. Beau strolled around the perimeter and returned to his wife and friend with his assessment. "There's just enough room for a small snake to get under the door and out into the rest of the building. Possibly, it could've gone up a wall into the HVAC system."

Trip couldn't resist eyeballing the ceiling. "God, I hope not. If that happened, it could be anywhere."

"How long was it here before the boy remembered he'd forgotten it?" Marianne asked.

"At least three hours," Trip replied. "The kid left around three."

"I don't know how fast snakes move," Beau added, "but that would be enough time to get as far as the front door, if it knew where it was going."

Marianne studied the cage. "There's no food left in here, but it's possible the animal wasn't aware of its sudden freedom until it finished its meal. It may still be in this room, if it only took its leave recently."

"My wife, always the optimist," Beau said.

Trip explored the rest of the room. "But a good supposition. Could you all move away from the door?" Sure enough, once the area had been cleared, they noticed a storage closet. "Anyone got a flashlight?" he asked before pulling on the knob. One of the women handed him her key ring, to which a small pocket light was attached.

Trip opened the door, then slowly moved the light up and down. After a few seconds, he stopped, closed the door, switched off the light. "Marianne, you're brilliant! He or she is curled up in a pail on the floor."

"That's the second time this week a Bonner has called me brilliant."

"Beau, would you find the maintenance guy? He should have a pair of work gloves he can use to return the thing to its home. Meanwhile, I'm going back to the auditorium to get this show back on track," Trip said. "Beau, come find me to get your own headset once you're done here."

Trip reentered the auditorium and addressed the group that had gathered in the front seats. "Drama's over, everyone. The runaway has been found and is being relocated to his proper home. So we can get back on schedule." He shot a glance up on stage. "And my wife can come down from her perch."

"That's not funny, Trip," she called. She'd been afraid of snakes, particularly garter snakes, since her childhood, when one had the audacity to climb up her wrist when she was picking strawberries. The live bracelet had glided away just as fast as he'd appeared, but not before she'd backed up and fallen over a wheelbarrow that had no business being there and sprained an ankle. Bruised her backside as well as her ego. She hated looking so weak, but this had been with her all her life, and she didn't see how she'd change now.

She dropped off the table one foot at a time and made her way backstage. Where were they? Ready for the fifth act. "Marianne? Can you hear me?"

"Of course, I can." Now that she'd turned it on.

"Time to bring in the rhythm dancers. Are they still there, or did they scatter with news of the snake?"

"Some are here. I'll have the leader round up the rest. We'll be there shortly."

Marianne's optimism knew no bounds. Two of the three who'd left the room were in the ladies' bathroom. The third was out in her car. Marianne didn't show up with them until four minutes later. "Sorry about the interruption, everyone," Sydney said. "Tomorrow night you'll have to proceed with the show, no matter what. I hope you memorized the route you took to get in here, because we can't have you mistaking that first door as your entrance. It comes right into the auditorium."

The rhythm women all nodded understanding, then lined up for their entrance. Sydney was impressed by what she saw from backstage. All these women were over seventy-five, but they'd been exercising together for several years and had begged Trip for a chance to show everyone their stuff. Not wanting to disappoint, he'd included them with no small amount of trepidation. He could relax now. They were terrific, and the audience would love them.

"I never would've believed it without seeing them," a woman's voice said behind her. Trip was still doing a sound check on the rhythm dancers' music, so Sydney didn't need to cue the next act just yet. She turned to find Annalise McGraw no more than three feet from her.

"Annalise. What brings you back here?" She remembered to turn off her headset.

"Cole is coming up on the program. I thought I should be here in case he needed me. Hope it's okay?"

"Sure. I should have realized, but I'm still familiarizing myself with the various acts and their order. Trip rearranged a few just last night. What is Cole doing?"

"You've never seen him do his thing? He's a ventriloquist."

"Really? I had no idea."

"He really wanted to do this, do his part for the town, even though it's getting more difficult for him."

Was Annalise trying to tell her something without actually saying it? "Oh? The throwing his voice part or operating the, uh, whatever it's called?"

"The dummy. It's okay to say it. Actually, motor mechanisms still come with relative ease. He just gets mixed up at times. Forgets where he was in the act. I'm here to cue him offstage."

Cole forgot things? Was there a socially acceptable way to ask someone if their spouse had dementia? "That's perfectly okay. Where would you like to stand?"

Annalise chuckled. "As close as I can hover without being seen. I don't want to embarrass him. He's still not ready to talk about his condition."

This was Sydney's chance. She hoped she did it right. She lifted a brow. "Oh? Is there something I should know as the stage manager?"

Annalise's eyebrows furrowed. "I'm sorry. I thought you knew. Cole is in the early stages of memory loss. We're not ready to put a more specific name to it yet. With early detection and proper medication, we hope to stave it off as much as we can. In the meantime, Cole's trying to live as normal a life as possible and has encouraged me to do the same with my organizations."

"Thank you for telling me. Let me know if there's anything I can do as stage manager to make it easier for him."

"Bright lights sometimes throw him for a few seconds, so if your husband could tone down the lights when Cole enters the stage, that would be great."

"I'll tell Trip now."

"Before you go, you should also know that Cole will stay with me in the overflow staging room. There will be fewer people there, although he's still the politician, always wanting to shake hands with people and say hi. I'll get him backstage in time. It may seem like we're late, but I'll wait until the last minute, so he won't get confused."

Sydney turned to leave, but Annalise had one more thing on her mind. "I'm telling you all this because I want Cole's performance to be special for him. But I hope you'll keep what I've told you to yourself and your husband?"

Syd was torn. The others needed to know Cole may have been shaving his golf scores as a result of his condition. If Paul had confronted him, Cole might have confided the real reason. Even if he didn't confide in Paul if confronted, that was no reason to kill Paul. But Annalise needed assurance that her husband's malady would stay secret as long as possible. "I'll respect your wishes as long as I can. But if this thing progresses, the sooner those who know you and care about you learn what's happening to him, the easier it will be for both of you." She hoped that would be the case.

The rest of the rehearsal went fairly well with the exception of two of the non-performers: Marianne and Beau. After successfully teaming up to locate the snake on the loose, Marianne remained in the primary staging room, checking on the secondary room only as those acts were due backstage. A specific location hadn't been assigned to Beau so he could roam and help out where needed.

Sydney was grateful for his presence every time he turned up, because she always had an assignment, most of which he deemed beneath his ability, so he'd vanish as soon as he finished. But the primary staging room was another matter, especially if Marianne happened to be gone momentarily. Beau readily took over, although he didn't have Marianne's list, which caused him to send in one act before Syd was ready for them.

"Marianne? You're way ahead. The juggling trio doesn't need to be here yet," Syd complained.

"I didn't send them. Did they come on their own?" Marianne said into her headset from the secondary staging area.

"I sent them," Beau said.

"You?" Both women replied in unison.

"Yeah, they were just screwing around in here, so I told them to go find you, Syd."

"There are a couple more acts ahead of them. I'm sending them back. Be ready. They're not happy."

Marianne burst out of the secondary room and stomped up to the primary room. "Beau," she gestured from the door, "can I see you?"

When he wandered over, she let him have it. "Why

did you take it upon yourself to release the acts? That's my job."

"Sorry, babe. You weren't here. They appeared ready to go."

"*They* don't get to make those decisions. Nor do you. *I* make those calls."

"Whoa! I had no idea I'd overstepped my bounds. I'll leave you to your precious staging area." He tore off, leaving her feeling vindicated and crushed at the same time.

A few minutes later, Trip called Marianne on her headset. "You and Syd are managing the lineup of the acts so well, I'm pulling Beau off duty in the overflow room. I need him here with me."

"Uh, sure, Trip." Well, that was one way to keep her husband out of her way, although she suspected, like Trip, Beau was now *assisting* from a comfy seat in the auditorium while she and Syd were doing the real work. Syd had been so right predicting how this project of Trip's would go.

Chapter Twenty-three

"You didn't all have to come," Kat protested as Sydney and Marianne drew up chairs around Micki in the salon where Kat was getting her pedicure. For the moment, she was simply soaking her feet. The nail technician was still with someone else.

Marianne examined the nail color chart. "We're not here for long. Trip wants us at the community center by four. But we couldn't go there before checking on you."

"So far, I've been massaged, given a facial and suffered through an eyebrow trim. After this, it's a manicure, then the really *fun* part, my hair and makeup."

"I'm glad you're both here," Micki said. "I learned something the other day at mah jongg and have been debating ever since whether we should pursue this avenue. It seems that the Schwimmer daughter, Lilith, hadn't been getting along with Daddy. I didn't get the reason, but apparently before her father's death she called Olivia daily, sometimes more, and whenever the call came during mah jongg, Olivia excused herself to go talk rather than have her call back later."

"That doesn't give us much," Sydney replied. "I know several mothers like that."

Micki nodded. "True. I used to be that way with my own mother. But it was the part about Lilith's animosity toward her father that got my attention."

"We can't exactly go to Olivia with this," Marianne reminded them. "Especially if, God forbid, Lilith is the murderer. Olivia would rather take the rap for her daughter."

"But think about it," Sydney continued. "If Olivia suspected her daughter the least bit, she wouldn't have asked us to investigate on the sly for her."

"Unless she wanted us to come up with some red herrings," Micki added.

"All of which are slowly evaporating," Marianne said.

Sydney pulled her chair closer. "Speaking of which, I think we can write off Cole McGraw also. I learned something from his wife last night during the dress rehearsal—Cole is doing a ventriloquist act tonight—that makes me think there may be a medical reason why he has supposedly changed his golf scores."

"Really? Do Beau and Trip know?" Marianne asked.

"I don't think so, and Annalise asked me to keep this to myself, so I can't tell you more."

"I'm sorry to hear that," Kat said. "The medical part, that is."

A woman in a pink jacket and matching pants appeared with a carrier full of manicure/pedicure products. "Ms. Faulkner? Are you ready?"

Sydney and Marianne came to their feet. "Guess that means we should leave," Marianne said. She placed a hand on Kat's shoulder. "Just relax and enjoy the rest of your salon experience. We can't wait to see the results."

"I'll have your dressing room ready for you by the time you arrive at the community center," Sydney added. "Have fun."

"Do you think she'll relax?" Marianne asked Sydney as they walked to Syd's car.

"That's supposed to be Micki's job, provided Micki remembers her role as supporter and stops bossing her around."

"Kat can take care of herself."

Syd opened her car door and climbed in. "I guess so, but I think there's more happening between her and the sheriff than she's let on to us. I get the feeling she feels caught in the middle between our investigation of Schwimmer's murder and her growing attachment to that guy. Something we couldn't foresee when we started all this."

"Do you think she's anxious about talking to Candy Carruthers tonight?"

Syd pulled out of the parking lot. "A little, but my guess is she's worried about how this makeover will go over with Formero. Will he like the new glam as much as he seems to be attracted to the old Kat?"

"I hadn't realized things had gone that far."

"I didn't mean *that* far," Sydney quickly put in. "But where did that idea of redoing her dining room come from? Kat's never cared much about the décor of that house. The dining room means she's thinking about entertaining. Most likely she's never had a dinner party because she didn't have a dinner partner. Perhaps that situation is beginning to change."

Marianne sat back in her seat. "Then we simply have to let nature take its course, and if it fizzles out, better now than later."

They drove in silence a few minutes.

"We have a few hours before we have to report in. What do you want to do?"

"You don't want to go home and grab a nap?"

"I would, if I thought I'd be alone, but I'm sure Trip will be there hyperventilating. He needs this time by himself to come down. I know. Let's treat ourselves to tea."

"Without the other two?"

"Yes. Just you and me, for once. We haven't been to Tina's Tea Party in ages. It's just the lift we need today."

It didn't take Marianne long to decide. "Okay, then. For the next hour or so we don't discuss the Schwimmer case or the follies."

"Good idea. It's been so long since we've just talked about our lives, it will be nice to get caught up."

Ten minutes later, they were seated at a table in the cozy tea room reviewing the lunch menu. "As much as I enjoy a good cuppa on occasion, I like lunch here more," Marianne admitted. "Looks like Tina's added a couple new entrees."

"Did I hear my name mentioned?" A red-haired woman garbed in a floral, tea-length dress covered in a dainty white lace apron hovered next to them.

"Hi, Tina. How've you been?" Sydney asked, smiling up at their hostess.

"Life is good these days. My son is doing well in college. Business is better than ever, for which I have you ladies and your friends to thank. Many new customers have told me you recommended this place."

"We only recommend places we enjoy," Sydney told her. "Tell us about these new items on your menu." Tina filled them in on the new chicken-vegetable cassoulet and Southwest tamale and corn casserole. Marianne tried the first and Sydney stuck with her usual, the Florentine quiche.

As they waited for their meals to arrive, they drank blackberry-flavored hot tea and snarfed down the rosemary-infused muffins. "I know I suggested we put the Schwimmer case on the back burner, but hear me out first on just this one thing, okay? By my count, we're down to three possible suspects, not counting the daughter. Do you agree?" Syd asked.

"Three, huh? Well, there's still Hanes Carruthers. Hopefully, Kat can uncover something from Candy tonight. Then there's Peri Dawson. She may have confessed her love for Paul Schwimmer to Kat, but women in love can also turn against the object of their affections."

"Especially when there's another woman involved. Enter Shelly Ludwig. She's number three."

Syd buttered her second muffin. "Money or love?"

Marianne had a question of her own. "How much do you think the sheriff has learned about these three?"

"I have no idea, other than he did look into Don Martin's case. So perhaps he's followed through on the other names we gave him. We'll never know if he was already aware of them. Plus, he hasn't arrested Olivia yet. So maybe our snooping helped."

Marianne stirred her tea, even though it didn't need it. "Three weeks ago, I'd never had firsthand knowledge of a murder in my life, except in the mysteries and thrillers I read. Now, I discuss this one with you and Micki and Kat almost daily to the point that I've forgotten we're talking about a man who is no longer alive because someone cut his life short. It makes me wonder what kind of person I'm becoming."

"It bothers me, too, that at times I sound so callous about his death as we discuss suspects. But I don't think I'm a different person. I'm doing this, and I think you and the other two are, too, because I want to help a friend who I believe is innocent and doesn't deserve to be considered the one who took her husband's life. She's lost enough."

"Such serious faces," Tina said as she put a dish in front of Marianne. Her assistant did the same for Sydney.

"Not anymore, Tina. I'm all smiles anticipating this meal," Marianne reassured her.

Two hours later, with their stomachs full, having also shared a piece of homemade chocolate cake for dessert, they made their way to the car.

"That was nice. I'm glad we pampered ourselves by coming here," Marianne said.

"We'll have to bring Kat and Micki back with us, once this Schwimmer thing is over. If it ever is. If I recall, Kat promised to treat us to a tea party after she won that big hand in mah jongg."

"I hate to break the mood by going home, but we can't avoid it any longer."

⌐╫⌐

"Knock, knock, we're here to see the new Kat Faulkner," Sydney said from outside Kat's dressing room. She'd allowed her friend ample time to arrive and get set up before coming to check out the makeover.

"I'm here too," Marianne called.

"Enter at your own risk."

Their friend stood before the room's three-way mirror. She wore the silver lamé gown she'd purchased at Yvonne's. The dress hugged her body, revealing curves even these friends didn't know existed. She even showed some cleavage. Sexy. All this was breathtaking, but it was the face and hair that had them applauding. Her dull gray hair had been colored silver gray and cut short. Not the pixie cut discussed earlier but a modified bob that came just below her ears.

"You look fantastic!" Marianne gushed.

"You will steal the show," Sydney added.

"I don't look too, uh, overdone?"

"You're supposed to look out of the ordinary," Marianne said. "The salon earned its money."

"Okay, I'll take your word for it. I can't very well change much at this point."

Sydney checked her watch. "Your roommate should be arriving shortly. Are you ready?"

Kat expelled a long breath. "As I'll ever be."

"I'll go look for her," Sydney volunteered.

Before Syd reached the door, Kat called to her. "Is this your way of keeping me from obsessing about my appearance?"

"Okay, I'll admit to that, although you were also the best person for the job."

Outside the dressing room, the two friends studied each other. "Think this will work?" Marianne asked.

"We'll soon find out."

"Guess I'd better report in to my folks."

They high-fived each other. "See you later," Marianne said and hurried away.

Sydney went looking for Candy Carruthers but kept her eye open for the sheriff as well. She located him just inside the front door. "Good evening, Sheriff."

"Rick tonight."

"Rick. Once the show starts, if you get a chance to slip into the back of the auditorium, I just thought you'd like to know that Kat's number is ninth in the lineup. She's rather nervous about how she looks, so if you see her, you might want to reassure her."

"Uh, thanks. I'll keep that in mind."

Just then, she saw Candy Carruthers coming up the front steps and excused herself to greet the woman. "Candy. I'm glad I found you. I wasn't sure you knew where your dressing room was, since you couldn't be here last night."

"Thank you so much, Cindy."

Syd smiled. "Let me help you with your things." She reached for the costume bag Candy carried, but Candy held on to it, handing Syd a small tote instead. "And it's Sydney."

"Sydney, my apologies."

"We've put you in our backstage dressing room with Katrina Faulkner. She's to go on a few acts after you, so she'll be there the whole time."

"Oh, good. I could use some help with my costumes."

Sydney excused herself as soon as she'd introduced Candy to Kat. "Oh, wait. Here's my music. Could you see that the right people get it?"

"Sure." If she didn't, there'd be no act. Now it was Kat's turn.

Chapter Twenty-four

"What a beautiful gown," Candy said as soon as Sydney left the room. "I wore something like that to one of my husband's fancy dinners."

"Thank you. I'm a cabaret singer, so I got this for my act."

"Where do you sing? I don't think I've ever heard you."

"I just started at the hotel downtown recently."

"I'll have to drag Hanes into town to hear you."

Here was her opening. "Hanes? That's your husband?"

"Right. I take it you've never met him? I don't get into town often, but he does."

Kat's job was to play dumb and pull out whatever info she could with her questions. "Where do you live?"

"About ten miles south of town. His family, Hanes mainly, owns The Big C Ranch, although we also have a house here in town. Hanes keeps it for when he has meetings here."

"Seems like an expensive proposition, unless he's here frequently?"

While they chatted, Candy proceeded to unload what looked like five pounds of makeup onto the room's only dressing table. Fortunately, all Kat now needed after her makeover was lipstick and a little powder. "Usually once a week. Sometimes two nights in a row."

"That's a lot of time apart. I'm surprised you don't live in town."

Candy pulled a couple of pairs of very high-heeled shoes from her tote and set them on the remaining space on the table. "I'd like to. It gets kinda lonely out there, but Hanes feels he needs to be near the herd, even though he has more than enough crew to tend to it."

"Do you ever come into town with him on those nights? The town offers all kinds of evening activities."

Candy shrugged. "I've suggested as much, but he isn't keen on it. His meetings tend to run late and are very hush-hush, so he doesn't even like me calling him except for extreme emergencies."

What kind of weekly meetings would a rancher have that ran late? If she uncovered only this info tonight, it would still be worth it. Maybe they could stake out the house and see what happened.

"I have no idea when I'm supposed to go on. I had to miss dress rehearsal last night because I went with Hanes to a meeting of some water group."

Water? Wasn't that supposed to be the issue between Carruthers and Schwimmer? "Sounds interesting."

Candy made a face. "You've got to be kidding. Hours and hours of listening to reasons why people needed access to water. Very boring. At least Hanes got his request granted, so the trip was worth it."

"I never realized access to water was a problem."

"Very much so. Fortunately, Hanes was able to get our neighbor, Paul Schwimmer, to extend his lease before Paul's untimely death. Yesterday was simply to get the agreement approved by the board."

Paul had worked out a deal with Carruthers? If that

was the case, there was no longer cause to suspect him of the murder. "Congratulations, then."

"So, once I get dressed, what happens?"

"Sydney Bonner, who brought you in here, will check back before your time to go on. Do you have a question? I can go find her."

"I just need help with my costume. It has a lot of hidden closures that need attention."

"I can help. What needs to be done?"

Candy unzipped her bag and removed something red and gold and sparkly. Once she held it up, Kat could see it was an evening gown...of sorts. Hard to tell with all the fringe and bangles. Candy didn't appear to be what one would call a refined presence on stage. Well, fine, since that was what Kat was striving for. With a little sass on the side.

After a quick knock on the door, Sydney stuck her head in. "Everything okay back here? I meant to check with you sooner, Candy, since you weren't here last night, but I got tied up with the third-grade dance team."

Candy stood stock still, her face a study in surprise. "Third grade, you said? As in young children?"

"Yes," Sydney replied. "Is there some problem?"

"I, uh, can't go on, Mrs. Bonner." Candy stuck the red number back in the bag and zipped it up so fast, part of the fabric got caught in the zipper. She struggled to free it, only to make things worse.

"What? Why not? What is there about third graders?"

Candy was breathing so heavy she had to stop a moment to compose herself before explaining. "If they are part of the show, I assume their friends will be in the audience as well."

"I, uh, guess. Why?"

215

"I'm an exotic dancer, Mrs. Bonner. Stripper, if you will. I take off most of my clothes in my act."

Eyes wide, Sydney and Kat couldn't speak at first. This couldn't be happening. How had Trip ever let this get past him?

"You understand, don't you?"

"Uh, yes. I just don't...how did this happen?"

"I never would have contacted your husband about appearing tonight, except the announcement said this was a *follies*. That word must mean something different to you all than it does to me."

"Like in Folies Bergère?" Kat asked. "Oh, my."

"Oh, my, indeed," Candy repeated. She returned to the pesky zipper.

Sydney came over to her and took over nudging the teeth of the zipper free. "Isn't there something you could perform instead without, uh, removing your clothes?"

"My singing and dancing are mediocre at best. My audiences never care, because they're too busy watching articles of clothing come off one piece at a time."

Sydney turned to Kat, pleaded for her help with her eyes.

Kat took a step closer to Candy. "What if the two of us sang together? You could appear as part of my set."

Candy attempted a smile, but it was half-hearted. "That's so thoughtful, but even if I agreed to join you for a song, I have nothing to wear. My costumes are a bit too revealing and could show even more if I don't watch the hidden closures carefully."

Kat swallowed. "I brought an extra, in case I didn't like how I looked in this one. You appear to be about my size. You could borrow it tonight."

Behind Candy's back, Sydney mouthed a silent thank

you. Letting someone else wear her brand-new dress was very generous.

"Oh, I couldn't, but thank you."

"I assume your husband will be out in the audience," Sydney said. "Why disappoint him? Try on the dress. If it fits, then say yes, you'll do it."

While Candy was making up her mind, Sydney's headset sounded. "Syd? I need you out front," Trip demanded.

"I'll be back to hear your decision as soon as I see what my husband wants," Sydney told her. She almost ran from the room. Wait till she told Trip what he'd almost done to his precious follies.

Trip wasn't out front. Instead, she found him seated at the back of the auditorium, a hand across his forehead. Rick Formero stood close by. "Trip! What's wrong?" Syd cried.

"I found him in the men's bathroom emptying the contents of his stomach into a john. He won't let me call the EMTs, and he doesn't appear to have a fever. But he clearly isn't able to direct this show tonight."

"What have you eaten today?" she pressed.

"Not much. I'm fine, Syd. I just need to sit here quietly a bit."

"Answer me. What have you eaten?"

"Beau and I had time on our hands, so we ordered a pizza. Well, Beau ordered it, and you know him."

"He ordered everything on it." Trip could no longer indulge in the same eating orgies he enjoyed in his twenties. He knew it and usually watched his diet, but when he and Beau got together, something about male egos kicked in, and he wouldn't admit his shortcomings. Beau should have known better. This had happened more than once in the past when the two of them took leave of their senses. The thrill of producing this show had probably been replaced with show night jitters, so Trip had given in to his boyish whims.

"You should probably go home and go to bed. Rest and more barfing time are usually the cure for this."

"I can't go home. Who'd run the show?"

"Isn't that what Beau's supposed to do as your backup?"

"Beau? Think about it, Syd. He'd flip out at the thought of being in charge. No, you're the only one who can take over for me."

"Me? I was backstage last night. I haven't seen the show from out here."

"All you really have to do is cue the music and the lights. Whoever takes over for you backstage will get people on in time."

Syd did some mental calisthenics. She could ask Marianne to handle backstage. She knew most of the acts. Beau could take Marianne's place in the staging areas. With the help of the headsets, Marianne could direct him from backstage.

No need to tell Trip about the mix-up with Candy Carruthers now. If Candy agreed to pair up with Kat for a number, Syd could handle that out front.

She turned to Formero. "Could one of your deputies run Trip home? I don't think he should drive."

"I'll find someone. Don't worry about this guy. Go take over as director."

Trip turned mournful eyes toward her. "Thanks, Syd. You're the best."

"No more eating when you get home, unless it's dry toast and tea. Okay?"

She turned to leave.

"Good luck," Formero called.

In the backstage dressing room, she learned that

Candy had agreed to do one number with Kat. They'd never rehearsed together, but they'd wing it. Somehow. Syd took Kat aside and thanked her again, then updated her on the change in directors.

"Syd! I'm so sorry for Trip, but that's a tough job to throw your way at the last minute."

"I don't want to dwell on that part right now. It has to be done. If you two are okay here, I need to find Marianne and Beau. We have about an hour before the curtain goes up."

Before she set off to find Marianne, Kat grabbed her hands. "If anyone can take on this job at the last minute, it's you, friend. You'll do fine. And don't worry about me or Candy."

Sydney dashed off, realizing she couldn't worry now about anything else other than getting through this night and ensuring the production went well.

Marianne was just as supportive as Kat. "You can do this, kid. You shouldn't have to, but that's a topic for another day. And since my husband was only all too willing to take over my job here, now he'll get his chance." She chuckled. "What a night!"

What a night, indeed. Syd hurried off to find Beau. She could have called him on his headset, but this needed to be done in person, especially if he was hurt Trip hadn't named him as his replacement.

"Who's gonna do my job in the lobby and at the back of the auditorium?" was his first question.

"Sheriff Formero is around to handle anything that might arise. You're needed much more in the staging areas. Good thing you already have your own headset."

"What happened to Trip? Sudden bug?"

"No, his stomach is rebelling from the junk he fed it all day."

"Oops. Guess I'm to blame for that." He had the grace to look embarrassed.

"Which we'll discuss later. For tonight, we focus on the show."

He offered a mock salute. "Got ya, ma'am."

Two more stops, to check in with the sound and light people. "Everything's set," the guy handling lights said.

"A couple small changes." She told him about striking Candy off the lineup but adding her to one of Kat's numbers. "I have no idea what you have lined up for Kat, but if you could modify the setup slightly when Candy comes out, that would be great. Don't go too dark. She wasn't here last night for dress rehearsal, so she doesn't know the stage."

That addressed, she set off to find the woman doing sound and music and repeated what she'd said to the lights guy. "No problem," the woman replied. "Tell Trip to get better soon. He's really lucky you could take over for him."

"Save that assessment for after the show," Sydney replied. "I've never done anything like this. I'm glad we have such great technical people like you to help."

For all the drama and last-minute changes, the show went remarkably well. The mic didn't work until someone in the audience showed Sydney how to turn it on. And one of the singers came in a couple of measures too late for her song, but she quickly caught up. Kat's numbers were the showstoppers. The lighting on her silver dress made her appear absolutely ethereal. When Candy joined her for their duet, the audience listened spellbound. To everyone's surprise and delight, including the two vocalists, their voices blended beautifully.

Later, as audience members were leaving, several people sought out Syd to tell her how much they enjoyed the show and to ask after Trip. Sydney sidestepped the real reason for his absence, gluttony, and simply attributed it to exhaustion from putting the show together.

As the line of well-wishers dwindled, Rick showed up with a money bag. "These are the proceeds from tickets purchased tonight. With your permission, I'll take it back to my office and lock it away in my safe for your husband."

"Thank you, Rick. I'm embarrassed to say I hadn't thought of it, there've been so many other details coming at me."

"Assumed as much. Least I can do." He paused. "Do you suppose Katrina is still in her dressing room?"

"Probably. I haven't seen her otherwise."

"I wanted to tell her how well she did. She looked really nice tonight."

"I'm sure she'd like to hear that."

"Syd? Your headset back on?" Marianne asked.

"Just turned it on again, in case you or Beau needed anything."

"Beau would like you to stop by our place when you're done here, unless you need to get home to Trip. He wants to debrief while things are still fresh in our mind."

"Sure. Why don't you let Kat and Micki know too?"

She made a quick call to Trip to tell him how things had gone and let him know she was stopping by the Putnams'. An hour later, she turned the building over to the maintenance staff and breathed a sigh of relief as she trudged to her car.

Chapter Twenty-five

"Who wants a glass of wine?" Beau asked.

"I'd love one, but I'm already dead on my feet," Sydney replied. But she did accept a bottle of water.

Once everyone had a beverage of some sort in hand, Beau raised his glass. "To Trip, in absentia, for putting together one hell of a show tonight. And to Syd, who stepped in for her guy at the last minute and made magic happen."

"Hear, hear," the others called.

"Magic, huh? Well, thank you all for pitching in and helping me get through this."

"Trip'll want to call us all together again to go over the night, but I thought we could use a little time just to come down," Beau said.

Micki rubbed her feet. "I'm just glad it's over. I haven't danced this much in years."

Marianne held up her glass again. "Kudos to Kat. Not only do you look spectacular, but you saved the day for Candy Carruthers."

"Yeah," Beau said, "what happened there? She was supposed to have her own slot in the show."

"Just how much did you and Trip vet her credentials when she showed up the other day?" Marianne asked. She went on to reveal what Candy's act would have been. "She's the one who caught it and voluntarily withdrew."

"I'm glad she decided to stick around and sing with me," Kat added.

"How about you, allowing her to wear your new gown before you wore it?" Sydney said.

"That was the least of my problems. She looked great in that black number, didn't she? Her husband certainly liked it when he came backstage to congratulate her. Even offered to buy it from me. By the way, I learned something else about him too." She didn't go on, and the other three women seemed to study their hands, waiting for Beau to catch on that his presence was no longer necessary.

"I can take a hint. I'll be going to bed myself now. Good show, ladies."

Once he was gone, it was time for Kat's report. "I hope I didn't insult him."

"No, he's used to our private sessions. So, tell us what you learned about Hanes Carruthers," Marianne said.

Kat recounted her conversation with Candy and how they'd come around to the subject of water rights on the Hanes property. "According to Candy, Paul Schwimmer and Carruthers settled their dispute before Paul's death, so now Carruthers will have access to water for several years to come."

"That's what Candy and Hanes were doing in Tallahassee yesterday. Getting the state's approval of the agreement," Sydney surmised.

Micki drained the last of her wine. "In other words, Carruthers had no reason to kill Paul. At least over water rights."

"Did you tell the sheriff what you learned from Candy when he came to congratulate you?" Sydney asked Kat.

Kat angled her head. "How did you know that?"

"He saw me first and told me he was on his way to see you."

"I considered telling him but thought we should do it together tomorrow, once we've all rested." She paused, bit a lip. "Plus, I didn't want to change the mood. He was very...complimentary." She offered a shy but knowing smile.

Micki nodded. "He liked the dress, didn't he?"

"Very much. I think I'll wear this the next time I sing. It seems to generate lots of attention."

"Didn't I tell you? Do you still feel strange about the hairdo?" Micki asked.

"Getting used to it. Just as long as I can take care of it myself."

Micki rolled her eyes. "Like it would be such a sin to get it done every week?"

Sydney sat back in her chair, stretched her legs out. "I'm beat. Someone decide when we'll get together next and where. I'm heading home to my recuperating ex-director."

Though they would have preferred to meet at Kat's, where they presumed the sheriff would feel on more neutral ground, Kat shied away from the idea because if things did continue with him, she didn't want him to associate her place with their investigation. Micki's condo was chosen instead.

"I'm glad you allowed me a couple hours to pick up. I ran the dishes, made my bed and otherwise made the place more presentable than usual," their hostess told them when they arrived.

"I wanted to avoid my house and Syd's, because our spouses will probably be around today. They're too tired to play golf," Marianne explained.

"We brought coffee and doughnuts," Sydney said, holding up a bag.

"Good, because I was too busy cleaning to make coffee or go shopping."

The sheriff arrived about then. Micki answered the door while the other three took their seats next to each other, which would force him to stand or sit away from them. A safe distance, or so they hoped. He took the chair they'd positioned across the room.

"Mornin', ladies. Thought you'd be sleeping in today after all your efforts for the follies."

Sydney, though tired, took the lead once again. "We have information to share with you, Sheriff, and wanted to do so expeditiously."

"Appreciate the gesture. What do you want to tell me?"

"As you recall, the day we met you at Olivia Schwimmer's house, we gave you the names of the three men who we saw as possible suspects in the murder of her husband. Shortly thereafter, we provided two more names; these were women we believed to have been having affairs with Schwimmer. Since then, you eliminated one of the men from the list. Don Martin. We now believe you can eliminate the other two men, Hanes Carruthers and Cole McGraw."

His eyes narrowed, his expression growing troubled. "Thought I told you, warned you, to stop investigating Schwimmer's murder posthaste."

"Which we did," Sydney continued. "But certain facts

came to our attention as a result of our work on the follies this week, which we want to pass along to you. We waited until now, because we wanted to get through the follies first."

He scowled but then blew out a resigned breath. "Okay, I'll buy. What are these *certain facts?*"

The three women turned to Kat. "As luck would have it, Candy Carruthers wound up sharing my dressing room with me last night."

"As luck would have it?" he asked.

"She was a late entry on the program, and Sydney wanted me to look out for her, since she wasn't able to be there for dress rehearsal. Anyway, we got to talking about the reason why Candy couldn't be there." She related how the Carruthers went to obtain the state's approval of their extended water rights agreement. "Bottom line, the reason for Hanes Carruthers murdering Paul Schwimmer no longer exists."

"That's it?"

"You already knew," Micki guessed.

"More or less. Didn't know they'd gotten the state to sign off on the extension. But I have to say, you were spot on identifying this water access issue as a potential motive for murder. I had my team on it right away."

"Why didn't you tell us?" Marianne asked.

He offered a superior look. "You don't have a right to such information, especially after I'd told you to drop the whole case."

"Do you know about his weekly trips to town?" Kat asked, his show of arrogance goading her into revealing more. "He comes alone. Candy is not invited. Sometimes he's here more than a day. Most likely, he's having an affair with a local, but you might want to check it out."

"We have. It's not an affair. The guy really loves his

wife. He told me last night as he was leaving how grateful he was that she hadn't embarrassed herself with that strip act. He comes to town for poker. She hates the idea of his gambling, so that's why he hasn't told her."

Micki was incensed, her nostrils even flaring. "You mean he pays taxes on a separate residence just so he can sneak away each week and play poker? The nerve."

"He inherited the house from his mother. He's not doing anything illegal."

"Not even the poker part?" Marianne asked.

"They're on private property, and the stakes are penny-ante. Not worth our time, as long as it stays that way."

"I guess this meeting was a waste of your time," Kat said, her shoulders sagging.

"You haven't told me about the other man you suspected."

"I'm not sure I can tell you much," Sydney began. "Cole McGraw, as you recall, has a reputation for shaving points from his golf scores. Most of the guys who've played with him have either overlooked this or have finessed their way into other foursomes and left others to play with Cole."

"Sad but not reason enough to arrest him," the sheriff commented.

"Right, until Paul Schwimmer had to play with him and threatened to expose Cole's habit. Rumor had it that Cole had been considering running for the state legislature. Suddenly, his problem could be a liability."

"Go on. We haven't been able to get much on this guy."

"He has a medical problem that is behind the score changing. I found out from his wife the other night but promised her I'd keep this to myself as much as possible.

I suppose one could argue his condition might have caused him to anger more easily than others and take it out on Paul, except his physical condition—upper body strength, in particular—would preclude such an action."

Marianne shook her head. "Poor guy. I had no idea."

"But please keep this to yourselves," Sydney pleaded. "It will be become public knowledge soon enough."

The sheriff rubbed the back of his neck. "So, all three men are now off your radar?"

The four women nodded.

"What about the two women?"

"You and I talked about Peri Dawson," Kat reminded him. "She finally admitted to having an affair with Paul, but she didn't show any anger toward him. I came away with the impression she really loved him and missed him now that he's gone."

"She is a real estate agent, after all," the sheriff said. "I'm not saying they're dishonest, but they have been known to exaggerate or downplay to get a sale. Maybe she was deliberately leading you on."

"Maybe. Or maybe he didn't love her back or love her as much. For a few seconds, we even thought she might be having an affair with Carruthers when she brought me a hot investment opportunity in some development land and then refused to tell me where it was or who was offering it."

"How did that connect to an affair with Carruthers?" he asked.

Micki answered this part. "I'd heard through parties who will go unnamed but I consider reliable sources that he'd been unloading property due to financial problems. Before Dawson revealed the married man in her life was Schwimmer, Carruthers seemed a possibility. Otherwise, how would she have known about this deal?"

"Perhaps he hinted about it at his poker game," the sheriff suggested.

"Dawson was part of those?" Micki's voice shot up.

"Apparently your research didn't uncover that little tidbit." He actually sounded smug.

"No, we didn't," Sydney admitted. "But we're done considering Peri Dawson. We'll leave it up to you whether you continue to consider her a suspect."

Micki picked up a couple magazines that had fallen to the floor and stacked them on top of more magazines on the coffee table. "Any word yet on Shelly Ludwig, or whatever her name is?"

"Only that no Shelly Ludwig has left on a cruise from any Florida port in the last month."

"Did you check for a Miranda Ludwig?" Sydney asked. "Or in other U.S. ports?"

"Yes and no."

"So, she could have gone on a cruise from a port outside Florida, but it's unlikely."

"All we know is that she has disappeared. We haven't been able to pinpoint exactly when, but it appears to have been around the same time as the murder."

"Have you learned anything more about her?"

"We've learned plenty, most of which I'm not in a position to share with you ladies. You already know she works occasionally at the florist shop and where she supposedly lived, although she rents under the name Miranda. She was born in the northern part of the state, graduated from high school up there. Sticks pretty much to herself, although she's been seen with several different men around Ocala. None of whom we've been able to identify as Paul Schwimmer."

"What else?" Micki wanted to know.

"That's all I can tell you."

Micki blew out a breath. "We already knew a lot of that."

The sheriff pulled at his collar, but then straightened his shoulders. "I shouldn't have to remind you, but I will. I'm not reporting to the four of you."

With most of their list of suspects dissipating, Micki continued to hold on to this one for fear of losing it as well. "Actually, you are, in a way. You report to the citizens of this county, right?"

"Of course, I do. But that doesn't mean you are entitled to all the intel I currently have at my disposal." He came to his feet. "Thank you for making me aware of what you learned about McGraw and Carruthers. The only other thing I can share with you is that Shelly Ludwig remains a possible suspect and we're still tracking down her whereabouts."

Though not the least bit happy with what little he'd told them, Micki performed her hostess duties and walked him to the door. "Thank you for coming."

She returned to find the other three sitting in silence. "I'd say we've come to the end of the line," she pronounced.

"My thoughts as well," Marianne replied. "What say you, Syd?"

Sydney considered. "I agree with Micki. The only thing that could keep us involved would be if we're contacted directly by one of the people we've interviewed and given new information. Even then, we're supposed to call Formero."

Kat sat forward. "Then I suggest we visit Olivia and tell her our investigation is over. Perhaps she should hire her own private investigator, if our efforts haven't been enough."

"I don't look forward to that little get-together," Micki said. "But I guess it has to be done."

"Look at it this way. No more seeking suspects. No more follies. We have our lives back. We should plan an excursion just for us," Syd said.

"We just went shopping in Naples," Marianne reminded her.

"That was for Olivia. Let's go to the Atlantic coast this time."

Marianne studied her. "Why do I not believe your heart is in that idea?"

"I'm still trying to talk myself into it. But give me a day to get used to it. I'll even drive."

"You drove the last time," Micki replied. "It's my turn."

"When?" Kat asked.

Sydney pulled out her phone and studied the calendar. "We're heading into the weekend. How about Monday?"

"Perfect," the rest agreed.

"But first," Syd put in, "we meet with Olivia."

Which they did, later that afternoon. "Thanks for seeing us on such short notice," Syd said at the door.

"I expected to hear from you long before now."

"We've had some loose ends to tie up," Marianne told her. "Plus, we've all been involved in the follies the last three days."

"Oh, yes, I heard it was a success. Congratulations to your husband, Sydney. I would have gone under other circumstances, but I'm not yet ready to be seen socially."

"Of course," Syd agreed. She ran through the names of potential suspects they'd turned over to the sheriff. "Since he prohibited us from undertaking any further investigative efforts, we couldn't pursue any new leads."

"In other words, you haven't come up with anything more."

"Actually, more information has come to us." Syd proceeded to lay out what they'd learned about McGraw and Carruthers. "Although we haven't been able to rule out either of the two women, there's no more we can do."

"That doesn't mean the sheriff isn't investigating them," Marianne added. "He and his office have the resources and legal authority to check into things we can't."

Olivia dropped into a chair, wrung her hands. "How does that help me?"

Although she sounded ungrateful, she was mainly scared. Sydney attempted to appease her. "But he hasn't arrested you yet, Olivia. If he had enough evidence, you would've been in custody long before this."

"But he could still arrest me any day."

Kat came over to her and took her hand. "That's true, but that doesn't mean it's inevitable. You know you're innocent, and so do we. Plus, you now have Colette Brownley defending your interests."

By some silent signal, all four prepared to leave.

"Don't give up hope," Kat said as she passed by their hostess.

"We're pulling for you," Micki added.

Marianne took Olivia's hand and squeezed it.

"I'll be right there," Sydney called to the others. She drew Olivia aside when it was just the two of them. "Remember that jacket with what you said was a jam stain?"

Olivia lowered her eyes. "Sort of. I think I told you I took it to the dry cleaner."

"You lied to me, Olivia. Lilith told me at the reception that the two of you didn't stop at the dry cleaner that day you went to the funeral home. I still don't think you killed Paul, but fabrications like that don't reassure me of your innocence."

Olivia swiped a palm across her mouth. "I'm sorry, Sydney. The truth is it was blood. My own. I cut my hand on a nail sticking out of our sofa earlier that day and somehow managed to get some blood on my opposite sleeve. I wasn't rational after I learned of Paul's death, or I would have realized my blood could be readily distinguished from Paul's. I burned it as soon I could escape Lilith's observation. Then I realized that would sound even more damning. So I made up the story about the dry cleaner when you asked."

"Thank you for coming clean with me."

"You believe me?"

Sydney nodded. "It's so convoluted, it must be the truth. I've believed in you all along, but this one little item didn't wash." Sydney turned to leave. "One more thing. Even though the four of us are at a standstill, that doesn't mean you can't continue your own investigation, that is, if you hired a professional investigator." She didn't give Olivia a chance to reply but instead slipped through the door.

Chapter Twenty-six

Sydney slept in on Saturday morning. It had been one full week. She needed the extra winks. Trip, back to his normal self, had kissed her on the top of her head and told her he'd be out in the garden. This was heaven. Then her phone rang.

"Sydney Bonner? This is Wanda Jones from the florist shop in Ocala. You said to call if I got any more information about Shelly Ludwig."

Syd went from groggy to alert in a nanosecond. "Right. What did you learn?"

"That she's back in town. I don't know for how long, but she's coming in to work this afternoon. The folks and I are going to my cousin's wedding, so she'll be here on her own. Thought you'd like to know."

"Yes, yes I do. Thanks. And enjoy the wedding."

"Tall order. Just another excuse for my parents to ask me why I'm still single." She hung up before Sydney had time to think of a comeback.

She started to call Marianne and then remembered their promise to the sheriff. Okay, this time she'd be a good little citizen and call him instead. But when she did, she learned he was out of the office, and when she pushed to leave a message, she was told although it was his day off, one of his deputies was available.

"I'll, uh, call tomorrow. Thanks."

She called Marianne. But her call went to voicemail. Had Beau finally agreed to take her to that movie she'd been wanting to see? "Marianne. Call me back as soon as you get this. Shelly Ludwig is back."

Next, she called Micki. Once again, voicemail. Oh, right, today was that lecture on investments at the university. She'd have the same luck calling Kat, because she was supposed to go with Micki.

That left only Trip. But was she ready to tell him about their investigation?

"Why are you looking so perplexed?" He'd come back into the house and come all the way to their bedroom without her hearing him.

"Huh? Oh, I'm supposed to do something today, but I can't recall what."

"Have some coffee. It'll come back to you. Meanwhile, I'm off to play golf. I'm filling out a foursome because one of their regulars is sick."

"How about you? You've been sick yourself."

"I'm back to a hundred percent today. I'll even treat you to dinner to show my appreciation for taking over my job the other night."

It would take more than one dinner to pay her back. Still, with him playing golf, that left her no one she trusted to accompany her. But she couldn't let the woman get away.

She dressed quickly, fixed a piece of toast and a cup of coffee for the road and took off. On her way, she left messages for Marianne, Micki and Kat telling them what had happened and what she was doing and asking them to come after her if she didn't call back by six.

What would she say? She couldn't very well ask the woman if she knew Paul. What excuse would she use for visiting the shop this time? Was another houseplant in her future? Then it hit her. All she had to do was engage the woman in conversation and sneak a couple of photos of her to send to Marla Trudeau. Even though Marla had said she didn't clearly see the woman Paul had kissed, perhaps seeing a photo would jog her memory.

She entered the shop pretend-calling Marianne, the idea being she'd have her phone handy when the photo op presented itself. "Okay, see you later this afternoon. Bye."

No one was up front, but a young woman with short black hair soon entered. "May I help you?"

"Is Mr. Jones here? He's done floral arrangements for me before."

"Sorry. Mr. Jones, his wife and daughter are all away at a wedding. Perhaps you could tell me what you're after, and I'll leave Mr. Jones a note so he can call you on Monday."

Since she'd already planned her *arrangement* in her head, Syd related the details. "I've never seen you here before. Are you new?"

"No, although I don't work here that often. I fill in as needed."

"Oh. What happened to the other woman who was here from time to time? Sheila?"

"Shelly. That's me."

Sydney did a fake double-take. "No! Really? I could've sworn you were blond."

"Oh, I was. I just decided it was time for a change."

"Even if I decided to make so dramatic a switch myself, I doubt my husband would be happy about it. He doesn't like change. How did your man react?"

Shelly blinked, then swiveled away to check something in a folder on the counter. She turned back wearing a faux smile. "I'm single."

"Then you can style it any way you like, I guess."

The shop phone rang, and while Shelly spoke with whoever was on the other line, Sydney sneaked several shots.

Shelly finished the call sooner than Sydney anticipated. "Did you take a photo of me just now?"

Caught. "You got me. I, uh, really like that cut flower arrangement over your shoulder. Thought we could do some of our garden flowers like that." She offered her best smile and hoped Shelly would buy it.

Shelly angled her head to the side. "I don't think so. I may have been on the phone, but I saw you aiming your camera directly at me."

Foiled again. She rolled her eyes apologetically. "Okay. I have a friend who'd look good in that cut. So, I snapped a few pictures of you."

"You could've asked." Shelly's tone was fast becoming less friendly.

"I should have. I apologize. Why don't I, uh, buy a dozen roses to make up for my behavior?"

Shelly narrowed her eyes and came around the counter to stand just a few feet from Sydney. "I'll sell you the roses, but I don't think your friend's hair was the reason for the photo either. What do you want, lady?"

Syd backed up a step, frantically trying to come up with a response. Somewhere in her brain she remembered the mantra, "a good offense is the best defense." Since she was out of options, she'd give it a try. "Did you know Paul Schwimmer?"

Shelly's eyes went wide as she, too, backed up a step. "Paul? Who?"

"Paul Schwimmer."

"I don't know anyone by that name."

"Really? You were seen in car with him in a local parking lot."

"Who told you that?"

"It's not important. Were you aware he died three weeks ago?"

Shelly didn't say anything, just stared at back at Sydney.

"No reaction? You apparently already knew."

"Murders are rare around here, particularly in the dopey town of Serendipity Springs." Shelly's response put them one step closer to admission.

"I didn't say he was murdered, nor mention where it happened."

"I read the papers too."

"On a cruise ship at sea?"

Shelly blinked again. "Who told you that?"

"I was in this shop over a week ago asking for you. That's where your boss thought you were. The thing is, none of the ships that sailed from any Florida ports in the last month have any record of you being aboard. I think you were camped out somewhere waiting for the heat to die down, although I'm surprised you came back so soon." A thought occurred. "Unless you ran low on funds. That's it, isn't it? That's why you agreed to work for the Joneses this afternoon. You don't have much cash on hand, and you don't want to leave a trail of credit transactions."

"What's with you, lady? What business is it of yours what I've been doing?"

"Did I mention you were seen kissing him in that parking lot? Not just a gentle peck on the cheek either. You definitely had something going with him. That was about a month before his death. What happened in the interim? Did Paul grow tired of you? Or did he refuse to leave his wife for you?"

Shelly's gaze moved about the front of the store, as if seeking an escape. Drops of perspiration that weren't there a minute ago dotted her forehead. She gripped her hands so tight, they were white. Sydney almost had her. Just a little more prodding.

"No, you knew about the wife, and you probably knew all along that he didn't plan to leave her. He liked his role in the community too much. Nor did he want to risk losing his land in a property settlement in a divorce."

Shelly still didn't reply, but her stare had become one of panic.

"Even though he was cheating on his wife, you didn't expect him to cheat on you, did you? And then, quite by accident, I'm guessing, you saw him with a woman who wasn't his wife."

She was treading on thin ice, but would there ever be a better chance to get this woman to confess? And by now, every fiber of her being told her this one was the real deal. She should get out of here immediately and let the sheriff handle it, even if Shelly ran off again.

But for some stupid reason she didn't listen to those fibers. Instead, she plunged ahead. "What did you do then, Shelly? I'm guessing you waited until he was out for a run along the path around Serendipity Lake. Then you confronted him, demanded to know who the other woman was. Maybe he told you, maybe not, but he refused to act guilty, beg your forgiveness. He even dismissed you and went back to his run. You were so angered by his lack of remorse, you followed him, grabbed the first thing you saw and hit him with it." She paused for effect. "How'd I do?"

Before Sydney knew what was happening, Shelly scuttled behind the counter and withdrew a handgun from her purse. "I'd say you went too far. You should've stopped while you were ahead. Now, you're forcing me to deal with you."

Sydney stared at the weapon, her brain not yet accepting the idea that someone was aiming a gun at her. At first, she was too astonished to be scared, but fear quickly poured through her veins, cementing her feet in place. "I was merely speculating on your actions. Thus far, there's no real evidence to prove you murdered Paul Schwimmer. Kill me, and you've admitted your guilt."

"Maybe so, but I can't allow you to tell anyone else your theories."

"Others know I'm here and are on their way right now."

"I don't believe you, but I'm not taking chances. Come around here, and don't try any funny business. I'm much younger than you and can easily take you down."

She didn't have much choice with that gun pointed at her. Sydney inconspicuously checked out her surroundings as she made her way around the counter to the area reserved for staff. Lots of pottery, ribbon and tissue paper. A pair of scissors rested on the desk. She did a fast calculation of the amount of time it would take to grab them and...what? Stab Shelly? Could she do that?

She didn't have the chance, because Shelly made her keep on going to the cooler, where the cut flowers were stored.

"Go in."

"In there? I'll freeze."

Shelly offered a vicious smile. "That's the idea. Even if your friends are on their way, you'll be an icicle by the time they find you."

Sydney swallowed. Hard. What could she do to stave off this march to doom? Like Shelly said, she could hardly best the young woman physically. The scissors were a lost cause. What about her phone? Would it work in the cooler?

Shelly had the same thought. "Give me that phone. Your purse too."

Sydney did as bid. Now she'd have to find some other means of escape.

"Sorry, no chairs in there. When you get tired of standing, you'll have to lie on the floor. You'll be all ready for the funeral home's van by the time they find you."

As soon as Sydney walked in, Shelly closed the door behind her and propped a chair against the door.

Sydney watched all this as if in a trance, like she was already frozen. She should be coming up with a plan to get out of here. And a Plan B and C. Several shelves holding containers of various cut flowers and greenery lined the wall. Shelves on the other side held a few arrangements. Probably for pickup this afternoon. Hopefully soon. But then she saw the lights go out. Shelly must have closed up for the day, customers be damned.

Fortunately, there was still enough ambient light to see the rest of the cooler. The door was half glass, so she could also see part of the area behind the counter. All she had to do was find something in here to bash against it and break the glass. But she couldn't find anything big enough or strong enough to do the job.

Still, she had to try. But on closer inspection, she discovered all the containers were a reinforced type of corrugated cardboard. Nothing heavy enough to penetrate the glass.

She was glad she'd continued to wear a watch, rather

than depending completely on her smart phone for the time. Too bad she didn't buy one of those smart watches when Trip suggested she get one. Maybe she could have sent some kind of message from one of those.

How long had she been in here? Five minutes? Ten? She made a note of the current time for future reference. Future. Ha! How much more future did she have?

How could she get out of here? Couldn't break the door. Couldn't communicate with the outside world. About all she could think of was mental telepathy. Wouldn't hurt to try. First, she thought of Marianne. Maybe the film had ended by now and she'd checked her messages. "Come now, Marianne. Don't wait until six."

She sent the same message to Micki and Kat. Trip also. He'd be so hurt if he ever learned she sent her thoughts to him fourth, but Trip knew nothing about the Paul Schwimmer stuff. How angry would he be, if she died in this cooler and only then he learned about her latest activities? He wouldn't be happy, that's for sure.

Good girl. Throw a little humor into this experience. If you live long enough to think back on it someday, this part about Trip will give you a chuckle.

The longer she huddled there attempting to think good thoughts, the harder it became to stay awake. Was there some kind of gas these flowers emitted, something that made a human sleepy? If she got out of here, she resolved to learn more about the operation of a florist cooler.

Somewhere in the background she heard noises, indistinct. She blinked her eyes open. The light outside suddenly flashed on.

She tried to stand, a little wobbly, but she wasn't frozen in place. It took effort, but she made her way to the door. "Help, help!"

A man in some kind of uniform glanced her way and bounded over to the cooler. The chair was removed, and a few jiggles on the latch later, the door was open and she fell into his arms.

"I don't know who you are, but you are truly a lifesaver. I would have frozen in there had you not found me."

"Patrolman Stanley Reimers, ma'am. Actually, I don't think those things get cold enough to freeze a person, or they'd freeze the flowers, but it musta been uncomfortable for you. How'd you get yourself locked in there anyhow?"

"I didn't. I was forced in there by the woman who works here. She's a killer and now on the loose. You need to find her."

The officer scratched his head, apparently unable to grasp what she'd said.

"Stanley? Did you find... Who are you?" A woman about the same age as Sydney moved into view.

"Who are you?" Sydney returned.

"Eleanor Tiffin. This shop was supposed to be open until five this afternoon. Did you decide to close early? I need the arrangements for my dinner party tonight."

Sydney understood Tiffin, but words wouldn't come.

Patrolman Reimers replied for her. "Find a chair for this woman, Mrs. Tiffin. She's been locked in the cooler and needs to warm up. Do you have a blanket in your car?"

"Uh, sure."

Within minutes, Sydney, wrapped in the woman's blanket, was sipping coffee Mrs. Tiffin made for her. Meanwhile, the officer was busy on the phone, explaining to his superiors what he'd found when he'd gone to investigate Mrs. Tiffin's complaint that the shop shouldn't be closed so soon.

"Her name is Shelly Ludwig, but she also goes by Miranda and probably other aliases. Her hair is short and black. I'd estimate she's in her early thirties, and she's uh, quite well put together," Sydney told him. "I took pictures of her, but she took my phone.

"Syd? Are you in there?" Micki called. She and Kat found their way to the back area. "What happened? Where's Shelly?"

Sydney updated them. She was just finishing when Marianne and Beau arrived, so she went through it again for them.

"Why did you come here on your own? You could have been killed," Marianne chastised.

"I'm only going to say this once, because it's too humiliating to repeat." She went through her confrontation with Shelly, ending with Shelly pulling a gun on her. She left out the cooler part, figuring they'd find out about that soon enough.

"You were on the trail of Paul Schwimmer's killer?" Beau asked. "Since when did the sheriff's department assign its cases to civilians?"

All four women exchanged guilty looks. "That's a good question, Beau," Marianne finally said. "One I'll answer for you on the way back to town."

"Speaking of Sheriff Formero," Micki put in, "where is he in all this? Didn't you call him?"

"First thing, before I called any of you. It's his day off, and I wasn't ready to share the information with anyone else. I regret that now, but at the time, I thought I could just drive up and confirm Shelly was back in town."

"Apparently your efforts went well beyond that," Kat surmised. "Did she actually confess to Paul's murder?"

"Not in so many words, but she didn't deny it when I

described what I thought had happened. That's when she pulled the gun and took off."

Patrolman Reimers returned from his phone calls. "There's a BOLO out for this Ludwig woman using the description you gave me, Mrs. Bonner. Sheriff Formero is on his way here. We'll need you to stick around to go over things with him."

"Can we stay with her?" Kat asked. "She appears to be quite calm about this, but we know her. Underneath, she's falling apart."

Falling apart? How did she know that? "I'd like that, if it's okay?"

"I, uh, suppose. At least until the sheriff arrives. I can't speak for him."

Formero arrived within fifteen minutes. He didn't look happy, even though they finally knew the identity of the murderer. "I can't wait to hear your rationale for coming here on your own, Mrs. Bonner."

"I tried calling you, Sheriff, but they'd only let me speak to the deputy in charge."

"Surely he would've told you to let him take care of it?"

"I, uh, haven't dealt with anyone else in your department, so I tried to find my friends instead." She told him about her calls and messages to the other three women.

"All right, we'll put that aside for the moment, since your coming here is a done deal. Now, tell me everything that happened. From the start."

She repeated her story again, filling in more details, since the sheriff was more aware of the backstory than the local police. "You made a huge leap describing how she murdered him to her, since you had very little evidence."

"She seemed truly surprised that anyone was on to her, so I used her state of mind to convince her we had it all but sewn up."

He simply shook his head. "Once the locals are done with you, I suggest you head home. Can one of your friends drive you?"

"I'll go with her," Kat volunteered. "I rode up with Micki."

The next hour went by in a blur, with Sydney going back over everything that had happened several more times. Finally, she was released, and she and Kat headed back to Serendipity Springs, Kat driving.

"We were so worried about you as we drove to Ocala," Kat said once they were on the road. "It's not like you to take such chances, Syd."

"I know, I know. I guess I've become more obsessed with finding Paul's murderer than I was willing to admit to you guys or myself. Even when I could see in her eyes that she'd figured out why I was there, I wasn't scared until she pulled the gun. Then I just about lost it. I've never been around guns before, let alone had the business end of one pointed my direction."

"Do you think they'll catch her?"

"I don't know. Her looks have changed considerably, but I'm guessing she took her own car, thinking she had plenty of time before anyone found me. Thank goodness for that Tiffin woman. She was bound and determined to get her floral arrangements, and for that tenacity, I'm grateful."

They didn't speak for several miles. Each of them tried to get her mind around all that had occurred in the last several hours. Finally, Kat spoke. "We did it, Syd. Or, you did it, but our investigation netted the real murderer."

"Olivia was so let down the other day, I hope we renewed her faith in us, now that she's not facing arrest."

Kat's phone rang. She put it into speaker mode.

"Katrina? This is Rick. Just wanted you and Mrs. Bonner to know we caught Shelly Ludwig, and she has confessed. Her story pretty much mirrors Mrs. Bonner's supposition. She killed him in a jealous rage when he told her he'd just been stringing her along. We're looking for the bloody log now. She must have pitched it far from the path, since we've been unable to locate it in our previous searches."

"That's such a relief, Rick. Thanks for letting us know. We can rest easier now."

"Tell Mrs. Bonner and your other two friends we're not done discussing your role in this case. But for now, let's just celebrate a positive conclusion."

"Our day of reckoning is still at hand," Kat told Sydney once the call ended.

"You'd think he'd be a little more grateful for our help."

Kat shot her a concerned look. "You took a big risk checking out that woman on your own. He's still concerned about what could have happened."

"I've learned my lesson."

"Oh? And what would that be?"

"Never leave you guys behind."

Epilogue

"**M**ah jongg!" Clarissa White called. "I've been trying for this hand for some time."

"Sorry, Clarissa, but I need that tile for my mah jongg," Olivia told her.

"But I called for it first."

"Doesn't make any difference, since I'm next in line to play and I have mah jongg also."

"Are you sure about that?" Bitsy Melzer asked.

"Check the rules," Olivia replied, adding the tile in question to her tiles to reveal her own mah jongg hand.

"Is that right, Sydney?" Clarissa asked Syd, who was seated at the next table.

Syd caught the knowing looks of Micki, Kat and Marianne and had to chuckle inwardly. Of course, Olivia was right. She was never wrong quoting a mah jongg rule. "Sorry, Clarissa, it's there on the back of the card."

"Here's my quarter." Julie's voice held a touch of resignation.

Clarissa didn't say anything. She just slid her quarter toward Olivia.

Bitsy, who'd thrown the winning tile, forked over her two quarters, her penalty for discarding the winning tile.

Back at Syd's table, the four of them breathed a collective sigh of relief. The old Olivia was back. Nit-picky, incredibly-good-at-mah-jongg Olivia Schwimmer and cause of the occasional headache was back.

That meant the four of them could play together again and resume their normal lives. They'd already planned their trip to Tina's Tea Party the following week. They weren't letting Kat forget her promise to treat them after her big mah jongg win a few weeks back, the same day Syd had overheard Olivia's distressed conversation with her husband in the parking lot of the community center.

"I've been wondering," Micki asked Marianne, "how did you explain our role in the Schwimmer investigation to Beau?"

"I told him that as friends of Olivia we'd provided the sheriff with the names of potential suspects," Marianne replied as she studied her mah jongg card.

"What about Syd getting herself locked in a florist's cooler?" Kat wanted to know. "Surely he was more than curious about that."

"I don't think the reality of her predicament has sunk in yet, since we got there after that nice patrolman rescued her. One of these days, Beau will want to know more, and I'll have to tell him."

Micki turned to Syd. "What about Trip?"

"Marianne told Beau I'd take care of that. And I will." Sydney truly meant to tell Trip. Someday. For now, let him bask in the success of the follies and count the days until the next *project* entered their lives.

"What about you, Kat?" Marianne asked. "Have you seen the sheriff since Ludwig was caught?"

"He's been busy wrapping up the case, but he did stop by yesterday. We had tea and discussed how to redo my dining room."

"Is that what they call it these days?" Micki teased.

"Micki!" The other three protested in unison.

"Oh, c'mon. This romance is moving so slow, we'll all be using walkers before he takes the next step."

Kat rolled her eyes. "He hasn't said so, but he's scared. Both because we seem to have bested his people in discovering suspects but also because he's afraid we tasted enough success to do it again.

"Again? Heaven forbid there be another murder in Serendipity Springs," Marianne replied.

Syd drew the tile she needed to declare mah jongg. But before she made her call, she replied to Marianne's statement. "Good grief, no! Our investigation days are over. Aren't they?"

Dear Reader,

Thank you for reading this book. If you liked it, won't you please take a minute to leave me a review with your favorite retailer? I had so much fun writing *Craks in a Marriage*, because it gave me the chance to recall pleasant memories from my retirement. Not murder, of course, but the great friends I've made through playing the game of mah jongg. You can learn more about my books at my website, www.barbarabarrettbooks.com.

Follow me on Facebook: http://bit.ly/2aXZvG9
Follow me on Twitter: www.twitter.com/bbarrettbooks
Follow me on Pinterest: pinterest.com/barbarabarrett7
Subscribe to my newsletter: barbarabarrett747@gmail.com

Craks in a Marriage is my first venture into cozy mysteries and the first book in the "Mah Jongg Mystery" series.

Barbara

Other Titles by Barbara Barrett

ROMANCE NOVELS

And He Cooks Too

Driven to Matrimony

Saved by the Salsa

Tough Enough to Tango

Not Your Mama's Mambo

The Sleepover Clause

Seduction on Wheels

Keeping It Casual

Paradise by Design

Don't Toy with Me

Change Up

Love in the Third Act

Excerpt from

Bamboozled

Second Book in the "Mah Jongg Mystery" Series

by Barbara Barrett

*C*athy wiped her eyes and then blew her nose. "Without consulting anyone, Dorcas added these creams and sun block to our offerings. They're not even produced by the essential oils company, but I'm still expected to promote them. I can't pick and choose what to sell."

"That's tough," Marianne said.

"That's not all. I can't get all the oils I need to keep in stock. Dorcas says she's experienced delivery problems, but I suspect she's holding them back."

"Whatever for?" Sydney asked.

Cathy ran a hand through her hair. "I think she plans to make a deal with another distributor somewhere else in the country. The oils have become that popular. She also raised her prices, which means I had to raise mine."

"Do you have a contract with her?" Sydney asked.

"Good question. Yes, I do, but the problems I've cited are written in general language which could be interpreted in her favor."

Sydney shot a glance at Marianne. They'd uncovered a good part of the reasons why Cathy was in such a state. "Given what you've told us, there doesn't seem to be anything we can do to relieve your stress."

Cathy attempted a smile. "Oh, but you have helped me. My frustrations have been building up for several weeks. This is the first time I've shared my problems with someone else."

Marianne joined Sydney near the boxes of creams and sunblock. "We should be going."

"If you need to talk again," Sydney said, "just call."

Cathy followed them to the door. "I don't think that will be necessary, but thank you for the offer."

Once they were underway, Marianne was the first to talk. "Looks like her husband was right to be concerned about her. I never would have guessed from her demeanor at mah jongg that she was under so much pressure."

"Nor I. Why does she put up with that woman?"

Marianne glanced back at the condo complex they'd just left. "Maybe now that she's voiced her feelings out loud she'll give some thought to quitting."

"With all that inventory in tow? She'd be walking away from a huge financial loss, unless she could get other sales reps in the area to absorb it."

When they arrived at Marianne's house, they both continued to sit in the car, wrapped up in their own private thoughts. "There's nothing more we can do at this point," Sydney said at last.

"I was coming to that same conclusion. But I hate it."

Just as Marianne was ready to leave, Sydney's phone rang. Sydney put a hand up when she heard who was on the other end. "Cathy? Did we leave something behind?"

"No, nothing like that. The sheriff came to my door shortly after you left. Dorcas Wiley was found dead about an hour ago. Supposedly, I was the last person to see her. You said to call if I needed you. I guess I'm the chief suspect."

A little about Barbara Barrett

Barbara Barrett started reading mysteries when she was pregnant with her first child to keep her mind off things like her changing body and food cravings. When she'd devoured as many Agatha Christies as she could find, she branched out to English village cozies and Ellery Queen.

Later, to avoid a midlife crisis, she began writing fiction at night when she wasn't at her day job as a human resources analyst for Iowa State Government. After releasing eleven full-length romance novels and one novella, she returned to the cozy mystery genre, using one of her retirement pastimes, the game of mah jongg, as her inspiration. Not only has it been a great social outlet, it has also helped keep her mind active when not writing.

Craks in a Marriage, the first book in her "Mah Jongg Mystery" series, features four friends who seek the murderer of another mah jongg player's husband before she is charged. None of the four is based on an actual person. Each is an amalgamation of several mah jongg friends with a lot of Barbara's imagination thrown in for good measure. The four will continue to appear in future books in the series.

Anticipating the day when she would write her first mystery, she has been a member of the Mystery/Romantic Suspense chapter of Romance Writers of America for over a decade. She credits them with helping her hone her craft.

Barbara is married to man she met her senior year of college. They have two grown children and eight grandchildren.

Now retired, she is a resident of Florida, although she spends her summers in Iowa, her home state. She earned her B.A. degree in History from the University of Iowa and her Master's Degree in History from Drake University.

When not in front of her laptop creating her next story, she plays Mah Jongg, knits, and enjoys lunches with friends.

Made in the USA
Middletown, DE
11 April 2018